The Happy Finish

The Happy Finish

Andrew Hook

The Happy Finish copyright © 2021 by Andrew Hook

All rights reserved. No part of this publication may be reproduced, stored in a retrieval system, rebound or transmitted in any form or by any means, electronic, mechanical, photocopying, recording or otherwise, without the prior written permission of the author and publisher. This book is sold subject to the condition that it shall not by way of trade or otherwise be lent, resold, hired out or otherwise circulated without the publisher's prior consent in any form of binding or cover other than that in which it is published.

Cover art by Edouard Noisette
(http://edouard-noisette.com)

ISBN number: 978-1-7398195-3-8

Printed and Bound by 4Edge

Published by:

Head Shot
85 Gertrude Road
Norwich
UK

editorheadshot@gmail.com
www.headshotpress.com

Light is meaningful only in relation to darkness, and truth presupposes error. It is these mingled opposites which people our life, which make it pungent, intoxicating. We only exist in terms of this conflict, in the zone where black and white clash.

- *Paris Peasant,* Louis Aragon

He sounds just too clever for us. What I mean is, you know, cops, we're not the brightest guys in the world. Of course, we got one thing going for us: we're professionals. I mean, you take our friend here, the murderer. He's very smart, but he's an amateur. I mean, he's got just one time to learn. Just one. And with us, well, with us, it's - it's a business. You see, we do this a hundred times a year. I'll tell ya, Doc. That's a lot of practice.

- Peter Falk as Lieutenant Columbo, dialogue from *Prescription: Murder* (1968 TV Movie)

1
Playing Hide And Seek With The Armadillo

Mordent once knew a kooky woman who flew on the astral plane. It was a ticketless journey. Her guides were animal totems: badger, moose, panther, zebra, possum, and the porcupine. He never asked why some animals were more important than others. Not because he wasn't interested - on a superficial level he was - but because such questions would evoke an evening's worth of conversation after which they would be too tired for sex. And considering Mordent was paying for sex, it was an expensive mistake to make.

Her favourite totem was the armadillo. She would sit cross-legged, shoulders hunched, and then bring her arms forward in an arc whilst Mordent unlaced his shoes and wondered what he was doing. Incense sticks burnt in long purple containers filled with rice grains. Amber lightshades imbued the room with a honey-glow. She would talk of the 'little armoured one' with its shell of cartilage and bone. It was as though their sessions took place in a lecture hall, and he wondered if prostitution didn't come naturally to her, whether she needed to incant some ritual for it to be palatable.

It wasn't a sensation that lent itself to the erotic, but Mordent had impulses with which he couldn't be choosy.

'The armadillo curls into a sphere to protect its vital organs when threatened. We can take this symbolically; the armadillo is encouraging us to assume this position to protect our inner selves.'

Mordent would remove his underwear, uncurl his penis into his hand. She would widen her eyes to give him confidence, although he often found it comical. Often he didn't care.

'Armadillos like water. They can walk underwater and even inflate their intestines so that they might float. Water talks to us about the *flow* of our emotions. How can the armadillo help loosen emotional tension? We can think of the armadillo as a way of release.'

Mordent's testicles weren't filled with water but they needed release. She would reach forwards and cup him, his balls shrinking slightly at the contact before his penis began to grow.

'Armadillos have the wonderful ability to detect items underground. They are superior at 'hide-and-seek'. Using the armadillo as a spiritual guide they can *find stuff for us*. Items either real or intangible. Encourage the armadillo to astral-travel ahead of you in life to seek and find that which is hidden from you.'

Mordent would watch as his personal armadillo played hide and seek within the confines of her mouth. She was the first of many whores that he would frequent during his life: experimentation was hard and fast until his bubblewrap peccadillo manifested itself and his preferences were defined. She would dart her head forwards quickly, withdraw slowly. The heady scent of the burning incense would tremble his stomach, until queasiness was overtaken by compulsion and an irrelevant race for life began.

She would spit into a tea towel.

'Those who hold the armadillo as a totem have a

natural defence system and can be incredibly protective. They're perceptive, attuned to their environment. They're smart, comfortable within their shell. Armadillo-people also have great memories, and adore the role of history-keeper. Inquisitive, introspective, thoughtful, grounded and keen to defend that which is precious....these terms best describe those with the armadillo as their totem.'

Mordent remembered her words now, standing in the cemetery, a curious twitch and ache almost genuflecting his genitalia in a thoughtful if not literal interpretation of the term. A cool breeze, not unpleasant, wended its way through poplar trees that lined avenues straight as the dead. Long black cars were parked like beetles with polished carapaces. Stick figures stood at a distance, perspective blurring their features and honing their shape. It was a nice day to be outside. On any other occasion it might remind him how good it was to be alive - and he was barely the most romantic of men. But today was different. Today was Hubie's funeral. And so today reminded him of how good it might be if Hubie were *still* alive.

Hubie, perhaps more than ever in his wooden overcoat, had been an armadillo.

And - contrary to his irascible nature, his eschewal of human relationships, and his malignant outlook - Mordent knew he missed him.

It was a death which might have been avoided.

Mordent felt himself culpable.

Unlike any of his sexual liaisons, it hadn't been a happy finish.

2
An Unhappy Finish

It had been Martens at the morgue who had broken the news.

'There's a guy been brought in who has your number in his cell. Thought I'd let you know.'

Mordent had been nursing injuries sustained from a battle he hadn't expected to win. His elation rose and fell with the pain, succoured through swigs of bourbon. He was stretched out on his sofa in an apartment he had only recently returned to. Not long back it had been ransacked and it still wasn't the way he wanted. Every morning he awoke and it didn't sit right in his memory, as though the Shoemaker's Elves had visited overnight and moved things left of centre. Even so, it was good to be home, good to have survived. Life as a PI wasn't without its dangers, but the return to normality had been by the skin of his teeth. He decided to look that expression up the next time he was online. He knew that he would forget about doing so.

Martens rang Mordent's cell. It vibrated in his pocket with the intensity of a fieldmouse.

'My number?'

'Yeh. And not only yours, but the numbers of all the good guys and all the bad guys in this fine city. Kovacs has expressed an interest.'

A thin residue of alcohol coiled in the pit of Mordent's stomach and began to rise, as though a snake stirred by a charmer. Martens' description had identified the body as clearly as if he had uploaded a photo. Still he had to ask:

'You got a name?'

'Hubie Errol Carpenter.'

Errol.

'You still there, Mordent?'

'Yeh, I'm still here. So what happened?'

'Took a dive into concrete. Some relationship issues. Room was locked from the inside so suicide is the likely verdict. I take it you knew him?'

Mordent nodded slowly. Then realised he was nodding and spoke.

'Just a guy I knew. In our parlance he was an informer. But he was more than an informer. He was a cipher, dealt in information - no doubt both ways. Kovacs can sniff all he likes but Hubie was clean. He didn't handle the stuff that he touched.'

Martens paused, waiting for a joke that never came. 'You ok?'

'Yeh, I'm ok. Some deaths are different to others. Thanks for giving me the heads up.'

'No problem, Mordent. Us outsiders have to stick together.'

Mordent hung up before he could think of a suitable riposte. Then he closed his eyes and remembered Hubie Carpenter.

They had been buddies as far as the term existed for Mordent, a natural loner. They had shared jibes and information. He had once worn his clothes. They had done drugs together one mermaid-filled evening when they had been in the same room and in different rooms. He had interrupted Hubie during coitus on many occasions, Hubie's predilection for the female form being only marginally less absorbed than Mordent's.

He'd had his ear bent by Hubie during the relationship issue that Martens had mentioned and he had believed he had resolved that issue. It turned out he was wrong.

Mordent lay on the sofa with his aching bones and wondered how much harder they would ache if he had fallen several floors. He wondered how it felt to fall. He realised he would never have to visit Hubie's derelict apartment block again. Small mercies came wrapped in the suffocating cloak of death.

Despite the prolific names in Hubie's address book the attendees at the funeral were few. Mordent recognised Hubie's girl, Catherine, but she wouldn't have known *him* without a gimp mask. She was leaning against a tall man who Mordent hoped was her father. In any event, he was glad it wasn't Ransome whose relationship with Catherine had inadvertently caused Hubie's death. Mordent held a conversation with Ransome shortly after Martens' phone call, wondered whether if he should have waylaid him when he had the chance. But as Ransome once said, *if it wasn't me it would be someone else,* and Mordent couldn't help but agree. Catherine had needs Hubie couldn't meet and even with his agreement the knowledge had pressed him towards death.

Along with Catherine a handful of solo males stood a respectful distance from the grave, hands in pockets, brokering no eye contact. Mordent assumed their provenance was from the same gene pool as Hubie's, or perhaps they were acquaintances from the track. Between the five of them their suits were approaching one hundred years old, hair colour edging towards gray, lines on their face a tree-stump indicator of age. He admired them for their bravery. It was the people who had stayed away, who had defected from Hubie's friendship, who – on both sides of the law – had something to hide, that Mordent reserved his distaste. If there was a time for honesty surely it came with death.

With the coffin in the ground Mordent watched Catherine bend to gather a handful of earth, her knees whitening through the stretch of black stocking fabric like twin headlights.

He wondered about the number of *whys* that ran through her head, whether she had any regrets; but knew that the tug of her desire would pull her back again and again to the inevitable. It wasn't her fault that Hubie had been such a good guy. It wasn't his either.

Mordent had made so many bad relationship choices that he wondered if there were any good choices. When was it that mankind decided to be monogamous? It was emotions that separated them from swathes of the animal kingdom, and according to the professionals were an indication of dominance, yet Mordent saw them as failings. Attachments led to conflicts of desire, transitory liaisons fulfilled a need but didn't abate connections. Overall mankind was caught in an emotional maelstrom of evolutionary making. There weren't too many amoebas jumping from fourth floor windows.

He watched as Catherine turned her head in his direction. It seemed she might speak, yet deciding Hubie's past life was also in her past she moved away with her chaperone towards one of the black vehicles. It swallowed her delicately. The last Mordent saw of her was the point of her right stiletto as it lifted from the ground, in the slow motion display of an automaton. He stared at the space it had inhabited for some moments during which the vehicle pulled away.

Turning back to the grave he found the other mourners had left. He walked to the edge. Surrounding grass was discoloured by biscuit-crumb sand, wooden boards which had covered the hole overnight lay alongside as though an invitation to walk the plank. He crouched, observed the casket. It's polished surface and handles seemed an unnecessary extravagance for something consigned to the earth - as though it were a time capsule ready to be opened fifty years hence, containing trinkets of a bygone age.

He briefly wondered what items might be buried alongside himself: a Photostat copy of his badge whilst on the force, his PI license, a gun, a bottle of bourbon (empty, of course), a handful of jazz records, a pastrami sandwich on rye, his birth certificate and some bubblewrap. Not much to indicate a life. Egyptian mummies put him to shame.

Mordent trapped dirt in his hands and then let it sift through his fingers. Words were supposed to come at a time like this. Sentences which meant more than the standard liturgy given by the priest. Paragraphs which expressed genuine regret, emotion, even love. Yet what use was it speaking to the empty air? Hubie could no more hear him than he could hear the worms rubbing their non-existent hands at the thought of their upcoming feast. It was all body and no soul.

Still, words bubbled on his lips perhaps to assuage guilt.

'Hey Hubie. Wasn't expecting to find you here. You could have talked to me. I was open. Ransome was sorted. Just one call and all would have been ok.'

Then he stopped. There was stuff he needed to say but as he heard his voice he realised he was going through the motions. A social necessity. One time he read that human emotions were on a seven second spiral. That naturally they defuse after such a short span, but our minds perpetuate them by replaying the same details. We are trapped in a circle of hell of our making. Mordent didn't want to live that hell. He stood and threw a handful of dirt onto the coffin. Hubie had made his own bed, and now had to lie in it – however uncomfortable that might be.

As Mordent turned away, men with shovels stopped leaning against a nearby tree and commenced their work. One of them whistled as he did so. Mordent didn't recognise the tune.

3
A Meeting Of Minds

Mordent didn't make it back to his car. A few hundred yards from Hubie's grave a tall thin woman stepped out from behind one of the tall thin poplar trees. She wore thick-rimmed glasses, a pale beige suit, tan stockings and shoes. Her hair was mousy, as if built by mice. If a trace of a smile ever flickered across her features Mordent knew it would crack the layer of foundation caking her skin. Her lips were also painted beige. She looked like a secretary in an accountant's office, but her presence stopped him in his tracks as effectively as a traffic warden bent over his illegally parked vehicle. He thought of stepping to one side, but knew such movement would be mirrored. It was clear she had been waiting for him to conclude his business at the grave.

'Mr Mordent?'

It wasn't a question. Mordent nodded.

She reached into a beige clutch bag and pulled out a calling card. Printed in black on a pale fawn background was the name *Emmeline Edwards*. Other than a cell phone number there were no further details. Mordent turned the card over in his fingers like an amateur magician before pocketing it inside his jacket.

'Emmeline?'

'After Pankhurst. My mother was a feminist.'

'And you?'

'I make no distinction between the sexes. I think the days for extremes are long gone.'

'Others would disagree with you, but we seem to be cut from the same cloth.'

'I wouldn't go that far, Mr Mordent. I am aware of your background. We use different tailors.'

Mordent looked closely but there wasn't a trace of a smile.

'So, how can I help?'

Emmeline gestured with a nod of her head to a small dark green Chevrolet parked to her rear. Like her, it had also been camouflaged through poplar tree perspective. 'Shall we? I prefer to discuss matters in private.'

She moved with the elegance of a giraffe towards the car which appeared too small to accommodate her legs. Rather conspicuously she opened the rear door and slipped inside, whilst Mordent followed suit and slumped through on the opposite side. Her legs bunched up against the back of the driver's seat, almost parallel to her chin. It looked comical but it wasn't comical. That was the difference. Mordent swung his door closed and the world folded with it, was condensed to a moment of silence which passed between them inside the vehicle.

Emmeline held out her hand. 'We haven't been formerly introduced. If we're doing business together I think certain formalities should be kept.'

Mordent took it. Her fingers were long, slender and cold.

'Business?'

'It's good that a private investigator is full of questions.'

'Perhaps you could get to the point?'

Then she did smile, and Mordent found he was

correct, a hairline crack of foundation breathed into existence then settled again.

'My offer, Mr Mordent, is to provide the service from which you previously turned to Hubie Carpenter. I am in the information business. I am discrete, efficient, and unobtrusive. I work from a much better area. I know everything you want to know before you know you need to know it. I do not keep the company of whores or horses. I am reliable, candid, and friendly. I provide information for a fixed fee no matter the duration of your query. I am Miss Emmeline Edwards.'

Mordent considered her spiel. 'I've never heard of you,' he said.

'Exactly.'

Again, a ripple of a smile fluctuated her powdered skin like a snake under sand.

'Whereabouts do you operate? There's no address on the card.'

'I prefer to come to you. Or we make an arrangement over the telephone. I've found it easier not to divulge my address. I've found being a woman can give men ideas.'

'Isn't that a bit sexist?' Mordent decided to play the feminist card.

'It's biological, Mr Mordent. And it works both ways. But when you're a strong woman in a vulnerable situation it won't matter how strong you are if your opponent is stronger.'

'And the evolutionary urge is hard to fight?'

'Exactly. We are all complicit. Every man I look at I am subconsciously or otherwise evaluating their sexual potential. Just as every man does when he views a woman. We look and accept or dismiss, from one to the other. And if we are already in a relationship it makes no difference. We remain with that person because we decide not to swap with every other person we come into contact with.'

'That's very direct.'

'It pays to be honest. You'll find me the same way in business. Do we have a deal?'

Mordent considered his options. He hadn't considered where he might get his information since Hubie had died. And Hubie had been homegrown, coerced into his role by Mordent following a burn-out in his personal life. There were trust issues to be had engaging a replacement, yet there was something about Emmeline that appealed in an asexual way. He realised with that thought he had automatically rejected her as a future partner, and that pushed a second thought out of his mouth:

'Have you accepted or rejected me?'

It seemed she had been waiting for the question. 'Both. I've accepted you professionally and rejected you personally.'

The slight was pushed aside by the honesty.

'Then,' Mordent said, 'we have a deal.'

They shook hands.

For Mordent, beige was the new black.

4
Pop!

Mordent once had a liaison with a girl called Lola White. She was considerably younger, sexually deviant, and her record collection confounded him with its edges and beats.

One evening she sat cross-legged on the floor, her wrists still bearing the handcuff-marks of his regulation issue. He was in the force during those years and Lola found his equipment came in handy when satisfying her needs. Unusually for their relationship they were teetering to a domestic situation, she was trying to convince him that punk took precedence over jazz. But also that they were essentially the same: a fluid cacophony.

Out of an album featuring brightly-dressed band members in test tubes she removed the inner sleeve of X-Ray Spex's *Germfree Adolescents*. She discarded this and placed the black vinyl on the record deck. Mordent's ears weren't attuned to the type of noise that blasted forth, although he allowed a grudging approval of the saxophone which was unlike anything he had heard in pop music and in its discordant sounds did hold a connection to jazz.

Sat on Lola's bed, wearing a shirt, socks, and little else, he regarded the discarded tissues used to wipe his semen from her face and found the part-transformation to a father listening to their child's record collection disconcerting but not entirely unarousing.

He picked up the inner sleeve, read through the lyrics which resonated themes of alienation in an increasingly commercial world, but then let the words drift aside from his vision as he realised the background on which they were printed was bubblewrap.

Mordent ran his hand over the sleeve. It was a photograph, but the image was so clear he could imagine pockets of trapped air indenting the skin on his palm. There was something erotic about it, he realised; on the face of it, nothing, but imbued with the residual glow of their recent fierce sex he considered it through red-light tinted glasses. He resolved to bring bubblewrap into the equation the next time he was suffocating Lola. He was sure she would have no objection towards it.

Their relationship was swift and torrid. It literally burnt out. When Mordent attended Lola's funeral it was in a professional capacity. It was ironic that she wasn't cremated.

But the bubblewrap seed had been planted. From encasing it around Lola's head and quickly popping it until an air-hole was achieved before she passed out, to the sound itself becoming an erotic stimulant, a trigger, Mordent became obsessed with the plastic material with its protruding air-filled hemispheres and wherever possible introduced it one way or another into his sexual behaviour. Having found it impossible to replace Lola with her rapacious needs and open mind, and his subsequent conquests utterly less accommodating, it had fallen upon the escorts in the city to satisfy his request. Over time, even those relationships had ended in acrimony or death, until he found Astrid who understood him perfectly. In sexual terms their meetings were akin to finding home.

Generally, however, he kept the obsession to himself. He'd bought a *mugen puchipuchi,* a tiny electronic Japanese toy that simulated the noise of bubblewrap popping, but that was exclusively to annoy people. And he didn't celebrate Bubble Wrap Appreciation Day, celebrated on the last Monday in January, finding that such a gimmick detracted from the totality of his immersion in the material as a fetish. When it came to the *air cap* he was all wrapped up.

He needed a release after the funeral and Astrid was at the forefront of his mind. He had booked her beforehand, anticipating the need. Parking close to her apartment he walked up the stone steps and pressed her buzzer. With the button vibrating under his fingertip he imagined her clitoris, something he had seen but never touched. Their relationship was devised by precise limits of his making, and sometimes it was better to maintain the erotic than to fulfil the pulse. It kept him in a permanent state of desire for her.

The door opened without further communication and shortly afterwards he was let into her apartment.

'How did it go?'

Unlike the other whores he had frequented Mordent had allowed aspects of his personal life to seep into Astrid's. In her hand she held a glass of bourbon. He took it and drank.

'He was buried. That's the long and the short of it.'

'And how do you feel?'

'Tense. Angry. Frustrated. The usual.'

'It's difficult to understand?'

'With a suicide there's no closure. You can hide the body under a mound of earth but the questions remain. *Why did they do it?* and *Could I have done anything to prevent it?'*

'Don't beat yourself up. Those answers are never known.'

'You and I know that's easier said than done.'

She poured him another shot of bourbon. 'On the house.'

Mordent downed it. When she smiled he found the ghost of Hubie edged to one side. There wasn't even the trace of an accusing finger.

'Shall we...?'

They took their drinks into the bedroom and Astrid waited patiently as Mordent sat on the duvet and slipped off his shoes and socks. When he removed his shirt she didn't gasp as she saw the fresh bruises, but admired them as they reflected dully in the strip of red fairy lights which wound their way across the head of the bed.

'You been playing away?'

She bent closer, traced her fingers over the marks on his back. Mordent hadn't had either the will or inclination to view them, but he assumed they were impressive. Even after a week it appeared they hadn't faded.

'You could say that. You should see the other guys.'

'More than one? Impressive. You've been working out, as well.'

He shivered under the lightness of her touch. It was rare that she was so tactile.

'There was a storm coming. I had to be ready for it.'

She laughed. 'Such corny dialogue.'

He grinned. 'I know.'

He knelt on the floor whilst she tied his hands behind his back. The ball gag fit snugly in his mouth.

Opening her dresser she removed a fresh roll of bubblewrap. One of the bubbles popped as she dug into the Scotch tape that bound it with her long red fingernails. She wore a smart dark blue suit with a skirt that stopped just before her knees. She didn't need to be dressed like a tart to turn him on, in fact the opposite was the case. Her sheer professionalism added to the experience, gave it a greater edge.

Carefully she wrapped the bubblewrap around his torso. It was tight when he breathed and the sensation of it against his bruises was not dissimilar to massage. She fastened it out of sight and then knelt to face him. He noted she held a long, red-bladed knife, the point of which appeared incredibly sharp. She tapped one of the bubbles with the tip, just above his right nipple. He looked into her eyes and they looked back - a direct gaze, a naked kiss. Her ruby-rouged lips parted and her voice was low and soft as she spoke:

'Imagine my husband fucking me in this room, Mordent. Imagine me bent over the bed with my skirt hitched up over my thighs and my panties moist with expectation.'

She pushed the blade into the bubble. *Pop!*

'Imagine him alternatively spanking then caressing my ass, using greater and greater force each time, as he punishes me for seeing so many clients such as yourself. So many clients.'

Pop!

'Imagine his work colleagues introduced into the room, my husband shouting how I've shamed him, how knowledge of my work has bled into the street. Imagine as he invites them to share me, how my wrists are held taut, how their loosened belts lift welts on my skin, how their cocks are fed into my open mouth, as I am repulsed, engorged, and excited simultaneously.'

Pop!

'Imagine the degradation your favourite whore suffers as she is used by these men, and imagine that I am thinking of *you* throughout the ordeal, imagining your cock growing in my hand as it does now, as I am filled to the brim under sufferance.'

Pop! Pop!

She didn't get any further into the fantasy. Mordent released himself into her palm, a glycerine-like discharge, the edge of the blade scratching the surface of his skin.

5
The Only Normal People Are Those You Don't Know Well

Work was light.

A couple of weeks after Hubie's funeral Mordent stood looking at the city from his office window. Dusk had fallen. As though the city were contained within an hour glass darkness pooled at its base whilst the sky above remained bright, a pale blue halo held by a shimmering of smog. Droplets of night filtered through the stratosphere, built the evening from the ground upwards. In an hour or less the night would gain complete control like a lid closing on a saucepan. And then the heat would become trapped and would fester within the minds of those unable to sleep, within the minds of those who had nothing better to do than aggravate the quiet citizens of the city.

This happened daily: three hundred and sixty five nights a year. And from it Mordent found employment: the missing and the missed, the bodies and the buried, the shenanigans of husbands or wives who believed their activities were cloaked by darkness, petty crime and petty criminals, offering his services wherever they were required. It was a bits and pieces life. His job was to pick up the detritus left by the refuse trucks driven by the police, those items that fell off the back of those lorries and which were too minor or marginal to be bothered with. Mordent fed on those scraps and they fuelled him. They paid for his meagre apartment and his equally meagre life. It was all that he had but he was content with it. Life hadn't grown him into a person who could do anything else.

He considered himself normal: yet he had killed, whored, existed in extremity, been attacked, and had fraternised with all strata's of society. From the window he saw other people inhabiting their lives, and from an outsider's viewpoint *they* might be considered normal: individuals moving from work to home to play, who ingested television programmes, raised children, were monogamous, and were unobtrusive in their manners and actions. Yet Mordent knew this was a fallacy, that within each *ordinary* person there was an extraordinary person manifest and waiting to break through. That it was, in fact, *extraordinary* to be ordinary, and that those who most people considered normal were in fact the extremes. Being normal did not constitute normality, it was a consensual construct that held no basis in reality. As Mordent had heard it said, normal people were those you simply didn't know very well.

There had been a case in England where a guy had been sentenced for cannibalistic thoughts, despite never having acted on them. Whilst he had in theory chatted to a pre-pubescent online, that child had never been identified and Mordent expected that the individual had likely been an adult masquerading as a child. The internet allowed the extension of fantasies from beyond an individual's head, yet in many cases they remained that: fantasies. He wondered when George Orwell's *Thoughtcrime* had become an actual crime. He wondered what it meant to be normal.

Heels click-clacked in the stairwell behind him as the workers in the temp agency along the corridor headed off for the night. He resisted the urge to collect their silhouettes as they passed by his glazed office door. He wondered about their lives and what normality they might contain; what hopes and fears they had. Human existence was a piece of elastic that was always stretching.

And, once stretched, could never regain its shape.

Hubie popped into his mind once again. He thought of him more these days than he ever had when he was alive. It wasn't as though he had taken him for granted, more that he hadn't needed deeper involvement. They *weren't* buddies, despite the occasional clamour for companionship. That role was an artifice to continue the guilt. Mordent had no buddies: only ex-colleagues, ex-girlfriends and an ex-wife. The only true friend he had was an establishment.

Morgan's Bar.

Grabbing his car keys from the scratched surface of his desk he headed into the night, becoming absorbed like ink within ink, staining the city with his uncomfortable presence.

Morgan's Bar was a haven of iniquity. Much as Hubie had dealt with the good, bad and the ugly on equal terms, so did Morgan's bar. Unlike *Cheers*, it was a bar where *no one* knew your name; apart from the proprietor, the ubiquitous Morgan, who kept information close to his chest. Mordent had drowned a few sorrows in the bar, and rarely celebrated. It was a place he visited when he needed inspiration or consolation. When drinking was best done publicly.

This evening it was quiet, the numbers of bums on seats scarcely enough to keep it open. Although Mordent wondered if it would ever close. What would happen when Morgan passed his sell-by-date. He hoped he would be dead by then. The absence of Morgan's Bar was anathema.

He eased onto his usual stool, facing the upended bottles and the glass mirror which reflected little more than a metre beyond him. Morgan had a grubby tea towel pushed into a glass. It was only for show. He had to be doing something even when it wasn't busy. Mordent wondered if he were open for chat.

'How's it going?'

Morgan gestured with the elbow of the arm leading to the fist inside the glass. 'Quiet.'

Conversation over, Mordent sank into an auburn haze within the glass, the bourbon nestling in his stomach like a cat making comfy on a sofa. That sensation - an almost spectral feeling - was as close to normal as he ever felt. He luxuriated.

6
The Fear Institute

Another day, another dime.

Mordent's feet were on his desk. There was a split forming on the left-hand shoe, a crease repeated by the movement of his foot which had weathered the leather he had failed to polish and was now threatening to grow beyond a crack. His right-hand shoe also bore a crease in the same position, yet hadn't begun to split. He was contemplating what this meant about the balance of his gait when a shadow appeared on the other side of the glazed glass of his office door. A hand raised for a knock.

The knock determined the type of client he might expect. Many held back, gave only a tap in fear of glass fragmenting under a blow. This meant an effeminate knock might be elicited from even the burliest of clients. Women tended to evoke their stereotypes, rapping with just one knuckle. Some elected to knock the wood below the glass, which was perfectly adequate but off-putting. Mordent wondered whether to knock at a height anywhere other than natural created a kind of frailty within the client. The best knocks were given by those who were confident, though they were not necessarily the best clients.

On this occasion the tap was tentative yet sure. The client unafraid of breaking glass, yet respectful of its resonance. There was money in that knock, and

Mordent shifted his feet from the desk and swept the pack of cards he used to play patience into an open drawer which also contained his gun.

'The door's open.'

A fop-haired youth, barely in his twenties, entered the office. Mordent wondered when his clothes came back into fashion. He wore a green tweed jacket with leather elbow patches, almost-matching moleskin trousers, and a lighter green bow-tie resplendent against a paisley shirt. Frankly, he looked ridiculous; just as those with inherited money often were, having not required the wherewithal to make their own way in the world and existing on a hand-me-down culture which was chic fifty years ago.

If the youth were a duck at a fairground shooting range he would be 60ft in diameter and Mordent would be holding an elephant gun. Easy money.

Mordent stood and held out his hand. Introduced himself as the youth shook.

'Benedict Holmsworth.'

There was a trace of a British accent which Mordent believed was affected. Benedict's appearance had been cultivated to impress those who weren't in Mordent's line of work. Mordent, therefore, was unimpressed.

'And how can I help you, Mr Holmsworth?'

'It's about my uncle, also Benedict Holmsworth.'

That figured.

'And how can I help him?'

'In some respects, it's rather late for that.' The youth sat and crossed one leg over the other, establishing that he felt at home. 'Have you ever heard of The Fear Institute?'

Mordent took a while to shake his head. The kid had the upper hand. 'I don't believe so.'

'The Fear Institute is an organisation determined to eradicate phobia. My uncle abhorred rats. It's not uncommon. I imagine there are few of us who love them - the wild variety I mean, not pets. Pet rats aren't really rats are they? Just overgrown mice. It was something he had fought against for a long while: not just actual rats, because we don't see many of those nowadays. But the *thought* of rats. He became fixated with the belief that humans are never more than six feet away from a rat. Have you heard that view?'

Mordent shook his head again.

'He found the statement via Robert Sullivan's book, *Rats: A Year with New York's Most Unwanted Inhabitants*. Have you read it?'

Head shaking was becoming *de rigueur* in Mordent's office.

'Sullivan references a 1909 book entitled *The Rat Problem* by WR Boelter. This was an English work in which it was estimated there were an equal number of rats to the human population. It was - at best - a speculative guess. Recent studies indicate that in theory standing at any given spot in an urban area you are at most likely to be 164ft away from a rat. Not quite the ring that 6ft has, but close enough; and in any event, for my uncle, it seemed to be fudging the issue. He wouldn't be budged on 6ft.'

Mordent resisted the urge to glance around his office space. According to the rental agreement it was 12ft by 12ft. If there was a rat it was likely to be him.

Benedict ran on: 'He wasn't an uneducated man, but brilliant minds often become fixated by the minutiae. These fixations become obsessions. I do believe he hadn't even considered rats before picking up that book. No childhood traumas, no visible presence in our property. Yet the seed of the rat problem took hold of his mind and towards the end it was all he could think of.'

'And the Institute of Fear?'

'Not the Institute of Fear, Mr Mordent, but the Fear Institute. There's a subtle difference. The Institute is run by a Mr Copernicus Fear. Just like Mr Bunn is a baker or Dr Rash might be in medicine. The name itself is a misnomer in reverse. Whether Mr Fear decided to examine the concepts of phobias because of his name is up for question, it was never raised in mine or my uncle's dealings with him. Coincidence is a funny thing that plays tricks in men's minds. But the bottom line is that it is not an institute *of* fear. Do you understand that subtlety?'

Mordent fought the urge to nod, then remembered there was money involved and nodded all the same. 'This is all very interesting Mr Holmsworth, but how does the Fear Institute fit with your uncle's rat obsession?'

Benedict sighed. 'My uncle was not so self-contained that he couldn't see the root of his oncoming madness. He contacted the Institute so they might rid him of this phobia, this obsession. He wanted them to help.'

'And did they?'

Benedict leant across the desk, both hands gripping the edge. 'Mr Mordent, my uncle was scared to death. I need you to investigate Copernicus Fear.'

He sat back, content with his dramatic presentation. Mordent wasn't convinced.

'You want me to investigate because of your uncle's fear?'

Benedict sighed. 'Please listen. They scared him to death. To *death*. They killed him. And not only killed him, they charged him for the privilege. He poured money into the Institute and they took his life. That's why I need your help. The police haven't listened.'

The young man's face grimaced with frustration.

Mordent named his price, plus expenses.

7
The World Revolves

Mordent knew a joke about Copernicus but it wasn't very good.

Copernicus's exasperated parents said to him as a teenager: *When are you going to realise the world doesn't revolve around you.*

Benedict Holmsworth had left Mordent's office satisfied that work was going to be done. Mordent was less sure of the fact. The meeting had been strange, to put it mildly. He pulled the cards from his desk drawer and shuffled them, enjoying the rough feeling in his palms as the cards settled as individuals into a smoother whole. If only solving cases was that simple. If you could take all the information, shuffle it within your head, and receive a clear and compact solution whose conclusion couldn't be disputed. Instead, it was more like fifty-two card pick-up. He dealt the cards on the table, some face-up, some face-down. Then began to overlay them in familiar patterns.

According to Benedict, his uncle had suffered a fatal heart attack. It didn't appear that the cause of death was in dispute. There also appeared to be no financial abuse in relation to his uncle's support of the Fear Institute. It wasn't so much as an open and shut case as an unopened one. Yet Benedict was convinced the Institute was culpable in relation to his uncle's death, and with money involved far be it for Mordent to dismiss him without skimming some off the top. He took that as fair play when dealing with the monied classes. He wasn't a communist, but redistribution of wealth when it came to his own needs was paramount.

The trouble with people with money was that they *did* think the world revolved around them. It was clear to Benedict that his uncle had been murdered because his uncle couldn't have succumbed to the normal internal forces which affect us all. Heart attack? *Unthinkable.* The more Benedict remonstrated that the elder Benedict had no previous history of heart failure the more Mordent ceased to listen. Yet he had to make a start somewhere, and in addition to the cards on the table there was another card he had to play when it came to shuffling information.

'Emmeline Edwards.'

Her voice sounded different over the phone, less beige more honey.

'It's Mordent. I'm hoping you can supply me with information.'

'These are my terms: incoming over the telephone, outgoing in person. COD. Does that work for you?'

'You know it does. Have you ever heard of the Fear Institute?'

'Is eraser theft daylight rubbery?'

Mordent snorted. 'I didn't expect you to have a sense of humour.'

'Expect the unexpected and you'll fulfil your expectations. What information do you want?'

'The usual, background. There's a guy who runs it, Copernicus Fear, whose name sounds as screwy as the organisation. I want the lowdown on him. I want to know if there have been any deaths connected to the institute which might be considered unexpected. I want everything and anything you got.'

'You shall have it. I will get back to you with a time and place.'

'Thanks.'

Mordent found himself about to comment on the tone of her voice but her handset had already been replaced in her receiver. He didn't allow himself time for a double entendre, but dialled another number instead.

'Marsham?'

Marsham was a rising star on the force whom Mordent had left as a supernova. Marsham had been complicit in not bringing Ransome to justice, leaving him somewhat culpable over Hubie's death because of it. Marsham didn't know the ins and outs of that little ménage a trois, but he did know he was beholden to Mordent and even if he hadn't already been attuned to him he most certainly was now. Mordent knew he could rely on Marsham for anything.

'Hey Mordent, that you buddy?'

'Yeh, how's it going?'

'Going fine, Mordent. Going just fine.'

'Giving Kovacs a run for his money?'

'I wouldn't go that far.'

'Sure you would. You're the dark horse coming up fast on the inside lane.'

Marsham laughed. 'Not in this climate.'

'There's official promotions and unofficial promotions. Kovacs plays it by the straight and narrow and you play it the way I used to. You'll get to where you're going in the end.'

Marsham chuckled again. 'You got it all sewn up. But you're not calling just to chew my ear. What's up?'

'Information, Marsham, information. What do you know of the Fear Institute?'

'The Fear Institute? Nothing, off the top of my head. You want me to look into it?'

Mordent gave him the same spiel that he had given Emmeline, although when Marsham didn't hang up he didn't mention the honeyed voice. Marsham had something to tell him).

'Listen Mordent, something weird happened here the other day. We had someone ask for you. I wasn't going to mention it. Family stuff is family stuff right? Weren't even sure if she were legit. But maybe I should have told you, I dunno.'

'Someone asking for me?'

'Yeh, a female, like I said.' He paused. 'Name of Berenice.'

'Rings no bell. She have a surname?'

Marsham paused again. 'Yeh, she had a surname Mordent. It was yours. She said her name was Berenice Mordent. Your daughter.'

The world revolves and we revolve with it.

After Marsham had hung up Mordent stared at a piece of paper on his desk upon which he had written eleven numbers. The permutation of those eleven numbers wasn't infinite but might well have been. Yet in the current coalesced format they represented sperm, the permutations of an equally perplexing discharge which might have created a baby. Mordent had no knowledge that he had ever fathered a child, and found it puzzling that she claimed to carry his surname, but the bottom line was that he was now aware that *someone* out there was claiming parentage and even if it were false the realisation he might not be alone in the world hit hard. The numbers were as commanding as a string of DNA.

He put the piece of paper into his jacket pocket and pulled the bourbon bottle from his desk. For someone with nothing to do, it had been one hell of an eventful morning.

8
Misdirection

He took the long way home. The sun was heavy in the sky, a shampoo drop in a golden commercial. Light bounced off skyscraper sides like the sphere in a pinball machine, the descending sun striking points against the glass. In this district the streets needed some improvement. Mordent's car bumped up and down displacing scenery as though he were watching the painted opening credits to a 1920s movie. The cardboard façade gained further momentum as the quality of the light exaggerated angles, heightened straight surfaces and made them one-dimensional. Yet these mundane buildings were more Holyrood than Hollywood. Or at least, Mordent's understanding of it.

Misdirection focussed attention on one thing in order to distract it from another. A form of deception. Mordent continued to place his gaze on dappled reflections, oily sheens, the auburn transformations of striated leaves, moonfaced heads caught in the curvature of car door panels, roiling clouds surfing a negative sky, the imprint of lowlife boots like relief lines on maps as tramps sheltered in doorways, the diamante arc of puddles flipped skywards by spinning tyres, the flop of some hats and the curving brims of others, features in profile zipping past flickerbook style, paw prints like dominoes left by dogs on the sidewalk, myriad permutations of the melee of life which - as he came to think of it - were just as random as those telephone digits and the faint chance of sperm locating an egg.

Full circle, he pulled up outside his apartment and wearily climbed the stairs. His rooms were in disarray. Plastic trays stockpiled by the kitchen refuse bin. He couldn't remember which day they were due to be collected. Clear glasses containing various alcoholic residues resembled coloured tumblers. Odd socks were spaced on the floor like painted footprints leading children around a museum. He wondered when he had last done his laundry.

There was no excuse to be had from Hubie's death, that wasn't a coathanger Mordent could lay claim to. He needed a woman around the house, but the type of woman he needed wasn't the type he wanted. Experience confirmed this. During the brief period of his marriage, Maria had kept him in line. Without her it wasn't that he was lazy, or even particularly slovenly, just that there was no reason to be tidy. It was easier to remain in slop.

In slop.

Couldn't that define his life? A rambling shift from one set of circumstances to another, eschewing convention becoming a convention in its own right. Had he lived this way in order to not face facts? *Berenice Mordent.* The name swam around the goldfish bowl of his mind but wasn't gone in seven seconds. Where had she come from?

Misdirection. Whilst he was looking one way, something had happened another. Yet it wasn't only him. Society personified misdirection. Everything existed solely to deflect from eventual non-existence. It was a theory Mordent had for a while. Humans, being conscious, unlike other animals, were acutely aware of death. However to focus on death would be insane, so society was developed whereby humans created work, relationships, leisure activities, art, families, the whole shebang purely as a distraction, a diversion from the ultimate. Without a conscious understanding of death none of this would happen. Man's evolution was propelled by an aversion to the void, fuelled by abject certainty. And when you looked at all those activities closely, when you realised how useless it was to fanatically follow a football team, or write novels, or get married or conform to any of society's stereotypes, when all that looked back was the emptiness and expanse of the universe. It was impossible to look, yet it was impossible to look away.

Working with the dead hammered this home. Most people could go their whole lives without seeing a dead body. They were born, raised, educated, courted, married, had children, became old, and then died. Unless they viewed dead relatives lying in state it was rare that they came into contact with death. It was allowed to remain a nebulous concept, floating on the horizon like cumulous nimbus, a cloud forever nearer yet in perspective far away. By the time it rained, skin was too cold and too stiff for it to register. And that unceasing downpour continued for infinity.

But for those who worked with the dead - nurses, doctors, firemen, police officers, morticians, funeral directors - there was no escape from the pressing certainty of a future lack of soul. However, over time the intricacies and subterfuge of the mind took over - once you saw the first dead body, usually in a state of hideous disarray, then you had seen them all. Society assimilated thoughts of death into life, counteracted its depressing guarantee.

With one exception.

Transition.

Mordent had killed people, most bad, some good, most deliberately, some accidentally. Occasionally without the opportunity to establish whether they *were* bad or good, split second decisions which were literally a matter of life or death. Yet he wasn't immune to the transition, in the run up to the kill the mind was fogged, impervious to external forces similar to the sexual impulse which dominated until climax. But after that climax, after the kill, the mind uncoagulated, the impetus unspooled. After sex, this might mean your lover was viewed in a different light, no longer a sex kitten of insanely erotic intent but a middle-aged woman with bad teeth and hollow eyes. After a killing, assuming the victim wasn't immediately dead, the interstice between life and death was sadness. For unlike the state of life or death misdirected by society, moving from one state to the other with inexorable surety gave as much pain to the victim as it did to their nemesis. There was cold clarity to be had watching someone die.

Thinking of Berenice, Mordent was in that moment of clarity. And however much his mind attempted misdirection it was pulled back to the certainty of her existence. Maybe it was a prank, maybe it was someone trying to obtain information about him, maybe it was mistaken identity: Mordent believed none of those things. He knew - somehow - that it was real.

It began to rain with some intensity. Water sluiced against his windows as if he lived adjacent to a theme park's waterslide. He wanted to get out of the apartment, but Morgan's Bar was too easy. Berenice's number burnt a hole in his jacket pocket, but that was too difficult. Instead he powered up his PC and searched for something Astrid had mentioned. It wasn't too hard to find. Shaking his head, doubting his intentions, he pulled on his jacket, removed that piece of paper and left it on his dining room table, then exited into the night to merge with the raindrops like a character in a scanimation book.

9
Bubblewrap Sumo

A bachelorette party packed the club. They occupied four of the eight tables and despite the relatively early hour were in the throes of disrepair. The bride-to-be's lipstick was smeared and out of the five glasses in front of her only two were empty, one upturned. She had a face which looked like it had been sucked halfway down a plughole, and the noise that rose from the tables mimicked chickens in a wind tunnel. Mordent immediately regretted paying the admission fee, but having done so was determined to stay. Of the other tables, mixed groups bent heads together to ensure they could be heard. Dance music vibrated the carpet, helping to loosen each of Mordent's footsteps from the sticky surface as he walked towards the bar where all the stools were vacant. The vibration almost vacated his own stool.

He heaved himself upwards, the stool height designed to show off a female's shapely legs rather than his toad-like form. His feet swung an inch above the silver joist. The barmaid was the antithesis of Morgan, she wore a fluorescent green crop top and pale blue jogging shorts. Some would have damned her for playing on her sexuality yet praised her for not fearing falling into a stereotype. Mordent's task was to avert his eyes whilst ordering a drink. He failed at both, the words bobbling from his mouth like craft in a whitewater rafting disaster, whilst his vision was pierced by her large nipples that fairly glowed through the top.

It was evident they rarely entertained solo clientele. The barmaid was full of chat once she'd poured his drink.

'Not see you here before. You here for the sumo?'

Mordent nodded.

'I'm amazed how popular it gets. But it is a laugh. It is a laugh.'

She bounced on the soles of her feet to the music. The nipples were magnets from which Mordent couldn't draw his metallic gaze.

'You seen it before?'

Mordent shook his head.

'It *is* a laugh. We've got professionals on site, of course. They do the first few rounds, then we take people from the floor. You going to try?'

Mordent smiled. He was warming to the girl who treated him as an equal. 'No. I'm just here to watch.'

'Watch. Yes, watch. It is funny.'

She bounced along to the other end of the bar where a couple had entered, then served them drinks. Mordent's eyes roved over the tables, was drawn again to the topic of misdirection. Yet being in a bubblewrap sumo bar was infinitely preferable to whiling away a lifetime in a Parisian intellectual café surrounded by morose-types self-absorbed by death. And he was sure the waitresses were less appealing.

Astrid had mentioned the bar in passing. 'Of course,' she had said, 'I have no idea what it's like. Decidedly *un*erotic, I imagine, but you never know.' Mordent had made a mental note of the club's name, but hadn't really imagined he would visit. Needs must, though, and he regarded the former dance area with a circle demarked by thick rope hammered onto the floor with interest.

The barmaid was back at his shoulder.

'We've always had wrestling here,' she said. 'Beans. Mud. Girl on girl. Custard. Sounds great unless you've got the job cleaning it up. And it wasn't always great for audience participation. Sure they had the enthusiasm for it, but signing health and safety forms beforehand took the edge off it. This way, no mess, no danger. I don't suppose you've ever been wrapped in bubblewrap yourself?'

It wasn't quite a question, so Mordent didn't give quite an answer. She continued:

'You can't hurt yourself. It's next to impossible. So we've dispensed with the health and safety forms and everyone has a good time.'

She beamed. 'You still sure you don't want to try it?'

Mordent nodded to the tables hosting the bachelorette party. 'I'm sure you'll have plenty of takers over there.'

'As long as they don't get *too* drunk.' Her teeth were whiter than white.

Mordent asked the question he had been thinking ever since he'd walked up to the bar.

'Have you done it?'

'Once. Just to try out the suit. But I did do the baked bean wrestling with another girl who used to work behind the bar. I won because she couldn't stand the smell. Of course, I keep myself fit as well.'

Mordent was about to say he noticed, but then you couldn't tell with the younger generation. However open they seemed to be sometimes an off-the-cuff remark could be considered inappropriate. It was a peculiar quirk that in a society where everything was more open than it ever was, offence could be taken so quickly.

As it was, he didn't have the opportunity to answer. The barmaid went to serve three men who had arrived and almost simultaneously the music was muted and the lights were marginally raised. The show was about to begin.

A rotund man who looked as if he might be wearing bubblewrap under his tight-fitting black suit walked out into the centre of the circle. His oriental appearance was borderline racist. A Charlie Chan moustache curved to fine points several inches either side of his head, and a conical Asian hat gave him a lampshade quality. Despite the suit, he wore red and gold Chinese slippers on his feet. It was clear the furthest East he'd ever been was to an East Side buffet restaurant.

The more Mordent thought about it, the more he realised sumo wasn't associated with the Chinese. The man didn't seem to be bothered by this as he introduced the evening's entertainment in a mangled Asian accent.

Mordent wasn't sure what he had been expecting, but if he *had* considered it then he wouldn't have been disappointed. His disappointment only stemmed from the fact that he *should* have considered it.

Two skinny males encased in bubblewrap emerged from behind a screen which – at a stretch – gave them the body forms of traditional sumo wrestlers. Being semi-transparent even through multiple layers, he could see they wore nothing other than underpants. This elicited shrieks from the bachelorette tables despite the physiognomy of the contestants. To be fair, Mordent knew if he stripped to his underwear he would be met with similar shrieks. They had reached that part of the evening.

The costumes weren't costumes as such, merely roll upon roll of bubblewrap looped around various appendages. Where a sumo's belt might be, the bubblewrap was thickened. There was something decidedly non-professional about the whole debacle. If Mordent had hoped for something salacious it was clear he was on a loser. His eyes strayed vicariously to the barmaid tapping her fingernails at the other end of the bar.

Heads down, the wrestlers powered into each other, the dance music cranked up, the clientele fired up, and after ten seconds one of the wrestlers was pushed out of the ring. The faux-Chinese raised the arm of the winner - decidedly non-Japanese all round - and after the loser left the circle another contender entered the fray.

Mordent ordered then drained another bourbon as a succession of scrawny males did *battle* within the ring. After a while he realised that the contenders were on a loop, that there wasn't a procession of bubblewrapped opponents, and that maybe the winners were fighting winners and the losers fighting losers or maybe none of that mattered at all. He no longer cared.

After the nth bout he realised the barmaid was at his shoulder. When she spoke, minute hairs on his right ear vibrated and goosebumped that side of his body down his arm and into his leg.

'It'll pick up in a minute. They'll get volunteers.'

'It needs to pick up quite a bit for me to stay here.'

'Don't be like that. Have another drink.'

Mordent did.

Mr Chinese raised the arm of what appeared to be the final winner, and then asked for four people for audience participation. As expected, all hands were raised from the bachelorette table and despite the barmaid's assurance that those who were drunk would not be allowed to take part, the bride-to-be and three of her coterie were hauled behind the stage. Mordent steadied himself for a wait, the bubbles wouldn't wrap themselves, and sure enough several minutes of the increasingly execrable dance music pounded his ears before the first two were announced onto the stage. The barmaid was right, it was *more* interesting.

Bizarrely they had been stripped to their underwear. Or at least, Mordent assumed it was *their* underwear. It might indeed be the quality of clothing that the members of a bachelorette party might wear on a night where they could expect to have fun, or it could be the management's idea of what underwear would be more suited to the gazes of an attentive audience, either way it was cut low back and front although the inhabitants held no shyness for displaying their wares. When they faced each other Mordent felt the stirrings of an erection in his trousers, undampened by an alcoholic haze. This was clearly a different kind of fight.

Yet, as it began, their tentative forays simply served to indicate how *good* the men had been. Those battles had lasted seconds due to technique, not the lack of it. The females danced around each other, lunged and held back, even the barmaid could be heard sighing. Any sense of the erotic dissipated as beads of swelled sweat formed as clear bubbles within the confines of the suit and mascara ran like black treacle tipped into a waterfall. Eventually, one of them fell backwards out of the ring.

The bouts continued. Mordent had another bourbon. With each drink the age gap between himself and the barmaid diminished and became more of a reason than a deterrent. He decided to make a fool of himself, but when he turned around there'd been a shift change and he stared at the watery eyes of a middle-aged male polishing glasses as though he were Morgan's replacement displaced to the wrong bar.

Show over, Mordent stumbled from the stool, ploughed his way through the tables, then fell into the cool outside air which accentuated his drunkenness even as it cleared it.

He considered his car. Reconsidered it. The name *Berenice Mordent* floated into his head with a crushing sensation that the sumo hadn't averted. He leant against someone else's car. The stars had come out. After a while he realised he was looking up. He had slid to the pavement.

The noise of several pairs of stiletto heels rattled across the sidewalk like spiders walking on stilts. Mordent eased himself to a sitting position. The bachelorette party was breaking up. One of the girls who had been in a sumo outfit had forgotten to get dressed, she had her clothes in her right hand, bubblewrap in her left, and neither hand knew what the other was doing. Some of the group hailed a taxi and half of them split. Mordent watched as they tottered down the street, which he then realised was wet from rain. Damp had settled in his trousers and pooled around his genitals. He was in a puddle.

Heaving to his feet he thought about driving. Thought again. Then he beeped open the doors before crawling onto the back seat.

This was how he welcomed morning.

10
A Cursory Glance

It was cold in the vehicle. Mordent woke the wrong kind of stiff. His back ached from the chill and the alcoholic residue in his mouth was the antithesis of the night before. He had a violent urge to urinate. One arm had come part-way out of his jacket overnight and was held in a crooked position in a half-nelson behind his back. He fought to put it straight through the sleeve and the resulting blood rush pin-pricked his flesh, made him shake his arm until it felt dismembered.

He sat on the back seat, slipped his feet into his shoes. Condensation clouded the vehicle's windows, proof of his existence. He wiped the nearest side window with his palm. In the pale sunlight the façade of the sumo club looked like a seaside resort out of season, any glamour it might have held in hibernation. He supposed one of the exterior lights had malfunctioned at the club, a flickering blue sheen tried to bleed through the condensation of the windscreen but the water droplets refracted it into haze. Then he craned his neck and noticed a line of yellow police tape across the adjacent alleyway. There was an elbow of uniform, a glimpse of authority. He imagined only the condensation had prevented a knock to the door of his vehicle. He was sure his registration had been noted and there was little to be had in climbing into the front seat and driving away.

Not that he had anything to hide other than embarrassment.

Reaching over the vehicle's front seats he pulled down the passenger mirror and checked his appearance, not out of vanity but respect. His eyes were bloodshot. He looked - quite simply - like a man who had slept in a car. Strips of hair stuck up from his head as though gelled. He smoothed them down, then wet his fingers and did it again. He rubbed his hand over his eyes, extracted sleep grains. He removed his jacket, smoothed his shirt, then replaced it. He thought for a moment. From the glove box he pulled out deodorant that had rust around the rim, then removed his jacket again, unbuttoned enough of his shirt to stick his arm inside, and sprayed his pits. He popped the deodorant back in the glove box, replaced his jacket and checked the mirror again.

He looked like a man who had slept in a car.

Sighing, he opened the door and stepped stiffly onto the street, hampered by his fixed position overnight and the pressure in his bladder.

The alley was the best location to relieve himself, but this morning it was also the worst.

He recognised the cop by the police tape. It was Davey. The kind of cop that Kovacs - the chief - loved. The kind of cop who did everything by the book.

Where was Marsham when he needed him?

'Davey. What's going on?'

Davey looked him up and down, the way an electronic sensor might scan product.

'Official police business.'

'I can see that. So what's happened?'

Davey bristled, puffing out his chest, emphasising his officiousness. 'I'm not able to tell you.'

'Davey.' Mordent felt repeating the name might crack the surface. Might. 'You know me. I was on the force. Curiosity doesn't fade.'

'The operative word is *was*. You have no right to know just as any member of the public has no right to know. Should it prove in the public interest a statement will be released to the press which no doubt you'll read in the papers. At the moment, this remains official police business.'

Mordent raised an eyebrow as a figure dressed in a one-piece white overall and matching hat emerged at the top of the alley and into the CSI van parked near the flashing lights of the police vehicle.

'Looks like they're giving the game away. Why don't we play charades? Just tell me how many words and consonants and if I guess then its fair play.'

Davey advanced towards him. 'Back off.'

Mordent held his ground. Then something in Davey's expression changed. The machinations of some members of the force were fascinating to watch, and Davey's thought processes resembled the cogs and gears of a particularly slow piece of equipment.

'What were you doing parked there?'

'You want the truth? Sleeping off a hangover.'

Davey's eyes scanned the street. The sumo club was the only bar nearby.

'You were drinking there last night?'

'Yes.'

Davey was suddenly caught between asking questions and giving information away.

'What time did you leave?'

Mordent gestured to the car. 'I can't really say I *did* leave.'

'You know what I mean?'

'Are you questioning me officially, or just asking about my social life?'

Davey glanced down the alleyway. 'Neither. I'll have to let Kovacs know you were here.'

'Kovacs will love that. C'mon Davey. What's it all about?'

'I'm not authorised to tell you. Don't make it difficult.'

'Difficult. It's so easy. All you have to do is open your mouth and...'

Davey advanced again. Reflexively his hand went to his holster.

It was Mordent's turn to postulate. 'You make a move on me Davey and you'll go from commando to commode in thirty seconds.'

'You threatening an officer of the law?'

'I didn't say anything. You're the one who appears trigger happy. You know the penalty for pointing or discharging a firearm without due cause? I do because I've done it. You know what Kovacs is like for following protocol. You'll be out on your ear before you can say Jack Robinson.'

'Who?'

'Exactly.'

Davey mumbled something about doing his job. Mordent scratched overnight stubble. The argument had dissipated and Mordent was torn between leaving and wondering if his presence might be linked to whatever had happened. He certainly hadn't heard anything during the night, not even his own drunken snoring.

He leant against his vehicle. Davey was as defused as a dampened firework. He thought of engaging him again in conversation but knew he'd never crack. Truth was, he really *didn't* need to know what had happened in the alley. Crimes occurred hourly in the city. It was only his proximity which sustained a half-beat of interest. Yet something kept him there, old-fashioned curiosity or just an absence of inclination to go anywhere else. Something to occupy his mind was also a form of misdirection, he briefly allowed himself to acknowledge. So he remained leaning against the car whilst the CSI team did their work, Davey throwing him dirty looks from time to time just to keep his hand in.

Twenty minutes passed. The sun began to dominate the skyline, rising above the taller buildings and pressing its heat upon the day. Mordent felt himself warming up, loosening up. He stretched his arms and his back followed suit. It was as though he were growing into the day. He felt flexible, viable, as though he could handle anything. He started to shake off the dog that the name Berenice Mordent had leashed to him and decided he might even begin to pet it. Would it matter if he had a long lost daughter? If she was old enough to make enquiries then she was old enough to be independent. Suddenly the thought of existing beyond his years didn't seem so bad.

At that moment he recognised one of the CSI's advancing up the alley. Mordent waited whilst he divested himself of the protective overall, latex gloves, and paper shoes and folded them carefully into an evidence bag. Thomas Kearney. They had once worked together on a case which Mordent could no longer remember, but he did recall their easy camaraderie. Kearney lit himself a smoke and wandered over. It appeared introductions didn't need to be re-established.

'Mordent.' He stuck out a hand.

Mordent held it. 'Kearney.'

'Good to see you. What are you doing here?'

'Was just passing. How goes it?'

'Kinda routine. Just waiting for the pathologist so we can move the body. Suffocation.'

Mordent glanced towards Davey who was visibly seething but powerless along the chain of command.

'Nasty.'

'Pretty girl in just her underwear. Now this is the weird thing, the killer used bubblewrap.'

'Bubblewrap?'

'You know the stuff they use in packaging: bubblewrap. He'd wrapped it - excuse the pun - around her head. I say *he* of course, but that's just a figure of speech. Asphyxiated. Probably took some time. No marks around her neck, a few bruises on her shoulders, both sides. We've done a quadrant search but can't find a trace of much unusual. No signs of sexual contact but that's a cursory glance. The pathologist has been held up in rush hour traffic. We'll know more when he arrives. Anyway, good to see you again. You still keeping your hand in? I heard you were PI nowadays.'

'That's right,' Mordent said. 'Was good to see you again Kearney. Take care of yourself.'

Kearney nodded and flicked the end of his cigarette into the gutter. 'See you around.'

Mordent watched Kearney disappear into the CSI vehicle and then he took a look at his watch. He had the information he wanted - whether in fact he wanted it or not. Now there were more pressing matters. Literally, the force of his bladder. He smiled at Davey as he got into his vehicle and then drove away from the scene of the crime. In his rear view mirror he saw Davey make a note of his licence plate.

11
An Emotion Induced By A Perceived Threat

Mordent headed straight to his office. Ideally he would have bounded the stairs two at a time, but the cramps in his lower body curtailed his motion whilst he desperately attempted to appear normal to the secretarial temps who passed him by. When he finally reached the toilet and relieved himself it was as though he were draining the sixty percent water that made up his body mass, as though a plug had been pulled amidst his internal organs. The force was almost enough to lift him off his feet.

After that, he had to sit.

He wondered about the girl in the alley. Wondered what wouldn't have happened if he hadn't been so drunk. Was she another ghost who could point an accusing finger like all the others? Had he failed her?

He decided he couldn't be responsible for all the murders in the city. If anything was responsible, then it was the city itself.

City murders were different to country murders. They were no less gruesome but usually more inventive. Those who were murdered were less likely to be known by their murderers. Botched thefts were more frequent, drugs obviously so. And the cloak of noir which entangled the city during the hours of darkness was a co-conspirator in matters of violence. Country sky darkness was wide open; city darkness was closed.

There weren't many noir movies set in the countryside, and when they were the spaces were conduits for moving from one city to another, a period of respite - even in pursuit - where the darkness wasn't so dominant.

Mordent ran a finger along a gouge in the wooden surface of his desk. He couldn't recall its provenance. It *might* have been a knife wound, it could have been a bullet's channel. It was perhaps as innocuous as running a pen back and forth within a natural groove. From some clients it might have been a stare. Days were slow when all he had to focus on was this. He stood and walked to the window, misted it with his breath - created a fog where there was none. But the residents didn't notice and they went about their business as normal. Someone down there was the bubblewrap killer.

He turned the words over in his mind. No doubt the story would get into the papers and their determination to fix a name on a non-entity would glamorise the murderer. Mordent didn't want bubblewrap associated with death. On some days it was all he had.

His cell vibrated in his pocket. Mordent's awareness returned by degrees, like waking from a dream. He always set the phone to vibrate for this reason, a physical and subtle sonic nudge; something he couldn't mistake for the radio.

The display indicated Emmeline Edwards.

'Mordent.'

'Of course! I have the information you require. Shall we meet in say an hour's time? There's a tea room I'm familiar with. I'll give you the address.'

Mordent scrabbled open his desk drawer for pen and paper. The tea room was in an area of the city he rarely had cause to visit. The crime rate was low. Not surprisingly for a tea room. He could have sworn Emmeline blew him a kiss when she put down the phone, but it wasn't a beige thing to do.

He was half out the door when his phone vibrated a second time. Mordent spoke to Marsham as he descended into the bowels of the building where his car was parked in the underground lot.

'I've got you some information on the Fear Institute but it isn't much.'

'Fire away.'

'It was established about twenty years ago by Copernicus Fear. That's genuinely his real name. We haven't had any contact with the organisation on an official basis until recently when an allegation was lodged by Benedict Holmsworth, nephew of another Benedict Holmsworth - just to confuse things – that his uncle was somehow murdered by the organisation. This wasn't taken forwards because there was no real evidence for the claim.'

'You didn't interview?'

'Nope. Benedict – the live one – claimed his uncle was frightened to death. The coroner's report indicated a heart attack. We're not into spurious allegations. Kovacs took a look at it and closed it down pretty quick.'

'Anything unusual in that?'

'Nope. He's recently been signing off all these types of enquiries. You know what he's like.'

Mordent did.

'So that's it. Nothing else?'

'I checked out any previous on Copernicus Fear and nothing comes up. He was professor of some university back in the sixties. He's eighty-four years old. Nothing else of interest. So what's the deal?'

'Benedict Holmsworth is paying me your salary to look into his uncle's death.'

Marsham laughed. 'String it out for as long as you can. Those kinds of nutters have money to burn.'

'Maybe. Listen, there's something else. A death this morning I heard about. You got anything on that?'

'It was a long night Mordent. You've got half a dozen to pick from. Which one.'

'I'll pitch a guess it was the most unusual.'

'Easy. The guy found stuffed into a dog kennel with one of those pet cones around his neck.'

'Ok, not the most unusual but getting there.'

'Second choice would be the guy sliced from the waist down, with his legs staggered to form steps like in a Salvador Dali painting.'

'You're kidding me.'

'Nope.'

'Third choice?'

'It'd be third and fourth choices. The couple found in the refuse truck presumably having coitus when they were crushed to death.'

'You're making this up.'

'Not at all.'

'So what is the *less* weird?'

'The girl in her underwear suffocated by bubblewrap.'

'That's the one I was enquiring about.'

'Details are sketchy on that one. The club next door runs a sumo bubblewrap evening which apparently she took part in. They're trying to track down CCTV who was in the club that evening. That includes you, apparently.'

'So you knew who I was calling about all along!'

'Of course.'

'And those other murders?'

'All legitimate. She really was the least unusual last night.'

'And nothing further to report?'

'Nope. Did you want me to keep you informed? Although I'm not sure I can do that considering you're a potential suspect.'

'You're not Kovacs, Marsham.'

'Damn right I'm not. I'll let you know if anything else turns up. Pathologist confirmed suffocation after you left the crime scene.'

'The vicinity, Marsham, the vicinity.'

'Yeh, whatever. What *were* you doing there? Davey reckons you were asleep in your vehicle.'

'I was. Davey's not the brightest Roman candle in the box. And I doubt that *he's* ever slept in a car in his life. It was just a drunken night, is all.'

'And you didn't see or hear anything?'

'If I did, would I be calling you?'

'It was me who called you. Anyway, consider your interview concluded. I'll write a report on it although you might still hear from Kovacs.'

'He won't be able to keep away.'

'Maybe not, but he'll do it by the book. You can be sure of that.'

Mordent agreed.

He had waited at the bottom of the stairwell whilst speaking to Marsham. In the underground lot the signal often failed. Now he opened the heavy exit door and walked across the concourse. He was right about the city and the country. Murders were different here. They were unique and bizarre and often quite wonderful in a voyeuristic way. And they kept the police force entertained. Sometimes he wondered if they were committed for that purpose.

The interior of the car smelt like he had slept in it.

He opened the windows and stale parking lot air mingled with his afterglow, tyre friction burns and discarded fast food wrappers. He revved the car up the exit ramp onto the street, imagined its apex leading to a line of greyhound buses which he cleared with ease. Landing on his front two tyres he wove through traffic and caused another vehicle to jerk into a fire hydrant, sending a water jet to arc skywards, simultaneously putting out the fire on the car which subsequently exploded.

He wished.

Traffic was jammed. He thrummed his fingers on the dashboard to the melodic jazz from his favourite radio station. Each of the surrounding vehicles contained pockets of civilisation. The certainty that man lived both together and alone fascinated him. The number of lives with their individual mannerisms, habits, and thoughts was inconceivable, so it was much simpler to believe that it was impossible. Mordent could nail his life to five people, if that. Although, again, *Berenice Mordent* swam into his mind and he thought of the piece of paper holding her phone number sitting on his dining room table, begging to be actioned.

As he slowly made his way across the city adjacent cars turned aside and were replaced as though he were the central figure in a display of synchronised swimmers. The closer he came to his destination the smarter the cars were replacing those discarded. Eventually they thinned out and his progress was less impeded, although his vehicle which had an aura of quality on *his* side of the city, now resembled a dog turd on a red carpet. Parking a block away from the tea room he made the remainder of the journey on foot, strangely eager for another meeting with Emmeline Edwards.

She was already waiting inside. She wore a beige top festooned with tiny black hearts, like a cake discovered by ants. On the table in front of her was a large pot of tea, two cups in saucers, and two cakes filled with cream. She stood when he entered, as though the tinkling of the door bell animated her, and offered a lace gloved hand. Mordent took it, the sensation of the lace against his palm resembled a circuit board. He expected an electrical jolt.

The scenario was much different from climbing four urine-stained floors to arrive puffing at Hubie's apartment, knocking and waiting whilst he squirreled away a partially clad *lady* into his side room then reassembling his clothing before opening the door. Mordent wasn't sure if he found the difference comfortable.

'Mr Mordent.'

'Emmeline.'

'Shall we sit?'

He rested opposite on a wooden chair which squeaked as he drew it closer to the table. The tea room was sparsely occupied. All those occupants were female at the higher end of the social spectrum. He was reminded of British television shows, those fixated on the upper classes, a relationship he understood to be love/hate. Emmeline filled his empty cup and then asked if he wanted *one lump or two* before picking up sugarcubes in metal tongs and dropping them into his cup with a dash of milk.

The reflection of a smile flittered around her face. Mordent realised she was enjoying his discomfort.

'This isn't my usual kind of hangout,' he said.

'I know. Nor mine. But the internet is a wonder for finding new and curious places, don't you think?'

'You don't always meet here?'

She shook her head. 'When you're in my line of work its preferable not to be found in the same place twice. You can understand that.'

'Hubie had no problem with it.'

She leant forward. 'Hubie was a man.' She leant back. 'The feminists wouldn't agree with me but men are the dominant sex; actually, they would agree with me when it comes to the dominant sex for potential harassment. Because I'm a woman, some men would see no problem taking advantage of me. Hubie invited you into his home. I never will.'

Mordent wondered if he were disappointed in that, then realised that even the thought itself corresponded to the male stereotype. Emmeline seemed to eat into him that way. Modern life was so confusing.

Emmeline leant forwards and picked up one of the cakes. 'I hope you don't mind,' she said, 'but I buttered your scone for you.'

He nodded, confused. When he bit into the scone he found it soft and yielding, the cream and jam sweet - almost luxurious. He wiped crumbs off his lips with his fingers. 'I've never had one of these before. It's delicious.'

She smiled. 'Good. Now, shall I tell you what I know of the Fear Institute?'

Mordent nodded.

'Do you know what fear is, Mordent? Fear is an emotion induced by a perceived threat. It doesn't have to be an actual threat, just one that our brains believe to be. That's quite a significant difference. Phobias often stem from unnecessary threats. Spiders are an obvious example. Yes, some spiders are poisonous and some can kill, but people in climates with no deadly spiders can still perceive the creature as a threat and be scared of it. That's irrational. What the Fear Institute specialises in is dealing with those irrational fears. They provide a service where the fear is confronted. Are you with me so far?'

Mordent nodded. His cheeks stuffed with scone.

'The institute is run by Copernicus Fear. So quaint! It is his real name. He's in his eighties. It seems to be a labour of love rather than an actual business, considering his age. He's a retired university professor. One of my client's knows someone who knows someone who knew someone who was *treated* by the institute. They had a fear of woodlice. Insect fears are quite common, it seems. Anyway, he was cured. Hypnotism, apparently. Do you have a fear, Mr Mordent?'

He considered the question carefully. Having faced death several times he was no longer sure if he was scared of it. In any event, it was hardly an irrational fear – nor one easily eradicated. So what *did* scare him? He decided to throw a curve ball.

'I'm afraid that my view of the world as a noir existence, populated by black and white dames with silver guns, is not the real world.'

Emmeline smiled. 'You're a fantasist, Mr Mordent.'

'I prefer the word *optimist*.'

'My ex-husband called me an optimist and himself a pessimist. I preferred the terms fantasist and realist. Of course, we all live in the real world, but it is decidedly a real world of our own making. Which is also a fantasy. The two can co-exist, can they not?'

'I guess so.'

'Indeed, your noir fantasy overlays the reality of the world in which you live. But if you genuinely view the world through noir-tinted glasses – and haven't been joking with me – then you are indeed living both realities simultaneously. Has that something to do with quantum theory? I'm afraid I'm a little dim in my knowledge of physics.'

'You've got me on that one.'

'Well, anyway, it's immaterial. The world in which we live only exists as we imagine it. And in that respect so do our fears. I would suggest, Mr Mordent, that should you wish to investigate the Fear Institute that you invent a fear to present them to eradicate. Doing so will embroil you in their practices and you can investigate them from the inside out.'

Mordent sipped his tea. It had cooled and was sweet and weak.

'That isn't a bad suggestion. Have you any other thoughts on the Fear Institute?'

'It's a sham, of course. But a legitimate sham. There are plenty of organisations willing to take money from the gullible public who do so without falling foul of the law. Take the church, for example. Other than that, from my knowledge and the knowledge of those I have consulted, it seems harmless.'

Mordent drained the remainder of his tea. Speckles of leaf floated in the milky residue like the Viet Cong viewed from a helicopter over the Mekong River.

'Couldn't you have told me this over the telephone?'

She laughed. 'Of course, but how boring would that have been. I do need some kind of social life you know.'

Mordent raised an eyebrow.

'On a purely professional level,' she added.

Mordent called over the waitress and reached for his billfold. 'I'll get these.'

Emmeline put her hand over his. 'My treat.' She pulled out a beige purse and the waitress left with money in hand. 'Besides,' she added, 'I don't want you paying my fees in public. Consider this inaugural meeting on the house.' She reached into her purse again and pulled out a different business card with a bank account number on it - no other details. 'Just transfer any future fees into this account. It's easier that way.'

'You said before it was COD?'

'Sometimes you have to bait the line in order catch a fish.'

Mordent nodded. Doing business with Emmeline was proving smooth and interesting.

12
Kiss Me In The Monk's Quarters

Mordent washed the weak tea residue with a shot of bourbon in Morgan's Bar.

Outside, bright day hammered on the windows, pushing ethereal tendrils into the bar which then retracted like children touching flame. There were few clientele. Morgan was watching a gameshow on the television he kept muted in an alcove on his side of the bar. It wasn't public facing. Mordent imagined there would be uproar should Morgan decide to revamp; fancy it out with modern décor, a selection of wines, table service. He pushed the thought out of his head just as the daylight was forced back into the day. It wouldn't happen.

He thought of his discussion with Emmeline. Wondered whether the fear of a Morgan's Wine Bar and Bistro might be something the Institute could consider a phobia. His kneejerk reaction that he feared nothing was correct on reflection. He considered himself immutable in that regard. But the idea of phobias had always intrigued him, to the extent that one of his favourite television shows had been *Monk*.

Monk was a police procedural series which ran for eight seasons and Mordent was fairly certain he had seen most of those episodes. He enjoyed the *Here's What Happened* segments where Adrian Monk would reveal how the crime had been committed. These segments were screened in black and white. Mordent had always considered it a nod to noir. It didn't matter if it wasn't. He enjoyed them all the same.

When it came to phobias Monk would have been the perfect subject for the Fear Institute. He had three hundred and twelve. Mordent had once decided to memorise some as part of a mental exercise, so he knew they included but were not limited to odontophobia, mysophobia, trypanophobia, lactophobia, necrophobia, ophidiophobia, mycophobia, acrophobia, enochlophobia and liftophobia. He wondered whether to present himself as Monk to the Institute. Emmeline's suggestion that he self-refer was logical, and he could include their fee as part of his expenses. So long as he had no genuine fear there was no worry - as Benedict might assume - that he might be scared to death.

He ordered another bourbon. It coursed down his throat like a skier on fire. Maybe those phobias were too distanced from his reality to be effective. He remembered scanning a list of Monk's hang-ups online, drawing parallels with his own life, and in amusement wondering whether a certain item might be mentioned. But it was conspicuous by its absence: *bubblewrap*.

He smiled as he realised he had a way in to the Institute.

Downing the remainder of his drink he looked around the bar as though expecting a round of applause.

The bar stared back at him.

Kiss me in the monk's quarters.

He remembered saying this to his ex-wife, Maria, when she had dragged him along to the Zen Mountain Monastery in the Catskills during a period where she was *finding herself* although he hadn't known she was lost. As it turned out, it was Mordent who was lost, both on the journey there and on the way home when he realised Maria wasn't who he wanted her to be. They had wandered around the site one Sunday morning, the loose-fitting clothing Maria had bought made him feel like a sheet in the wind. They were on a tour rather than within a group accessing the formal programs, but Maria had been full of questions about participating in the *zazen* and attending a *retreat*. The only retreat Mordent wanted was backwards home.

During a break they had a few moments to themselves and that was when Mordent said, *Kiss me in the monk's quarters*.

It was nonsense and Maria wasn't amused. She pushed him away.

'You're not taking this seriously.'

'You're taking it *too* seriously.'

'Is there anything wrong with that?'

'For you, no. For me, well...'

'You're so selfish.'

'Can't you do this without me?'

And so the conversation continued within the tranquil grounds of the Zen Mountain Monastery.

Whenever Mordent thought of Monk he was transported to those simple wood and brick buildings with the open interiors filled with sunlight reflecting off the polished wooden floors like swimming pools in syrup, the A-frames resembling the apexes of man-made mountains pushing up from verdant green, the tranquillity of the Basho pond and the produce in the vegetable garden, the argument with Maria and the drive home when he determined he could no longer be faithful. Of course, it would be a few years later that she would discover this.

Adrian Monk held no connection as far as Mordent was aware to any monastery, other than language; just as Mordent's *Monk's Quarters* reference had been a pathetic play on words; a terrible insinuation. As he deliberated whether to order another drink he considered how his life had spooled around certain mannerisms and words, become entangled with people and places until he was positioned on a stool in a darkened bar with a potential daughter standing in the background, obfuscated by confusion and the steady passage of time.

The scrap of paper called to him from his dining table.

13
Kin

Mordent wrung himself dry after a shower. Water coursed down wrinkles in his body like rain finding a path through bark. He had slept since those drinks in Mordent's bar, wanted his head clear before he made the call which he now knew to be inevitable. Once dressed, he sat at his dining table, with the piece of paper in front of him, together with a glass of orange juice and breakfast: a bagel two days old.

Holding out his hands he found that they wavered. So unlike him. His heart was hammering too.

What would it be for this woman to be his daughter? What changes would that affect?

Still, he had to make the call. She was close enough to find him, he couldn't bury her and remain static. And if she sought him out he would backpedal, deny. Contact had to be on his terms.

It was early enough in the day for her to be at home, it wasn't too early to wake her. Clouds blotted the sky, soaking up moisture. It would rain later, with steady persistence, and the city would gather its noir hue and Mordent would be comfortable within it, a drop of ink within ink. Until then, sporadic sunlight illuminated then shaded him, the glare of a spotlight, his life in the frame.

Procrastinating no longer he picked up his cell and

punched in the numbers. It rang four times before it was answered.

'Hullo?' *Sleepyvoicequiet.*

A pause. 'Is this Berenice?'

'Yes, who is this?'

'Is this Berenice Mordent?'

There was gasp. It was primal. She was his daughter.

'It is, isn't it? It *is* Berenice Mordent.'

'Dad?' The word was barely a breath, but it passed through the phone and into Mordent's body taking his own breath with it. His stomach muscles clenched involuntarily, and with that squeeze he felt tears gather at the corners of his eyes. Wrung out again.

He opened his mouth but his throat was a cave sealed by a boulder.

On the other end of the phone he could hear Berenice crying, huge wracking sobs which made him want to put his arms around her in a way he had never wanted to hold anyone in his life.

It fucked with his head.

'I need to see you.' These were his words.

Empty space punctuated by gasps.

'I can't today.'

Mordent pulled it together. 'Tomorrow. Mid-morning? There's a deli called Bukowski's.' He gave the address.

'I guess I can do that.'

They were holding back. Everything demanded immediacy but it couldn't be rushed. Certainties needed to be established.

'This is awkward,' she finally said. Mordent considered her tone of voice, the way the words left her mouth, the choices she made with them. So much to discover.

'Let's leave it until tomorrow,' he said; then added, 'but call if you need to.'

'I will.'

'Bye.'

'Bye.'

He terminated the call.

Questions.

Questions.

Questions.

He pushed them out of his head and they pushed back.

He found he was sweating. He wiped his palms on his trousers and then drank some of the orange juice. It needed a little something.

He stood, swayed; sudden dizziness brought the sides of the building in on him as though it were reconstructed through computer generated imagery. He recalled the movie *Dark City*, an SF film with noir trappings, where memories and cityscapes were altered overnight by an alien agency attempting to isolate the soul.

His soul was isolated.

Beside his sofa was a half-empty bottle of bourbon.

He regarded it as his vision steadied and formed the object whole.

It was too early in the morning. He repeated the thought to himself: *it's too early in the morning*.

It *was* too early in the morning.

He was a father now.

14
A Pair Of Curtains

The previous afternoon he had made a different telephone call; one to the offices of The Fear Institute where he had booked himself an initial appointment to assess how they might assist with his phobia.

The secretary taking the calls was male. Conforming to his stereotype Mordent couldn't keep disappointment out of his voice. He was a product of an age that came later than noir but nevertheless still viewed women as broads and dames in a way he never considered derogatory but simply the parcelling of the flesh.

'Can I book an appointment?'

'Certainly. Let me take some details.'

Mordent provided a false name: Raymond Greener.

'And if it doesn't trouble you, Mr Greener, may I take a note of the phobia you wish us to cure?'

'It's bubblewrap.'

'Excellent. We have an appointment tomorrow afternoon if it would suit?'

Now, driving towards the Fear Institute, Mordent attempted to focus his mind on bubblewrap rather than the conversation he had with Berenice.

As promised, the clouds had filled like cotton wool dipped in ink. Rain wasn't forthcoming but the horizon darkened similar to a child closing the lid of a toy box during a game of hide and seek. Mordent hunched his shoulders accordingly, prepared for a deluge that wouldn't come, one that he was, in fact, protected from by the vehicle. Evolutionary habits died hard. Drivers popped on their lights, their beams emitting glows like a shoal of deep-sea angler fish of the bathypelagic zone. The city itself hunkered down, darkness absorbing the remaining light, and although he drove a straight line Mordent felt he were descending, sinking like a woolly mammoth into the tar pit of La Brea.

The Fear Institute was packed into an early brick building sandwiched between two modern carapaces in much the same way as St Patrick's Cathedral in Manhattan was squashed between skyscrapers. The windows looked authoritarian, a series of panes like frames in a film, elongated at the bottom with smaller panes above, segmented by heavy wooden surrounds. *The Fear Institute* was lettered halfway up the two-storey structure in what appeared to be Times New Roman font. A faux arch doorway was blocked by an oak door. It might have been placed there from Europe. It certainly looked placed there from somewhere.

Mordent found a nearby parking spot and waited. He was socially acceptably early, but took a few minutes to pull on the persona of his antithesis: Raymond Greener, bubblewrap phobic.

It wasn't going to be an easy task.

Leaving his gun in the car he wandered across to the building. The door was locked. He could see no bell but there was a heavy metal knocker in the shape of a wreath that he pulled back and released with a bang. The door was too thick to hear footsteps down a hall, and so when it sharply opened he was taken by surprise.

A tall, thin man, not out of place in the original Addams Family, pulled back the door as though emerging from behind a curtain. Mordent was reminded of the old Doctor Doctor joke:

Doctor Doctor, I feel like a pair of curtains.

Pull yourself together.

Although he preferred:

Doctor Doctor, I can't stop dressing in Saran wrap.

Well, I can clearly see you're nuts.

Perhaps this was appropriate considering the pseudo-medical nature of the Fear Institute. He wondered if Copernicus Fear was a doctor in any form of the word, or whether he had a string of letters after his name. In any event, it was clear that it wasn't Mr Fear himself who had opened the door.

'Can I help you?'

'I have 2pm appointment this afternoon.'

'Mr Bubblewrap?'

'That's me.'

'Please come inside. You must forgive me for not recalling your name, but here at the Fear Institute we tend to categorise people by their phobias. Those are much easier to remember than names.'

Mordent followed the man, skinnier than an atomic shadow, into the depths of the building. It was all dark wood-panelling and muted light. Mordent was sure this was to create an effect for the client, that of leaving the real world behind, a sanctuary where their phobias could be discussed, rather than the original layout of the building. There was something false about it which could be described as typically-American from disparaging European TV shows he sometimes settled on when channel surfing. He knew what it was - fake archaic. He thought of this as he watched the man's shoes clip the polished oaken floor.

'This way please.'

The man gesticulated into a small room and allowed Mordent to pass through, closing the door behind him. There was more wood panelling than the stockroom of a timber yard. Books were lined around all four walls, but as Mordent looked a little closer he realised the repetition of the colours of their spines indicated wallpaper rather than actual tomes. Behind a large oak desk a swivel chair faced away from him. He couldn't tell if it were occupied. He decided to stand with his hands in front of him, lightly clasped together, because either way he had the sensation of being watched.

'Years ago,' a voice began, 'I had a phobia of being ignored. It debilitated me. Hampered me in all my activities. I didn't know what to do.'

The voice was slow, measured and old. Mordent assumed it belong to Copernicus Fear. It came from the direction of the chair.

It continued: 'What was I to do? Nothing? You don't get christened Copernicus without being given a modicum of courage. So I advanced against the phobia, I made it clear that I wanted to be known, and soon enough I was. That's what you need to do, Mr Greener, rage against the machinations of your phobia. You will find the solution lands in your lap.'

The chair swung around, not quite as elegantly as the occupant intended.

'My name is Copernicus Fear and I am here to relieve you of your fear.'

Mordent stared at the diminutive individual held in the chair similar to a baseball mitt holds a ball. The performance contained an aura of amateur theatrics that seemed archaic and unnecessary. Mordent wondered how many times Copernicus had swung himself around in that chair, not only before an audience but in practice, getting the movement of his legs just right. Yet to smile would undermine his presence, so he advanced towards the desk and pushed himself firmly into character as a coin might make an impression in putty.

'Mr Fear, I'm pleased to make your acquaintance. I am Raymond Greener.' He stuck out his hand.

'Forgive me if I do not rise, Mr Greener, nor if I cannot reach your hand over the desk. Whilst the years have been kind to my mental faculties I'm afraid my flesh is not as supple as it used to be. Consider your hand grasped and shaken.'

Mordent nodded then took a seat. Copernicus Fear had obviously studied business management during his long life, as his visitor's chair was markedly smaller and less comfortable than the one in which he sat. Mordent was also lower to the floor.

'Now,' Copernicus flipped through paperwork on his desk which must have contained more than Mordent had given over the telephone, 'let me see. Ah, here it is. Bubblewrap. Mr Greener, in your own words please, could you describe your phobia to me?'

'I can't remember when it began,' Mordent said, 'but I was transferred from an office job to packaging. We were downsized. I had to take books off a production line, wrap them in that material, and then stack them inside boxes for shipping. Each time I stacked a book I had to press down on it - the boxes weren't really fit for purpose. I mean, they fit the size of the books, but the bubblewrap wasn't accounted for. There were six of us in the storeroom. Each time you pressed down one of those bubbles would go off. It was like gunfire in there. Bang bang bang. Eventually I could hardly bear to press down on the wrap due to the expectation of the burst, and then the actual touch of the wrap under my palms began to irritate me, the sensation of the imminent implode encapsulated by the feel of the raised nub of the bubble. Eventually I applied for a transfer but the trauma remains. I can't view bubblewrap now without shuddering. It might sound ridiculous but I can't even touch the stuff. It's impacting on other job applications and it's getting me down. Do you think there's anything you can do to help me?'

Copernicus leant back on his swivel chair which squeaked loudly. 'That's quite some speech, Mr Greener. I can tell you've held that back for some time. At the Fear Institute we don't differentiate between one fear and another. Bubblewrap, innocuous as it might be to some, can be terrifying to others. It's not all about rats and spiders, heights and slights. You'll find our methods can be used to treat anything.'

'At a cost, I presume?'

'Naturally. Jones will give you our fee sheet on the way out. I prefer not to get involved with that side of things. My interests are purely psychological, but the building needs to be maintained, salaries require paying, that kind of thing.'

Mordent chanced his arm. 'Do you take donations?'

Copernicus laughed. 'Who wouldn't? But we're not here to bleed people dry. If, in the unlikely event our treatments don't work then we refund your contribution. But we do need part-payment up front. We trade in information, and once you have the information there's no guarantee you'll pay us. Far better that we take payment in advance. We don't have the acumen to chase people for money.'

'Can you give me an idea of how this all works?'

'Empowerment over your fear. It has to come from yourself. A little bit of hypnosis if required, but that's just to jog you along. We are the conduit for your recovery, but you are the catalyst. It might all sound mumbo jumbo right now, but eventually it will fall into place. Are you with us?'

'What's the first step?'

'Jones will sort you out. Consider our fees. We can set up a program once we know you're happy with us. But as an initial task buy some bubblewrap on your journey home and keep it visible in your apartment. You don't have to approach it, but interact if you can. Consider your reaction.'

Mordent stood. 'I'll do that Mr Fear. I imagine my situation is a little unusual. What other cases do you have?'

But Copernicus Fear seemed to have been absorbed into his seat. He closed his eyes. 'You'll have to excuse me, I get very tired. Jones will see you out.' And he swivelled the chair so he faced the opposite direction. As if they were connected the door behind Mordent opened and Jones stood there, an automaton.

'Over here, sir.'

Mordent left the room, picked up payment information from Jones, then left the building.

He shook his head. The meeting had resembled a Victorian fake séance show. All smoke and mirrors. He hadn't expected much else, but on reflection he had doubted his expectations.

Even so, if the Fear Institute was a front then it would take some digging to find out what was behind it.

And that meant more money in the Mordent Bank.

Benedict Holmsworth would need deep pockets.

15
Nemesis Snemesis

He drove to the office. Rain came slow and fat, too static for wiper use, and droplets sat across his windscreen as though the glass were covered by a sheet of bubblewrap. Should he have been Raymond Greener he would have crashed his vehicle, but Mordent's mind became tuned to Astrid and the quickening of her fingers; an all too agreeable pop.

Images remained in his head as he parked his car, and were imprinted on the females that he passed in the corridor who worked for the temp agency. It wasn't his fault that the reproductive pulse throbbed so violently in his mind. He needed release but had gone beyond the age of finding it vicariously. He decided to make an appointment with Astrid for later that week. She was often busy, and he tried not to let that fray his mind: the thought of her with other men.

His office phone began to ring as he struggled with the key in the lock, then stopped moments before he picked up the receiver. He wondered if he were being watched. Then his cell vibrated the fibres of his trousers. He pulled it out: Marsham.

'How's it going?' Marsham's voice was light, with an undercurrent of need.

'Fine. You got more information for me?'

'Nothing of note. Just giving you a heads up.

Kovacs wants you brought in. He thinks you were holding back on the bubblewrap case. I'm supposed to be fetching you myself, but I'm sure you know the way. Got any plans this afternoon?'

'Nothing I can't shift for Kovacs.'

'Best to keep your nose clean, right?'

'If you say so.'

'You know so.'

Marsham terminated the call. For some reason Mordent felt he'd been hauled over coals. Maybe Marsham was getting edgy over the information he held, and with Kovacs rattling cage bars there were trust issues at risk. Either way, Mordent didn't mind paying a social visit. He could do with winding up someone after a couple of days which had begun with him asleep in a vehicle at a murder scene, led to him contacting an unknown daughter, and then dancing a pantomime with an eighty-year-old psychologist. He could barely wait to return to his car.

Rain was a firework explosion as droplets caught light just before hitting his windscreen. Mordent drove blind, more by instinct than sense. Dark slewed sideways like trampled charcoal rubbings, the rain further blurring his vision; like an aircraft his route signposted solely by red and white lights. Or as though all cars were subway passengers, rubbing overcoats as the silver bullet shot into darkness, wobbling them one way then another.

Mordent's soul shone in this atmosphere, feeding from the dark, from the night, from the scattered lights refracted through rainwater, from the hulking bulks of the surrounding vehicles, from the pedestrians blurred on the sidewalk in their many-coloured raincoats, from the *swoosh* of puddle splashes and the monochrome gleam of surface water, from implications unseen and adventures yet to come. He was held in this darkness in much the same way as Copernicus Fear was clutched by his swivel chair. The embrace of the familiar, the safety of the known.

He was waved into the police car park. Despite his absence from the force he was still treated as *one* of them by *some* of them. The police commissioner's parking space beckoned but Mordent wasn't quite so cavalier. Instead he parked beside Kovacs' familiar vehicle, forwent the temptation to glance inside as the weather danced raindrops on his head like Chinese water torture gone mad.

Front of office an old colleague, Bartholomew, was behind the counter, pretending to work whilst he surfed the net.

'Mordent! How the devil are you?'

'I'm good Bartholomew. How's the wife and kids?'

Their banter had been an in-joke for years, a ritual unchanged, despite Bartholomew never having married. Yet the last time he was here a gold band encircled Bartholomew's finger and Mordent was glad to see that it remained.

'The wife is just fine, Mordent. Just fine. Still no kids though.'

Mordent was about to say *me neither,* when he remembered that he did - in fact, in theory - have a kid; even if she were a kid no more. Bartholomew noticed the shadow cross his face but let it lie.

'I take it Kovacs is in,' Mordent asked. 'I saw his car in the lot.'

Bartholomew nodded. 'He seems to live in his office nowadays, he leaves here less and less.'

'I imagine that impacts his home life.'

'You should be here when his wife calls,' smiled

Bartholomew. 'You know Kovacs does everything by the book, but I believe his wife does too.'

Mordent laughed. Kovacs had, in fact, written a book - *Kovacs' Guide To Modern Policing Procedures* - and he wondered if his wife had done the same. *Kovacs' Wife's Guide to Modern Marriage*. Neither would be an interesting read.

'He should be expecting me,' Mordent said. 'Surprise him and let him know I'm on my way up. It's semi-official business.'

'I got wind of that,' Bartholomew said, 'it's all over the force.'

'Great. Eighth floor?'

Bartholomew nodded. 'He'll be expecting you.'

Mordent rode the elevator. He was reminded of that in Hubie's apartment block. This was the opposite. Pristine. Didn't smell of piss. It surprised him how Hubie reappeared in the quiet moments, the casual contemplation. Etched into the base of the elevator was the manufacturer's name: *Schindler*. Mordent smiled. He might know the contraption as an elevator, but the British would call it a lift. *Schindler's lift*. Life's coincidences amused him. When the doors opened he stepped straight out into Kovacs' domain. He scanned the office for the top of Marsham's head but couldn't see it. It was quieter than the morgue. Kovacs ran such a tight ship that even mouths were sealed.

Jamieson was by the water cooler. Jamieson was always by the water cooler. Should Jamieson die and go to hell, he would be found standing by the water cooler.

'Mordent.'

'Jamieson.'

They shook hands. Jamieson's was cold and clammy from the ice-cool plastic cup he had been holding.

'Word on the street is that you're a wanted man,' said Jamieson. 'Come down to earth? Bubble burst?'

Mordent couldn't detect an intention of irony so played it straight: 'Just in the wrong place at the wrong time.' He looked around. 'You're the only person I recognise here. All the others clear out?'

'Cleared out or driven out. Kovacs is the cattle driver. Your face fits you stay, it doesn't then you go.'

'So how come you're still here?'

'I keep my head down, Kovacs doesn't see my face.'

Mordent nodded. 'Still reading the good book?'

Jamieson laughed. 'It's useful when I'm on the john.'

They bantered a little more then Mordent noticed a finger bend the blinds in Kovacs' office.

'We're being watched. I'll catch you later.'

Jamieson nodded. 'I'm not planning on falling.'

Mordent saw the blinds retract. He strode across the second half of the office, rapped sharply on Kovacs' door, and then stepped inside without waiting for a response. Kovacs was only half-way back to his desk.

'Practicing your surveillance technique?' Mordent barked.

'I was watering my cactus if you must know,' Kovacs said, 'as well as keeping an eye on things.'

Mordent glanced to the window. A pool of water gathered in the pot holding the spiky plant.

'Anyway,' Mordent said, then added in his best Lurch voice, 'you rang?'

Kovacs gestured to the chair opposite his desk, then sat himself, riffled through a file. 'Let's keep this official, shall we?'

Mordent also sat. 'Of course. How often do you do these personal interviews?'

Kovacs bristled. 'When I need to corroborate an officer's story. Marsham says he telephoned you. That you confirmed you were asleep in your vehicle after a bout of drunkenness,' the word fell out of his mouth like a drunk itself, 'and that you hadn't seen or heard anything suspicious whilst you were incapacitated. Davey also reports that you had just appeared to have woken when he noticed your vehicle. What neither of them have elicited to place in their reports is what you were doing there in the first place.'

'I'd attended the club socially, the previous evening, and left a little worse for wear.'

'The murdered woman was found in her underwear suffocated by bubblewrap. According to staff at the club she had taken part in a bubblewrap sumo event which – allegedly watched by a man fitting your description, somewhat salaciously – occurred earlier that evening. It was reported you left the club shortly before the murdered woman's party. Anything further to add?'

'I spotted her leaving the club with her friends. Some of them caught a taxi, others didn't. No more than that.'

'Doesn't it strike you as strange that they might have left her in that condition? It was a bachelorette party I understand. Wouldn't they have looked out for each other?'

'Are you asking me what I saw or what I think? What I saw was that they were very very drunk. Maybe she ducked into the alley for a piss and her friends hadn't realised they'd separated. Have you tracked *them* down?'

'We're working through a list.'

'Do you believe I killed her?'

Kovacs looked him eye to eye. 'What do you think?'

'I think you'd like to think that I killed her but you know damn well that I haven't. I think you'd like to think you could involve me in some way which might mean my PI badge gets revoked, but again you're on a hiding to nothing. And I believe you know all of this and want me to know it too.'

Kovacs shifted in his seat, trying to get comfortable. 'You think you know a lot.'

'I know you don't know Suduko from Sadako.'

'What's that supposed to mean?'

'One's a number puzzle and the other is the entity from *The Ring*.'

'That's not what I meant.'

Mordent leant back. 'I've told you all I know. Maybe you can tell me some things.'

'This isn't a social chat, Mordent. It's an interview.'

'If it's an interview then where's the second detective and the tape recorder.'

'It's an informal interview.'

'I'm claiming police harassment.'

Kovacs stood, genuinely angry.

'I've entertained your bullishness for several years, both before and since you left the force. You want to get one up on me, you resent me for rising through the ranks and taking your job, you think you're smarter than me. None of this is true. And even if it *was* true, I'm behind this side of the desk and you're behind the other. Nothing you can do or say will change that. You're wrong that I want to take your badge off you. I hate to say it but you can be a useful - if not reliable - source. But you're also a loose cannon. And if you're present at a murder scene I need to know two things: one, what were you doing there and two, what do you know. In the unlikely event that's nothing then I want to know that too. This is me doing my job, Mordent, and I can do it well enough without wisecracks, cynicism or disparagement.'

He paused, reflected.

'And when that cooperation happens, then I'm happy to cooperate with you.'

Mordent nodded. He let the dust settle and then watched Kovacs return to his chair, as though he were aware he had remained standing during a theatrical performance after the curtain had risen following an interlude.

'So you're saying you're happy for the old *you scratch my back I'll scratch yours* scenario, so long as I scratch yours first.'

'You could put it that way.'

'Let's put it another. You're saying if your Uncle Jack helped you off an elephant you'd help your Uncle jack off an elephant?'

Kovacs scratched his head. 'An unusual way of phrasing it, but the principle is the same.'

Mordent smiled. Kovacs. Fish. Barrel.

He just needed to provide Kovacs with information in order to get some in return.

'So we're square. I was at the sumo club because I'd heard of the bubblewrap challenge. I'm researching bubblewrap because I'm undercover investigating The Fear Institute which provides treatment for phobias. I've chosen bubblewrap, randomly, as the phobia. I admit I got drunk at the club - these things happen, if not to yourself - and in order not to break the law through drunk driving and to ensure the safety of my vehicle I slept in the car. I saw what I saw. When I woke I questioned Davey out of a matter of professional interest. Then I went home.'

'And that's everything?'

'Everything.'

Kovacs made a few marks on the paperwork in front of him. Mordent imagined he was crossing *t*'s and dotting *i*'s.

'Now you've got to help my uncle jack off the elephant,' Mordent said.

Kovacs sighed. 'What do you want to know?'

Truth was, Mordent didn't need to know much at all. But if he didn't cash in this chip it would be lost to him.

'Have you had any similar deaths to the girl in the alley?'

'Bubblewrap deaths?'

'Suffocations, anything similar in the area.'

'Not yet.'

'Any sign of sexual interference?'

'None.'

'Looking like an isolated incident?'

'Certainly.'

'Any sign of robbery?'

'No.'

'Motive?'

Kovacs threw his hands in the air. 'Early days. For someone who has no connection to this case you have a lot of interest in it.'

'Just trying to rule myself out. Whilst I'm here, what do you know about the Fear Institute?'

'Never heard of it. Should I have done?'

'Probably not. Marsham gave me some info, but it wasn't much.'

'Marsham needs reigning in.'

Kovacs said this under his breath, almost involuntarily. Mordent thought of asking further. Thought again.

Kovacs stood. 'I expect you'll be going. You're not officially a suspect, but don't leave town.'

'What is this, the wild west?' Mordent also rose. He was at the door before Kovacs spoke again. His tone shifted.

'Little bird told me your daughter was looking for you.'

Mordent kept his back to Kovacs. Wanted to ask him if he had seen her, what she looked like.

'I ran a check on her name through our files. Nothing. Not with your surname, anyway. Maybe she's not a chip off the old block.'

Mordent had his fingers around the door handle. He was intensely aware of its presence against his flesh.

'Of course,' Kovacs continued, 'she might have given a false name. Or she might not be your daughter. You taken that further?'

Mordent turned the handle. He could feel the mechanism withdraw the bolt from its snug hole.

'Just interested me,' said Kovacs, 'as to how you might handle something like that.'

But he spoke to empty air. Mordent was walking back through the office, past the new guys, past Jamieson at the water cooler, past the open elevator, through the fire doors, and down down down the concrete stairwell, each step resonating within the amalgam of metal and brick until he broke through the door at the bottom like a circus dog jumping through a paper hoop and took a deep lungful of air in the parking lot.

It had stopped raining. The sky had cleared to a pale blue like a woman might unzip a grey dress to reveal a petticoat. Shortly, black nakedness would descend, but it was sufficiently twilight for Mordent to scratch a dime along the side of Kovacs' vehicle before he got into his.

Sometimes, violence was the only answer.

Violence or sex.

16
A Tropical Pulse

Mordent reversed out of the car park and tore down the street, waving at a traffic cop who looked up from a sandwich. Mordent drove too fast to identify the contents.

Darkness pulled in behind him as the sun set, as though his tow bar was hauling the night, a black blank canvas obliterating the pureness of the day and replacing it with an undercurrent of mortality. Mordent considered how life mimicked the day/night cycle. Only in life there were no guarantees. That girl in the bubblewrap, wrestling with her friend, would she have done anything differently had she known of her final night? Probably not been encased in the wrap; Mordent would have chosen otherwise.

With one eye on the black molasses of the road, wet from rain and superficially sticky, he kept his other on the phone in his lap, sent a text to Astrid on the glowing rectangle. It was rare she was available at short notice, but the urge was rising, the impulse strong. He decided that if he had no response within fifteen minutes then he would cruise and take his chances on the street.

He didn't often resort to casual prostitutes. Yet occasionally a shallow fuck satisfied the need. He defied any man who might say different. Or any woman, when it came to that.

His tyres bore a circuit of the city. Car headlights bit into his frame, the white teeth of wolves. Elongated shadows stretched trees to the horizon, forested the buildings. As he circled, prowled, Astrid gave no signal, the night drew closer until it was no more than a fist in a dark gloved hand.

He pulled up outside Bukowski's, his state of mind confused with the irony that he would meet Berenice there in the morning whilst he hoped for release tonight. The adjoining streets contained what remained of the red light district, those more desperate elements that hadn't been driven away to other cities or online where the choice was candyshop. Occasionally product drifted past the delicatessen's doorway, a reverse windowshop. Mordent pulled himself out of his vehicle and entered the building, ordered a ham on rye and planted himself on a plastic stool at the store front. Watched those in the world go by.

He was looking for a woman whose body - in an alternate reality - he might write on in marker pen: *I wish my car was this dirty.*

Car lights refracted off nearby buildings and shot skywards. Mordent was reminded of the myth of UFO's. As a boy, he imagined himself on Mars, a silver suit on a red planet. As an adult he didn't believe in modern fairytales; or rather, to do so became too dangerous. Better to deal with hard and fast realities than allow flights of imagination. Those journeys came to a crash all too readily.

He bit into his sandwich. There was a girl named Jessica he once met in this deli. He wondered what she was doing now.

More lights bounced off the buildings as cars swung to the right. Mordent remembered Hynek's classification for UFO sightings, specifically those related to *close encounters*. He had always applied them just as equally to dating women - who were, in his anachronistic mind, also alien creatures. He consumed his sandwich, chewed thoughtfully, ran an eye over the figures flitting against night's backdrop, and flicked through each of the encounters in his mind.

Close encounters of the first kind: a visual sighting, seemingly less than five hundred feet away, showing an angular extension.

Close encounters of the second kind: a physical effect. The interface between one object and another. In UFO reports this might indicate some interference in a functioning machine. With proximity to women Mordent found it meant interference with male intelligence.

Close encounters of the third kind: where an animated creature is present. Mordent took this to mean first date.

Hynek's encounters stopped there, but Mordent was aware of an extension to the scale which metaphorically applied to all the relationships he had had:

Close encounters of the fourth kind: abduction.

Like an unwilling seaman he often felt Shanghaied on voyages of the heart. Better to keep it simple, contractual.

He chewed his roll methodically.

It was best to keep emotion out of it.

Emotions were the problem, not the sexual urge, the tropical pulse.

He moved the remaining crumbs around his plate, then pushed it to one side.

Car lights shone. He wanted contact.

The temperature had dropped whilst he had dined. It drained some of the tension from his body. But the pulse was still there. He left the joint and returned to his car. Climbed into the womb. His engine started beautifully. With jazz from his favourite radio station on low he eased the car into traffic and crawled like a shark amongst plankton down the side streets near Bukowski's. His head fuddled, muddled by sensations which mentally blocked his thought processes. The sidewalk was almost bare. Streetlights were sparse. About halfway along, standing in shadow, a prostitute stood with a cigarette dangling out of the side of her mouth. The cigarette's position was downwards, the smoke curled down, her face was downturned, her whole posture was down. Mordent pulled up alongside and looked directly into an expression riddled with age before accelerating away. Even when hyped, he had limits.

Turning the corner another woman stood in view, one that didn't need shadows. Mordent stopped and leant across the passenger seat popping open the door. She slipped in, her short skirt riding to reveal stocking tops banded like a raccoon's tail. She smiled: a good start. Looked to be late-thirties. She had been around the block as much as Mordent had driven around the block, but in her favour it was a nice neighbourhood. Her voice was light, almost too girly, but hit the spot as she ran through her prices. Already a good idea.

Out of a choice of car or apartment Mordent followed her directions and parked opposite a faceless building with a door almost hidden in the brick. She buzzed herself in and Mordent followed. As soon as the door closed they left the dark behind, and a fluorescent haze reasserted reality with sharp lines and unforgiving angles. There was an elevator but she didn't use it. Mordent imagined the confined space held awkwardness, danger. Instead he followed her ample behind up two flights of stairs and waited patiently as she fumbled for some keys in her purse.

The edge began to drain. He felt like a homebuyer shown around a new apartment, or a child following in the wake of a distant relative. Both scenarios then mutated into fantasy and he realised with work he could turn them to his advantage.

As her head bobbed in his lap as though he were bouncing a basketball, her hair stiff with spray, Mordent imagined both the estate agent and the relative stripping behind closed apartment doors. His imagination filled in the blanks.

It had been awhile since bubblewrap hadn't been part of the game, but he exploded in a fusion of refracted rainbow lights; a gunshot medley.

The deed done, everything abated, he discharged himself onto dark-yellow streets.

17
Kith

Mordent woke with fur in his mouth, a crawling sensation; then spat out a spider. Rising, he entered the kitchen where he downed a glass of water, then a second. He carried a mop back into the bedroom, looking for Woody Allen's spider the size of a buick, but feeling more like Alvy Singer versus the lobster in *Annie Hall.*

The spider had fled.

Mordent opened the curtains. Usually he didn't close them against the night, but the thought of meeting Berenice in the morning had caused him to shut the world out. The city was pressed against the window, dirt rivulets paralleled each other where rain had slid against the grime. Mordent's apartment was so high up that the windows were cleaned by abseiling guys. They often weren't there. Across the morning sky, heavy clouds tumbled like blackened sumo wrestlers. Mordent pushed the thought out of his mind, where it roiled with all the others, watched silently as a tip of white light delineated the outline of one of the clouds, as if a child drew around it with a magic pencil.

The city: always different yet always the same.

He was naked. He stretched his arms back and tautened his shoulders, puffed out his chest. He held no illusions about his body: *adequate* was a good word to describe it. The leanness he had honed a month or so ago had gone slack following Hubie's death. *More* thoughts to push out his mind. But pushing thoughts was like kneading dough, the further back they went, the more came forwards. And Berenice was at the forefront of all of them.

He didn't need her. He knew this. If he hadn't have known of her then he wouldn't have wished her into existence. He had no gaps to fill, no evolution to prove. Just as he didn't need a steady woman he didn't need *any* steady girl. What could their relationship be other than hello/goodbye? He hadn't raised her. Had never seen her. Hadn't known of her in order to foster a hankering. He had probably *been* with girls of her age. Was she the only girl in the world he wouldn't consider giving a fuck?

Yet, literally, he *did* give a fuck. That was the peril of the English language. It tied you in knots by your own hand. Her presence could be a catalyst, carrying the force of a political assassination. But Mordent would rather have Watergate than Stairgate. She was obviously not a child, but might regress if Daddy were needed.

The clouds peeled further back, an exposed eyelid, a slit. A shaft of light plumed Godlike onto the street below and Mordent couldn't help but follow the beam, like an Irishman expecting a pot o' gold at the end of a rainbow, or a theatregoer watching for someone to enter a spotlight.

And as he watched, Mordent remembered Aesop's fable of the wind and the sun, where each bet who was the strongest by making a traveller lose his cloak. However hard the wind blew, the man pulled his cloak tighter around him, but when the sun shone he removed it gladly. The moral being that strength can be found in kindness not violence. Mordent always found that a gun was the sun in his hand.

He wondered if the tale would have been bedtime reading for Berenice. Wondered again.

He might get soft in his old age. That would be dangerous.

Into the beam of light walked a man who removed his hat. Mordent pulled his face from the window, hating the certainty of fate, then pushed it forwards again. The man had gone but Mordent was sure he had recognised him. From where, he couldn't quite tell.

He shrugged the thought. Wondered if he would recognise Berenice. Shrugged again.

After a few hours he was washed, ironed and dressed. When he entered Bukowski's he was a different man to the previous evening. His senses had returned, this time with an accentuated sharpness. His eyes were razors reaffirming that looks might kill. Again, the English language. The only *looks* that could kill were those sported by a peroxide blonde with bright red lips in a tight black dress, breasts like the ripest fruit on the tree, and with curves that would throw a rally driver. At least, from his point of view. He imagined women would also be slain by the male equivalent.

None of those dames walked into Bukowski's. Not that he was expecting Berenice to resemble *that* stereotype. He ordered a second cup of coffee on an empty stomach, turned his cell around in his hand with the movement that might keep an ant on the up-side of its world. He wondered whether to dial her, text her. He wondered whether to leave. Then, across the other side of the street, running between traffic, in a smart grey skirt suit, a woman escalated into view. Short brunette hair, curly at the edges, oval face, quick legs. Mordent knew it was her before she opened the door. When she turned she knew it was him.

The place was half-full. In retrospect, it was the

wrong place to meet. Berenice's mouth dropped open then closed again: the clichéd fish out of the clichéd water. Mordent pulled out the adjacent stool, let her sit. She was thirty if she were a day.

'I'm not sure what introductions are fit for this situation,' he heard himself say, as if from afar, 'but if I had any doubts they've just been erased.'

She smiled. If she had been a two-hundred-year-old painting those cracks would be touched up through restoration, but here in Bukowski's Mordent pulled out a clean handkerchief and dabbed with some affection at her face.

'Thankyou.'

The two words ran into each other. Something that language was wont to do.

'Can I get you something?'

'Twenty nine years two hundred and thirty two days.'

He could feel his senses shutting down, pushing her away. Then her smile returned like the beam of that morning's light and she said, 'Sorry, being a bitch. I'm like that sometimes.'

She smiled and suggested ham and eggs. Mordent left his stool and wandered over to the counter. Put in her order. Inside, another box ticked that she was his and there was nothing to fear.

Back at the stools they fell into an easier conversation.

'How did you find me?'

'My mother mentioned you once, at the end.' She paused, expected a question which didn't come, which Mordent saved for later. 'Just your surname and where you had met, what you were. I haven't been searching long. When I asked at the police station it was half-hearted, disguised. I never really expected to hear back.'

'But my surname. How come you carry my surname?'

'I don't; but I knew if I gave it I stood greater chance flushing you out. It intrigued you, didn't it? I knew that it would. That was why I gasped when you asked my name on the phone. It had to be you, couldn't be anyone else.'

'It could have been one of the cops at the station.'

'No, I knew it was you. It *was* you.'

'You don't know anything about me.'

'I know enough. Enough to make it worthwhile.'

'Enough to break your heart over again?'

She sipped her coffee. 'Don't give yourself credit for that. You never broke my heart. You can't miss something you've never had in the first place.'

'Now you're breaking *my* heart.'

'Honesty does that to people.'

'Is it right to be honest?'

'It is when you're starting afresh, when you're my age. When you're young it doesn't matter, lies and fantasy interact. But as you get older I've found you need the truth in it.'

As they spoke he found her eyes would dart to his and then away, like a bird returning over and again to a nest.

'Tell me who your mother was.'

'Clarice Lane.'

'Clarice Lane.' Mordent repeated it slowly, without recognition; slow enough to make Berenice think he was savouring it.

'You don't remember her, do you?'

'I didn't say that.'

'Remember her then.'

Berenice took another sip of her coffee. This time she held his gaze. He saw himself swimming in her.

'So you're right. The truth. I don't remember her. I don't remember the name.'

Mordent closed his eyes. His head spun with lack of food, too much caffeine. A hurricane might have rotated his stool until the seat lifted off the spindle and he came crashing to the floor. He felt sick, felt he had failed her, wondered if he had botched a test that she had been expecting him to pass.

When he opened his eyes he saw Clarice Lane.

The photo was old, faded, had been folded in half for some time leaving a white line across the middle, a crocodile tear. Clarice wore a white dress and had a white sweater slung over her shoulders, her arms dangling tanned-brown at her sides. In a suit that looked like it had been stolen from a dead man Mordent saw himself standing beside her, one arm across his chest, the hand of the other in his pocket. He couldn't take his eyes off himself. He had no photographs of his youth or his post-teen years. The only picture he had seen with any regularity was the staff photo he passed daily when he worked on the force. Looking at himself now he saw all the years that had fallen from him, the invisible years which a mirror didn't reveal because you looked in the mirror everyday. In the photo was a young man, early twenties, with much of life still in front of him. Mordent knew the next time he looked into a mirror he would see himself as an old man.

But, still, he didn't remember Clarice Lane.

Berenice folded the photo in half along the worn edge and snapped it back inside her purse. 'No doubt that's you, is there?' she said. 'But you still don't recognise my mother.'

'It's not that,' Mordent began, but he decided not to race through the list of women he must have slept with since then. The words teetered on his tongue like schoolboy divers at a communal swimming pool. He thought: how can I go about this. He said: 'I've aged so much.'

'If I can recognise you, why can't you recognise her?'

He shrugged, involuntarily. 'Since when have you had that picture?'

'Since a couple of months ago. Just before she died.'

'What happened?'

'Nothing dramatic. Cancer of the colon. It happens every day. Not something I imagine you see in your line of work.'

Disease is the big killer we do nothing to apprehend, thought Mordent. But he didn't say this. He said: 'We see death in all shapes and sizes.'

She shrugged, a pale reflection of his own, an echo.

'Aren't you going to ask what I want from you?'

'I think you got it. When you sobbed down the phone.'

'I'm not expecting us to be friends.' She gazed out of the window and Mordent saw them reflected back. The sky was open, limited only by their visibility. 'Listen,' she said, 'it's crowded here. Let's walk.'

She slipped her arm between his as they left Bukowski's and crossed the road. Familial recognition stopped Mordent thinking of her as any other woman.

They found themselves in the park, sat, watched pigeons and a grey squirrel.

'Mother said you wouldn't remember her and that you wouldn't know why. That photograph was the snapshot of one day. There was no before, no afterwards. She met you, you seduced her, she left. That's all there was to it. But in that space of time one of your sperm fertilised an egg and nine months later I popped out, fully formed, mouth open and fatherless. It's not your fault and it's not hers. You mind if I smoke?'

Mordent shook his head, yet inside fatherly thoughts twisted and shouted *daughter* and *cancer*. In his jacket pocket he pulled out a lighter and she shook cigarettes out for both.

'When you're young,' she said, 'life is simple. You live in your own little world. The older you get, the more that world expands, until eventually it starts closing in again. The rub? It's always just your little own world. Only once in a while do you affect someone else.'

'That sounds like my nihilistic tone.'

She shook her head, smoke S-bending in the movement. 'I'm not one for big words, big concepts. I say it as I see it. You know where I work? No, of course you don't. I work in taxidermy. You see enough death there to say *get stuffed*.' She laughed, coughed, then choked with it. Mordent watched as she went red in the face then regained her composure. 'In that kind of job you develop a matter-of-fact attitude. But I'm rambling. I'm excited and nervous and sick to my stomach. You must have somewhere to be right now.'

Mordent looked at his hands then put his arms around her. She shuddered. She was right. He did have somewhere to be. It was right here. Right now.

'Oh,' she said. Then she hid her face and let the tears flow.

It's started, Mordent thought. *It's started and there's no going back.*

18
15th May 19__

Mordent stood by the lake, skimming stones into the water. He didn't give a damn where the stones came from or where they were going. All he cared about was the number of bounces they made on the skein of the liquid surface. It was only later, years later, that he would regret their black descent.

He was two weeks in the force and it was his first day off. He was eager, hungry, reticent to be away from life. Across the other side of the lake the police station loomed large. Mordent wanted to skim a stone so far it would take off and hit the side of the building, to remind them that he was still there.

A fly alighted on the back of his neck and he hit it with the flat of his palm. Dead. Two weeks in the force and he had seen seven dead bodies, three of them in one location. A dead fly bothered him no more than a dead bluebird. Of course, those seven hadn't been the first he had seen; that one was buried in his childhood, literally, but counselling had put that to the back of his mind.

He bent to pick up another stone, heard a noise on the gravel, turned his head to view the feet of a girl in white pumps, white dress, white cardigan hung over her shoulders like an old woman's shawl.

Her face was pretty, unconventional. It was pretty unconventional. There was a quirk to it that intrigued him. He decided to get to know her better. Better than a snapshot glance.

She stopped at the lake, slipped her feet out of her pumps and wriggled her toes against the gravel. She looked his age, maybe a year younger. He bent and picked up two more stones, handed her one.

'Best of three?'

He realised she had taken the stone almost unconsciously, because when she heard him speak it was as though she hadn't noticed him. Her expression was so far away that it was in the next State.

'Sorry?'

'Best of three?' He pointed to the stone in her hand. Deciding actions were better than words he bent his arm back and skimmed the stone across the lake. After two jumps it hit a clump of weed and sank.

Life returned to her face slowly, as though a fish being reeled into a boat. A smile broke.

'Easy.' She directed her stone across the water. It didn't sink til the sixth.

Mordent bent again, selected four more stones; tried to ensure they were small and smooth, of equal weight.

But they didn't stop at three stones. They played for the next twenty minutes until they lost count of the score and Mordent found it increasingly hard to breathe when their fingers touched during the exchange.

'What's your name?'

'Clarice. What's yours?'

'Mordent.'

'Mordent?'

'My surname. Only if you know me longer will I give you my Christian name.'

She laughed. 'When you get to know me better I'll tell you my surname.'

'Deal.'

'Deal.'

They walked and talked for a while, Mordent's hand itching to slip into hers. Couples lounged on the grass in the sun. Some people were reading. A guy in a trilby fed pigeons from a bench, creating a semi-circle so it looked like he was recounting a story to an audience. Au pairs pushed prams as big as dog kennels containing barking children. By the bandstand, a spindly three-legged creature with a bag over its head flashed passersby. Clarice stopped, 'Would you mind if we had our picture taken?'

Mordent had thought nothing of it.

Yet he was awkward, didn't know how to stand. He wasn't used to it.

He was still standing when Clarice went over to the photographer and wrote her name and address down on a slip of paper. He watched as she paid, then felt guilty about it.

'Shall I buy you a drink?'

'Such a gentleman who asks!'

Her mood was getting brighter, more playful. Mordent began to wonder why she had been strolling alone. Why she had stood at the lake. He had told her he was a rookie police officer. Was she happier in his protection?

He felt happy protecting her.

He hadn't long moved to the city, was still finding his whereabouts. He didn't drink heavy, was a country boy used to the outdoors. There was some sophistication to Clarice that unnerved him. As they left the park he slipped an arm around her waist and she didn't move it. The street they wandered down wasn't the cleanest, dustbins overflowed and guys in big leather jackets smoked on apartment steps. Seeing a sign for a bar he stuck his head inside, but it was dingy and dark, uninviting. He couldn't take her there. He didn't imagine he'd ever frequent *Morgan's Bar* again unless it was to raid it.

She took his hand then. Guided him. 'Don't worry about that drink. I'm here for a couple of days. I'm rooming on the other side of the park. Come with me.'

There was a subtle switch in their roles as she led him back across the park. He followed her like a dog. He'd had his fair share of relationships and one-night stands. The city beckoned darkly in that respect, augmented his suburban fumblings. But an intoxicating power flowered around Clarice and took him with it. They almost ran up the steps to the crumbling brownstone, formerly majestic now just crummy rented rooms, and ascended a stairwell that clattered under their feet, echoing down as they rose, almost propelling them in the updraft.

Inside, she slung her white cardigan onto the floor. He reached behind her and unbuttoned her dress, her fingers equally frantic at his belt. Suddenly the tardiness of the day was rushed to this moment, preliminaries forgotten. Naked she moved him back to the bed, felt for his penis and held it in cool fingers as it hardened. She was already wet. Positioning him inside she rode him from above, his first experience. Pubis against bone. Over and again. The frisson of her flesh brought him swiftly to climax and they paused then switched. She gasped the second time he entered, deeper from the rear. Her behind was the colour of pumice, her sex blood from that stone. When they had finished she rolled over, almost catching him inside. Then she rose and pressed her breasts to the windowpane, stared manically at the city.

'Don't you just love it here? Don't you just *love* it?'

When she slept, Mordent gathered his clothes and changed in the bathroom. Quietly he left the apartment.

He did love it. Just a little too much.

19
Apply Some Pressure

Mordent had returned to his office by the time the phone rang. He felt calmer, more in control than he had since Hubie's death. The meeting with Berenice had gone well: no accusations, no recriminations. She genuinely wanted an adult relationship with him, parental baggage packed and already on the plane. When she left the park for her job at the taxidermist they made arrangements to see each other again.

She had laughed: 'I'll make you an otter you *can* reuse!'

Then she was gone in a smudge of traffic.

No way back, but no problem moving forwards.

After checking messages Mordent had left his cell on his desk. Vibrations jiggered it a slow foot sideways where it fell to the floor. He picked it up and checked the display. Martens from the morgue.

'Mordent.'

'Martens. I've got a cadaver you might be interested in.'

'Anyone I know.'

'You would have *wanted* to know her, that much is sure, but nothing clinically proven.'

'So lucky you're in a job where your hands *aren't* to keep off her.'

'Don't get nasty. That's all behind me. We've done that to death.'

'As the dead actress said to the dead bishop.'

Martens sighed. 'I'm serious, don't get smart.'

'No problem of that in your company.' Mordent sat on the edge of his desk and it creaked like a coffin lid. 'What makes you think I'll be interested?'

'We had a girl on the slab the other day, suffocated. I heard Kovacs had a chat with you about her. Found at the scene of the crime. Anyway, there's been a second one, similar circumstances. Thought you might want a look first before you put your foot in it and wake up at the crime scene.'

Mordent stood. 'Same spec?'

'More or less. There's traces of sexual contact but nothing violent. Neighbours say she worked as a prostitute so that's not unexpected. The papers run with this, they'll call him the bubblewrap killer. All packed up with nowhere to go.'

Mordent ran a hand through his hair. 'When did this one come in?'

'Early morning. I was working the graveyard shift.' Martens laughed and it wasn't pleasant, like a chainsaw underwater.

'Whereabouts?'

'Apartment on Denmark Street, back alley kind of place. Downtown. One of the old fashioned red light districts. Or so I'm told.'

'Can I come in?'

'Sure. I'm here for the next couple of hours. Should prepare my report by the end of my shift.'

'I'll be there shortly.'

Mordent stuffed his cell into his pocket, then rubbed his fingers together. He was sweating. He knew who the body on the slab would be, but had to see for himself. Things were getting weird.

The echo of his feet reverberated in the stairwell as he raced to the car lot. He tore onto the street like a strip of paper. Mid-afternoon traffic was light, a blessing. He had a feeling he was being set-up, but couldn't see how or why. Sometimes his body convulsed as though he were being given cardio shock treatment. His head - unfurred since his meeting with Berenice - furred once again. He made the journey through a series of minor mishaps and near mistakes. Car horns signalled his arrival at the hospital.

He used the side entrance and fire escape steps. When he entered the morgue Martens was bent over a cadaver. He had run through so many jokes about this that another would have come easy, but it wasn't that kind of day. Martens noticed the reticence.

'Hey Mordent. I've been holding this pose since our phonecall. Where's the quip?'

'Not today, Martens. Just show me the body.'

Martens moved away from the corpse. Cold and grey, she had had a lot more life in her when Mordent had been inside her the previous evening. In fact, when he had left her she had had some of *Mordent's* life inside her. He had paid extra for her to swallow.

'Recognise her?'

'You could say that. Where's the bubblewrap?'

Martens gestured to a side table, where a head-shaped roll had been cut off the body. On her face, as though she had been attacked by an octopus, were tiny sucker-shaped circles that corresponded with the wrap.

'You won't believe the effort I've made not to tamper with the evidence.'

'Huh?' Mordent couldn't think straight.

'The bubblewrap. Loved popping it as a kid. Just the feel of the air beneath the skein, the delight in applying some pressure, the give of the material and then the pop. I tell you, I've had to keep my hands on *her* to keep them off the wrap.'

'Sure, sure. You said on the phone there were traces of sexual contact?'

'Dried semen in her mouth. I've taken a swab. If it's someone known then we'll get a match. Evidence of other sexual contact in her vagina and anus, but not as recent. She was known to work as a prostitute, so I would have been surprised if there had been no evidence rather than the other way around. She hadn't suffocated with the semen still warm in her mouth though. Chances are her murderer and last client weren't one and the same.'

'Could you swear on oath to that?'

'I could speculate on oath given the information available.'

Mordent ran a hand through his hair. He wasn't sure how to handle this. He and Martens went back a long way, but it wasn't the kind of tentative friendship he had with Hubie. On many occasions it had been acrimonious because Mordent had held all the cards. Yet, needs must.

'My DNA is on the national database,' Mordent said, slowly.

Martens was distracted. 'So is mine. In this city, most everybody...Oh! *Your* DNA is on the database.'

'You got it.'

Martens leant over to the woman on the slab, gripped the sides of her mouth between his fingers, and moved them back and forth. The flesh made a sucking sound. 'You know,' Martens said, 'she's pretty enough to play with but I decided against sloppy seconds. I'm especially glad now I know they were yours.'

'Shut it Martens, I'm serious.'

'Apparently so.'

Silence hung in the room: a Mexican standoff as to who would make the first noise. As it happened, the corpse discharged some gas.

'For fuck's sake.'

'Chill it Mordent, happens all the time.' Martens paused again. 'Are you asking me to do anything?'

'I don't know. You get any prints on the wrap?'

'Nope. But it needs to be sent for further analysis. Why? Expecting yours?'

Mordent shook his head. He ran through a few things: his proximity to the two bubblewrap deaths – the second intimately so, a shopkeeper who could confirm – if ever asked – that he had bought bubblewrap on his journey back from the Fear Institute, and his meeting with the institute itself where bubblewrap was the main topic of conversation. The odds weren't stacked in his favour.

'You know,' Martens continued, 'if – and I mean *if* – there's anything I can do I won't be doing it out of the goodness of my heart.'

Mordent swallowed. 'It could be there's someone out to nail me. I need time, more than anything else.'

'I can delay my report, but I can't delay the samples being sent off to the lab. Delaying my report isn't going to be of much use to you.'

'So the alternative would be to spoil the samples.'

'To spoil the samples?'

'I don't have to spell it out Martens. We both know I once caught you in here with both hands full. That's why we've been chummy ever since. You help me this one time then the slate is clean. That won't be hanging over your head ever again. I might even lay off the quips.'

Martens removed his thin gloves and worried a fingernail.

'You kill her?'

Mordent shook his head. 'No.'

'You want me to spoil the semen sample?'

'If that's what it takes.'

'It's not that simple.'

'It never is.'

Martens sighed. 'Years ago we wouldn't be having this conversation, but nowadays science is a different game. Sometimes it seems even my job is in jeopardy from the suits in CSI. And their roles get augmented daily, their numbers increase just because *CSI* is more popular on TV nowadays than re-runs of *Quincy*. I spoil this sample, they'll get another. I'd have to virtually cut off her head to prevent them from finding a sample. It's not as simple as removing green spinach from between her teeth, if you get my drift. Not only that but they'll know I've tampered with it. That puts me at risk. You got an alibi for after you saw this girl?'

Mordent shook his head. 'I take it *home alone* doesn't cut the mustard?'

'You and I both know that's unlikely. Of course, they gotta prove you did it and – if you didn't – well it can't be *proven*, can it? Not that that's saved many people over the years. I dunno Mordent, you've got yourself a problem here. I wish there was something I could do.'

Mordent gestured over to the sample. 'Can you just spoil it, just the once, to delay things?'

'And how am I supposed to do that? Pour orange juice in the tube and mix it up? I tell you Mordent, this ain't the 40s, it's more black and white nowadays. I could pour cement in there and they'd still get your DNA out of it.'

'Lost in the post?'

'Lost in the post, he says! I could...' Martens

paused, 'on reflection it *could* get lost in the post. You've bought yourself a day, two at the most.' He wandered across to the tube and dropped it into a clinical waste bin. 'Strictly between you and me, right? And no more jokes about fucking the cadavers.'

Mordent patted Martens on the back. 'Let's keep the jokes, but no intent; no more threats to drop you in it. Let's keep the relationship purely professional, but losing the jokes, that'd be like losing a limb.'

Martens nodded. 'At least that albatross will be off my neck. I might pop into a taxidermist to get it stuffed.'

'Funny thing...' Mordent began, then held back on saying he knew somewhere who might do that. It was an imaginary albatross. He didn't know of anywhere that would stuff imaginary animals.

He turned his back to leave, but he couldn't turn his back on the situation. Before he knew it, Kovacs would run him in and go all procedural on the questioning.

'One more thing, Mordent,' Martens said. 'We touched on *Quincy*. I loved that show. I'll tell you a fact that might interest you. Quincy was a widower, although towards the end of the run he married a second time. His first wife had previously been shown in flashback, and the producers used the same actress for his new wife as they did for the old. The two unrelated characters' identical appearances was never mentioned on screen. I love it that sometimes stuff happens that doesn't need to be explained.'

Mordent nodded. 'I prefer *Monk*, myself; and he needed an explanation for *everything*.'

Martens grinned. 'Therein lies the difference.'

Mordent nodded again, brusquely. He left the morgue only marginally reassured that he had bought some time; but he didn't need to be a detective to know that Martens would retrieve that original sample and store it somewhere safe as an insurance policy should Mordent ever need to get rid of him.

That saved sample would be Quincy's second wife.

20
Snowball

Mordent gunned his vehicle over to Morgan's Bar, ducked inside the blackness like entering an octopus's inky heart.

He felt like one of Goldilock's three bears. Someone was sitting on his stool.

He took the adjacent seat, bristling and growling. Yet the dark couldn't quite sap the light of the girl beside him. She seemed solo, a speck of gold in an old timer's pan.

When she crossed her legs he thought about making a claim.

'Another snowball.'

She pushed an empty glass across to Morgan, who squeezed some fresh lime juice into the advocaat before shaking it and topping up with lemonade. It was the first cocktail Mordent had ever seen Morgan prepare. Once he had done, Mordent ordered a whisky.

The girl turned to him. She was no longer a girl. Mid-thirties if she were a day.

'They say a rolling stone gathers no moss, but a snowball does, don't you think?'

'I'm not quite following you.'

'Sometimes you start something and it gets bigger and bigger and before you know it you can't handle it any more. Like love, you know.'

Mordent sipped his whisky. 'I don't know much about love.'

'I don't believe you. Everyone does. They all know their experience of it.'

'Some people haven't had much experience.'

'Those are the people who know the most about love. The others only thought that they did.'

Mordent nodded. He watched her take her drink. He wanted her to remind him of someone, but he wasn't sure who. He only knew she didn't remind him of anyone.

'So is that what brings you here?'

After he spoke he realised he might as well have asked, *Do you come here often?*

She smiled. 'I might be a rolling snowball but I'm not about to be picked up.'

'It wasn't a pick up I wanted this evening. More of a pick-me-up,' Mordent said honestly.

'Life not treating you well?'

'I've had better times.'

'Is it something you can discuss?'

'Probably not.'

They both drained their drinks and ordered afresh.

She stuck out a hand, finger-cold. 'Grace'.

'Mordent.'

'Is that your first or last name?'

'It's the name I give.'

'Ah. So it would be your *Internet* name.' A smile enhanced her expression. 'So be it. You'll have to decide what kind of name Grace is. My first or last name or username.'

'From where I'm sitting it's a personification.'

'Let's not descend into compliments. I've found embarrassment a dead end to conversation.'

Mordent let go of her fingers.

'So what *does* bring you here?'

'Just a passer by, passing by.'

'Sinking snowballs like its winter already?'

'Ah. So it's a story you want; you need beguiling.'

'Not beguilement; succour. I need succour.'

'And you think I'm just the sucker to give it you?'

Mordent allowed a soft laugh; a bomb in a place like Morgan's. 'Those are my lines.'

She smiled. 'So as I said, it's a story you want. You hope that mine will make you forget yours. So be it. Have you ever been in a relationship with a much older or younger person?'

Mordent thought back. Lola White. A girl who had been drugged and then burnt to death.

'I have.'

'And how did that end?'

'Brutally.'

'And so it is with me. Rejection is reserved for artists and lovers, don't you think? But repetition doesn't make it easier.'

'So was he much younger?'

She laughed. 'You flatter me. No, he was much older. In his seventies. Does that make me bad?'

'Only if you want to be.'

Another laugh. 'You understand me without knowing me at all.'

'That's just the way I operate.'

'Ah, a surgeon?'

'If a surgeon drank in here I'd be worried for his patients.'

She glanced around. 'Yes. I didn't pick this establishment very well.'

'You were telling me a story...?'

'Oh, it's nothing much. Getting dumped by a man

that age for a younger woman smarts a bit, that's all. I'll be fine come the morning.'

'You want me to talk to him for you?'

'Gallantry in this day and age!' She laughed again. 'You know you wouldn't want to. I wonder why you ask. I'm not looking for a sympathy fuck.'

The word seemed incongruous in her mouth, but there was also an attraction to it.

'That wasn't what I was suggesting.'

She smiled. 'I'm teasing you - see, my defence mechanisms are kicking in already. Subconsciously I'm flirting to find a new partner. Don't look so worried. Tell me about this girl you knew. Older or younger?'

'She was younger.'

'Name?'

'I don't see the relevance...'

'C'mon, humour me. We'll never meet again. Honesty is the best policy. My man's name was George. That was his surname - *was*, hark at me! Single already - First name Ezra.'

'Lola,' Mordent said slowly, feeling the name roll off his tongue like a teenage gymnast, 'Lola White.'

'Lola White.' Grace was a female echo. '*Lola White*. Shall we have another drink?'

Mordent nodded, then waited whilst Morgan set them up. 'Last one. I need my head clear for twenty-four hours.'

'Sounds intriguing.'

'If it's *too* intriguing you'll read about it in the papers.'

They sipped their drinks, watched each other like an antelope keeps an eye on a crocodile at a watering hole. Both were the antelope. Both were the crocodile. Under other circumstances Mordent knew they might have hooked up, but the last thing he needed was a woman on the rebound. The last thing he needed was a woman at all.

Their differing stories remained untold. Mordent knew it was for the better. He watched as Grace asked Morgan to call her a cab. He wondered if Morgan resisted saying *You're a cab.* He realised it was getting late if he were slipping into Laurel and Hardy routines. It was time for him to get off the mule.

Just before her taxi arrived she said: 'So we exchanged half our names, and the names of our lovers. Shouldn't we exchange our full names?'

'My first name's Stingray,' Mordent said, reflexly.

Grace smiled. 'My surname's Snowball,' she replied.

21
Stand By Your Gun

Grace's taxi had long gone by the time Mordent stepped out of Morgan's Bar. He'd sunk another whisky, embroiled his mind in women. Grace had left a trace of perfume, a calling card. Lola hadn't worn perfume, but her olfactory memory was the stench of burnt flesh. That other whisky was needed to shake her out of his head.

His vehicle beckoned large on the pavement, a death trap. He considered walking, reconsidered a taxi, re-reconsidered driving. He might be over the limit but he had experience. He didn't want to sleep in his car again and wake up next to a murder.

Coincidences were piling around him like a child stacking blocks. Sooner or later they would reach optimum height and crash.

He fumbled for his keys in his jacket pocket. Found his forearm gripped as he touched them. Realised his other arm was also clenched. Found himself marched down the adjacent alley with his feet off the ground. Shook his head to reassert reality within his drunken haze. The alleyway closed in like a cone.

He was thrown against some metal trashcans that should have been replaced in the seventies. They made the sound of a musician tripping over a drumkit. Instinctively he reached for the gun in his holster, then saw the weapon dangling from the right index finger of one of the hoodlums.

'You looking for this, Bud?'

The voice was so gravelly Mordent expected small stones to shoot out of the mouth. It was too dark to discern anything other than shapes, the glint of his gun, the glints of *their* guns. He couldn't decide whether to remain on the ground. Standing might give him an advantage or be perceived as a threat. He decided to remain within the rubbish. It was more comfortable down there.

He realised he had mumbled a reply.

'We're the friendly guys,' said a second voice. 'A warning shot. You mess with Mr George's girls and he will mess with you. Capiche?'

Mordent wondered over the necessity of using the Italian word. The threatening manner imitated the Mafia, or rather the way the Mafia was portrayed in movies and pop culture. From the use of the word it was clear these guys had nothing to do with the Mafia. In fact, they were so far removed they weren't even second cousins in the family.

Still, they remained holding guns. He bit back a retort.

'Understood.'

The shadows' shoulders slumped. Mordent realised they expected a fight. They *wanted* a fight. He had folded too easily, like a long-snouted animal created by an origami master.

One of them stepped forwards, drew back a leg for a kick. Then appeared to think twice.

'For what it's worth,' Mordent said, 'I have other battles to fight. Tell your Mr George that I have no interest in his girls.'

The shadows conferred in a whisper.

'You're only supposed to scare me, right. Violence isn't the answer. One of you might get hurt.'

'Listen Bud,' the voice wasn't quite as gravelly this time around, as though some of it had been used to grit the alley, 'a warning's not a warning unless you believe it might be carried through. We back off now and the threat will have gone.'

Mordent edged backwards, stood. 'I'm drunk. Want to swing a few punches with a drunkard? There'll be no fun in it. You have nothing to prove. I know I'm outnumbered. I back off, we're all happy.'

The other guy spoke again. 'Mr George might want a souvenir of our visit. You got any fingers you don't normally use?'

'Well let's think. Evolution determined man's thumbs are opposable for a reason, so I can't really dispense with those. I need my pinkies for when I'm sipping tea with my Great Aunt, extended at a right angle don't you know. My middle finger gets a lot of use nowadays, in fact I get the feeling it's going to be in demand pretty soon. The rest of the fingers are beneficial when making a handshake or a fist. So, no, I can't quite say that I'll be able to lose one any time soon.'

'A wiseguy,' the second guy snarled.

'And you guys are not so wise,' retorted Mordent, picking up confidence. 'I bet you don't know your Rimbaud from your Rambo.'

'Huh?'

Gravel-voice advanced again, then a door Mordent hadn't noticed opened up beside him and Morgan appeared in the alleyway; a bag of trash in one hand and a baseball bat in the other.

'You need help?'

Mordent shook his head. 'These gentlemen were just leaving.'

The shadows looked at each other once again, then began to retreat. 'Just remember what we said.'

Mordent heard a clang as his gun was thrown against a trashcan. The alley lightened as the shadows departed.

'You gonna clean this up?' Morgan said. 'I don't want the authorities on me.'

'Sure.' Mordent dusted off his jacket, found himself thinking of a dust jacket. 'Just one question. The broad I was talking to earlier, in the bar, you ever see her before?'

Morgan shook his head. 'Nope. She wasn't there long before you arrived. Those guys connected with her?'

'Who knows.' Mordent righted the cans, returned spilled waste to their dark interiors, retrieved his gun from where it lay on the floor. 'Who knows,' he repeated, 'but I get the feeling one day I'll find out.'

Morgan shrugged. 'Just keep it out of the bar.'

Mordent nodded. As the side door closed he shuffled back up the alleyway. His right leg ached as did his right shoulder, but he couldn't claim to have been roughed up. The only puzzle was how the goons had been alerted. Grace said she had been dumped, maybe she hadn't been honest. Either way he had no means of contacting her. Unless she wound up dead he decided he wouldn't see her again. And *unless* she wound up dead then he had other fish to fry. Tonight had merely been a reprieve, a distraction.

22
Getting Stuffed

For the second time in two days Mordent woke with a mouthful of fluff, as though during his night time reveries he had been transformed into a long-haired pussycat with a rough tongue and a propensity for furballs. If only the metaphor were literal then he might dine out on the revelation that the miraculous were possible, however the interior of his mouth only *felt* as though it were furred and gargling in his sink soon undid the sensation.

The wondrous would have to go hungry for now.

He fixed himself some eggs over easy. Toasting bread he noticed it blue-shiny with specks of mold. He picked those bits out and they clung beneath his fingernails. As he ate they became dislodged and he consumed them regardless. The eggs broke perfect onto the bread.

It hadn't been more than a handful of days since he was kicking around for work. Now he had the Fear Institute to investigate, a daughter to chat to, the bubblewrap murders to ease himself out of the frame, and had been threatened by some rogues following a purely coincidental meeting. He wondered what the next twenty-four hours might hold. If he wasn't careful they might include his arrest.

What would Kovacs have on him, he wondered? Some sperm in the mouth of a dead hooker. It wouldn't

– couldn't – be enough to assume guilt, not on its own. But cumulatively, with his proximity to the first bubblewrap death, it didn't look good for his image.

He decided to make a few calls. He had agreed to pop in to see Berenice at her workplace later that morning. In the hour he had to kill he decided he could hold a service and bury it as well.

'Benedict Holmsworth.'

'Mr Holmsworth, its Mordent, the PI. How are you today?'

'Not in the habit of taking social calls from employees. I take it you have some information for me. Shall we cut to the chase, as I believe they say.'

Mordent held back on bile. 'I've contacted the Fear Institute, met with Copernicus Fear as though I were a prospective client. Nothing I've seen so far indicates they are in the business of death. I've also made contact with some associates who would have such information if it were *publicly* available. Again, nothing. So I'm keeping you up to date with my enquiries. Tell me, at any stage in your uncle's treatment, did his fear of rats abate?'

Benedict snorted. 'So you have nothing and expect me to supply you with something. Sounds like I could do the investigation myself.'

Mordent bit back twice. There was money involved. Money that might be needed for a lawyer. 'These things take time. I have another appointment with the Institute which could prove fruitful, but it would help if you could answer my question.'

There was a sigh. 'If anything, my uncle's fear of rats increased. I was not a fan of their treatments.'

'Did you uncle advise what those treatments were?'

'No. He didn't like to discuss it. Discussion exacerbated the fear, do you understand?'

'I get it. Well, I'll keep you up to date.'

'Please do. But only bother me if you have information. That's what I pay you for.'

The line went dead. Killed time. Mordent wondered if the other Benedict Holmsworth had been more hospitable than his namesake.

He considered calling Marsham, but didn't want to reveal his involvement in the second bubblewrap death. Even so, he wondered why Marsham *hadn't* called him.

There was another call he needed to make, but dialling Astrid's number yielded no answer.

He was starting to think that the twenty-four hours he had bought was as worthless as the paper it hadn't been written on.

He stripped and ducked into the shower. Water jets punctuated his skin like a nail impression toy, formed map reliefs and miniature cities. Pushing his face towards the stream he was reminded of bukkake actresses. Although *actress* might be even more of a push. He considered the lack of control, of being put in a situation where there was no turning back. The suffocated girls had placed him in that position. Metaphorically, he was open to abuse.

Less than an hour later he was held within the security of his vehicle; solitary confinement for the senses. Bright sunshine revealed windscreen streaks like retinal floaters. The outside world refracted, skewed, but was it any different through glass? Perception intrigued him. It was perception which could determine right from wrong, innocent or guilty. It was perception that underlined everything.

His perception of his first meeting with Berenice had been favourable. He wondered what she had thought of it.

The district where she worked was filled with quirky boutiques, their frontages painted garish colours, rare flowers attracting specific money-bees. He parked across the way from the store. Flanked by a shop specialising in umbrellas with Japanese manga motifs and a retro SF establishment, the taxidermists' windows were broad and open, welcoming not depressing. Over the top of the shop large letters were painted in a font Mordent assumed had yet to be patented: *Get Stuffed! 216 Owen Avenue.*

He crossed the street and looked at the display. Squirrels stood *en garde*, épées raised, their eyes piercing behind adapted masks. Toads held each other in languorous embrace. A fox peaked out from under a peaked cap, his black waistcoat containing a pocket watch and a rolled-up newspaper. Possums played possum. In the rear of the shop a bleached white polar bear stood on two feet, mouth open, teeth fierce, holding a badminton racket in one raised hand and a shuttlecock in the other.

Mordent knew he would like it there.

A tiny bell rang as he entered. The shop appeared deserted. All occupants in stiff repose. It wasn't dark or dingy but bright and open. It strived to be the antithesis of the stereotype.

Suddenly one of the figures moved, and Mordent realised that what he had taken in the periphery of his vision as an exhibit was in fact a bald man in his late thirties. Mordent believed - and didn't question - that he had remained deliberately still.

'May I assist?'

'I'm looking for Berenice.'

'Ah - the estranged father!' The man beamed like a curve painted on an eggshell. 'She's out back, up to her elbows in formaldehyde. I'll just let her know you've arrived.'

He slipped past the polar bear through a batik curtain and disappeared whilst Mordent looked around at some of the other displays. Two domestic cats sat playing cards around a green baize table. A mouse in a white dress lay tied to railway tracks as a rat twirled an elongated moustache. Other mice crowded around oversized footwear in a nursery pose of *The Old Woman Who Lived In A Shoe*. Behind the counter, small boxes were stacked several stories high. Mordent was about to examine these when the man returned to the room.

'She'll be with you in a moment. My name's Damian, by the way.'

He sat behind the desk, picked up one of the boxes, and pushed it into a Jiffy bag suitably addressed. 'We sell so many of these,' he said. 'Taxidermy kits. They come with pliers, galvanised wire, surgical gloves and a seventy step guide on how to turn dead mice into miniature ornaments. Minus the mice. We suggest local pet stores supply those.'

'Live?'

'No, not live. We're not in the business of death. The stores sell the mice as reptile food. Preferably fresh because they're more pliable that way. Mice are the easiest animals to work with, or chipmunks. But mice are almost bred for this kind of thing.'

Mordent nodded. Surrounded by dioramas of dead animals he couldn't believe any species would object to taxidermy as their final destination.

'How'd you get into this line of work?'

'Serendipity. I've got an affiliation with dead creatures. It might seem macabre but I've found whenever I touch an animal it dies shortly afterwards. I'm not always aware of this, of course, but a few coincidences arose and it's something I'm certain about. It struck me that if I were a person conducive to taking an animal's life then I am also the best person to restore it. And so my life's work.'

'That sounds a little freaky to me.'

'It does, doesn't it? And it is. It's best to accept such things and work with them. Each time I add a glint to an animal's eye it reassures me.'

'What's the biggest animal you've worked with,' asked Mordent, eyeing the polar bear.

'Oh not that one. That's display purposes only. But I was part of a team that restored a giraffe. I felt particularly guilty because I had petted it once whilst it was alive. I offered myself to the zoo as a freebie.'

Mordent was spared further questions as Berenice emerged from behind the batik. She gave him a quick smile and then provided Damian with a summary of her morning's work, before taking Mordent's arm and leading him out of the shop.

'There's a patisserie on the corner that specialises in kosher cakes. They're not the best, but I only have thirty minutes for lunch.'

'Damian works you hard.'

'Partly, but it's best to return to the subject without too long a break. I'm stuffing a beaver right now.'

If Berenice saw the double-entendre her expression didn't show it. Mordent realised that if he were talking with anyone else he would have raised an eyebrow, but he couldn't do that in his new role. The disparity intrigued him.

After a few minutes they were sat at a round table, drinking strong black tea and eating apple matzo cake.

'You like this work?' Mordent asked.

'I do.' Berenice smiled. 'I like working with the animals and I like the specialisation. I like it when I tell people what I do. You don't get that in many other professions. Do you like your work?'

'Like isn't a word I would associate with it,' said Mordent. In his mind's eye, a procession of people he had killed fell over one another like tipped dominoes. 'But it's something that I'm good at. And I really don't know anything else.'

Berenice sipped her tea. 'When I enquired after you at the precinct I had a mixed reaction. Some seemed openly hostile, but for others you were a favourite grandfather.'

Mordent laughed. 'Grandfather is pushing it a bit.' Then he realised they hadn't spoken about relationships. 'It is, isn't it?'

She smiled. 'I have no children and I'm not with anyone right now, but if I need someone to walk me down the aisle or bounce a child on their knee then you'll be the first person I call.'

Their conversation flowed freely and happily. Mordent couldn't quite believe it.

After her second slice of cake Berenice said: 'Are you able to tell me what you're working on right now?'

Mordent sighed. 'I shouldn't.' He sighed again. 'I've got a client who thinks his uncle was scared to death. I also think I'm being set up to take a fall over something else, but I really can't go into details on that one.'

'Ok.'

'I'm not planning on going anywhere.'

Berenice wiped her lips with a napkin. 'But it is a risky business?'

'You could say that. You cross the road and you take a risk. You get out of bed in the morning you take a risk. But the risk is always fifty/fifty - either something will happen or it won't.'

'That's a philosophical way of looking at it.'

'It's practical.' Mordent looked at his watch. 'Your thirty minutes are almost up.'

She nodded and they both stood. She took his arm again as they returned to the taxidermists.

'This is almost too easy, isn't it?' she said.

'Don't question it. Don't make it harder than it already isn't.'

Outside the doorway, in full gaze of the glass-eyed mammals, she kissed his cheek. 'Don't be a stranger.'

He touched her forearm. 'I won't.'

23
Hubble-Bubble

Astrid answered the fifth time Mordent called.

He stood looking out of his office building at rain sheeting down from the sky, as though a glazing company were refurbishing the clouds and all their product had slipped.

'Hello?'

'It's Mordent. You ok? I was having some trouble reaching you.'

'Yes, I'm ok.'

Mordent didn't need to be a detective to tell that she wasn't.

'I'll take you at your word. Look, it's not a business call, more a social call. I might be in a fix. Sometimes you're the best person to turn to. You remember the gimp mask incident?'

'Who could forget?'

'And you know the kind of work I do. You're one of the few people I feel I can turn to.'

'Where is this going? I'm a little busy at the moment.'

Mordent pulled up short. Was Astrid giving him the cold shoulder? And if so, why?

'They've been a couple of deaths recently that I think someone is trying to hang on me.' He paused. 'They involve bubblewrap.'

Astrid's response was quick, unemotive. 'Bubblewrap and prostitutes. I know.'

'You know?'

'Information like this travels fast in the trade.'

Mordent thought it over. 'But the first murder wasn't a working girl. She was part of a bachelorette party.'

'You think whores don't have friends who get married? Trust me, she was a whore.'

'Oh.'

Her voice softened. 'You didn't know that did you? I'm sorry I was a little brusque. My business is even more dangerous than yours. It's just that...' her conversation tailed away.

'...it's just that you wondered if I had anything to do with it?'

'There aren't many – if any – bubblewrap fetishists in this city.'

'That puts me in pole position for the murders.'

'That makes me a potential victim.'

Mordent laughed. 'Whether I'm guilty or innocent?'

'Whether you're innocent or guilty.' She sighed. 'I'm sorry Mordent, but I can't see you again until this is over.'

'I know where you live.'

'That's what scares me.'

'Really?'

'No. I don't know. If it's someone else involved then it scares me.'

'I didn't know the first girl as a client.'

'But that makes it clear you knew the second. I can't take the risk.' There was another pause, deeper this time, one Mordent knew came out of friendship rather than any professional connection. 'I'm sorry.'

She replaced the handset. Mordent continued to watch the rain, the drops like giant spermatozoa masturbated against the glass, sliding down the building and into oblivion. His life was becoming suffocated real fast.

He went back to basics. Hunting in a drawer for paper and pen he sat at the table and doodled something nondescript with the possibility of a face in the top left corner before starting a list of those that knew of his fetish. It wouldn't be a long list, but that would be the point:

Astrid
Simona
Juliette Darnier
Anna
Lola White

His brow furrowed as he struggled to remember others he might have visited, however casually. Then he drew lines through the already dead.

Astrid
~~Simona~~
~~Juliette Darnier~~
Anna
~~Lola White~~

Simona had been the first whore he had paid for the pleasure of bubblewrap, but she had been involved with someone he had once wiped out and then he had to take *her* out. Juliette Darnier had been linked to Simona for reasons he had never fathomed, but her revenge trip had been terminated by the police shortly before Mordent's possible emasculation. He had never been able to investigate the link in case the tables had turned on him.

Lola, of course, was long gone. Anna had been the stepping stone between Simona and Astrid. He couldn't imagine why Anna might hold a grudge, but then her possible involvement didn't mean she was a killer. As it stood, she was his only lead. He had no doubts that Astrid wouldn't have divulged his predilection.

Galvanised, he slung on his jacket, checked unnecessarily for his gun, and headed out to the wet streets, the miasma of the city.

It had been a while since he had frequented the district from which Anna operated. It was almost a clandestine complex: grimy on the outside, high-class on the inside. After twenty minutes sludging through rain the weather improved as he turned down the one-way side street that led - maze-like - to his destination. The closer he drove, the closer the sides of buildings hemmed in, until he could barely manoeuvre his vehicle between trashcans and he had to pull in both wing mirrors for safety. It was an area that didn't want to be found, expect by the most tenacious. Just after a final sharp turn, however, the road opened onto a large circular carpark. The pagoda at the centre of the maze.

The sun's promise after the rain couldn't lift the vista to anything approaching attractive. Steam rose from scabby wasteground, patchy areas of grass were beyond revival, old needles stuck up from the soil as metaphors for modern-day vegetation in a post-climate change twist. In a half-moon crescent apartment block buildings appeared run down, were richly graffitied. The whole area was stale, run-down, but it was a front. Behind the dereliction worked some of the highest class hookers in the city.

Some men liked the sleaze. From the carpark with

its Jaguars and Mercs no doubt many of the punters could have booked these women into the Hilton or the Marriott but that would be too easy. Some men wanted to go out of their way to get what they wanted, to take risks which they didn't need.

Mordent could understand it even if he couldn't afford it. He had found Anna here one year in desperation, but couldn't pay her prices for long. In any event, she was mechanical in her work, didn't provide the frisson he needed, and once Astrid was on his radar there had been no turning back.

A link from her to the recent deaths seemed obscure, incalculable. But what had Sherlock Holmes said: once you have eliminated the impossible, whatever remains, no matter how improbable, must be the truth. He had applied that once to a missing bath sponge and been utterly wrong, but these were different circumstances and it had to be worth a shot.

She worked from the second floor. Or he hoped that remained the case. The handrail was paint-worn, flecks of rust decked his fingers like gold-leaf on a Buddhist's forehead. Despite the handful of vehicles the buildings were quiet. Some of them, he knew, were soundproofed.

He stopped at 219. Disconnected déjà vu propelled him into the past, but the sexual impulse was absent. When he knocked he imagined the sound echoing from that past and into the present. When Anna opened the door she wore a familiar faded kimono.

Her expression was querulous; no doubt his memory of her was greater than her memory of him.

He leant against the jamb. 'Are you free? Can I have a word?'

'I don't...' but then she did. She stepped sideways and he walked through. The apartment was lush in decoration, dimmed light added to the effect.

'Perhaps I should have called,' he said, 'but I no longer have your number.'

'Sure thing honey.' She glanced at her watch. 'I have eighteen minutes free til my next client. You here for a quickie?' She looked around, as if searching for bubblewrap.

Mordent shook his head. 'That's not what I came for.'

He saw that she held a small device in her hand which would alert security if he was anything other than legit.

'You won't be needing that,' he said. 'I want information.'

She sat indecorously on the arm of a sofa, crossed her legs. 'My time is money.'

Reaching into his jacket pocket Mordent drew out his wallet, flipped, skipped, then selected a few notes. He lay them on the cushion beside her.

'You remember me?'

'I do now.'

'Remember why I used to come here?'

She slid her right index finger into the side of her mouth, then applied pressure and allowed it to slip out with a popping noise. Mordent noticed a couple of years hadn't been kind to her. And as her finger flexed out of her mouth a false fingernail shot across the room.

'I need to know whether you ever told anyone – *anyone* – about my fetish.'

'All client information is secure, honey.' She said it routinely, as though she were working in a bank. Mordent remembered that disconnection.

'So you have never passed on, under any circumstances, my bubblewrap fantasies? Not to another client, or another worker, or anyone?'

She shook her head. 'Discretion is essential in this

business. You know the class of clientele we get. My life wouldn't be worth it if I gave out information.'

He nodded. It had been a wasted journey. But he had needed to do something.

For a moment he wondered if he should warn her, whether the news of the bubblewrap deaths had spread. Then he realised both responses were negative. No one would have been able to trace him to her. She was only a dead end. She *wasn't* dead. And if she *had* known of the deaths she wouldn't have let him in.

Now he glanced at *his* watch. There were still ten minutes til her client arrived.

She looked across to the sofa. 'Put another twenty on there honey, and I'll ease some of that tension.'

He looked better in her mouth than her finger did.

24
Footwork

When Mordent had been on the force he was more effective on his feet. The security of a vehicle was just an object for police to hide behind. They already had uniforms as public barriers and their cars continued that theme. If he had wanted to get to the nub of something, to winnow out information from a reluctant source, then it paid benefits to arrive on foot.

Now he was a PI he didn't have the vehicle or the uniform, but obtaining information remained the same. Footwork could be defined as dogged perseverance, each step distinct, specific. Whereas a vehicle could run roughshod indiscriminately, walking bought time and thoughtfulness to the task. This was the clarity he now sought. He couldn't fail to be implicated in the murders, that much was clear. So he needed to use his knowledge to his advantage, and garner as much as he could to be used in his defence.

It was for this reason that he parked his vehicle some way from the sumo club. On reflection, he should have done that on his first visit.

Twilight had begun to fall as he had left Anna's apartment, the dim glow failing to enhance the appearance of the complex. On the stairs he had passed a man who kept his hat pulled over his eyes: politician, pop singer, movie star, Mordent couldn't tell. Even if he had seen his face anonymity would have been preserved. In that district, outing someone only meant that you were outed yourself.

Now he pushed open the door to the club. As he had hoped, the barmaid from the night before was working. She wore a fluorescent sky-blue crop top and pale green jogging shorts. A noise calling itself music blasted full-pelt from the sound system. She hopped from one leg to the next. Dancing or exercising Mordent couldn't be sure. The interior of the bar was empty.

'Hey, we don't open for another twenty minutes.'

Mordent had to lip-read this over the noise.

She knelt and turned the music down.

He opened his arms, palms outward. 'Door was open.'

She sucked in a breath. 'My fault. I keep getting told off for that.' She looked around, as if deciding whether to offer a drink. 'Hey,' she said, 'don't I know you from somewhere?'

He leant on the bar, tried to be as unpresupposing as possible. 'I was here the other night for the bubblewrap sumo. The night when the girl got killed.'

Honesty was sometimes the best policy. In this case it hit the button.

She smiled. 'Yeh, I remember you. I had to tell the police about you, I hope you don't mind.' There was no trace she held the slightest concern.

'Of course I don't mind.' He decided to show her his PI badge. 'I'm almost one of them myself.'

'Oh.' The word came out of her lips like a bubblegum bubble. 'It was a sad night. They've stopped the sumo. You know that?'

He shook his head. 'I didn't know. It was a laugh though, wasn't it?'

Nostalgia flitted over her features. 'Yeh, it was a

laugh. Now we're back to the beans. That was why I was exercising. Getting ready for my session later.'

Mordent couldn't help but admire a physique that could have thrown him over her shoulder and spun him around like a wrestler if she wanted to. His evolutionary impulses confused by role reversal.

'Is it ok if I ask a few questions? Stuff the police probably missed?'

'Yeh, sure.' She bent to take some glasses out of a washer and stacked them under the counter. 'Just let me get on with my work in case the boss steps in.'

'The girl who died. Had you seen her in here before?

She shook her head. 'I didn't recognise any of that party. We get a few regulars, but most of the customers tend to come in groups - and usually only once. It's a laugh, you see, but once you've seen it you don't need to see it again. Certainly once you've taken part you rarely want to do it again.'

'Did you notice anything unusual?'

'Not a thing. Was a regular night. You think someone here might have taken a shine to her? I'd left off before the end of the night.'

'I know. I noticed you'd gone.'

'I do weird shifts. The boss is flexible. I have a train to catch that runs at funny times. The guy who fills in for me works out back most nights.'

'Ok.'

She paused in her work. 'You know you were the only one in here taking a real interest in the scene. I had to pass that on.'

'It's fine. Don't worry. They know who I am.'

Concern floated from her features like a released helium balloon. 'Sounds odd, but I didn't want to drop anyone in it.'

Mordent shrugged. He wasn't sure how to respond.

'I've not always been on the right side of the law,' she continued. 'You know how it is.'

He nodded. 'That isn't always a bad thing.'

She grinned. 'Do you want a beer?'

He considered his options. 'That might not be a great idea. No offence.'

'None taken.'

The conversation stalled. Mordent took another look around the bar where all his troubles had begun. If that first death had been deliberately connected to him then someone had to have known he had been there or was going there. He lingered over that thought for a moment.

'Do you have CCTV in here?'

'We do, but the police took it.'

'No copies?'

'Not to my knowledge.'

'Ok. Was good seeing you again.'

'You too. Come back when it's busy. I'll flick a bean your way.'

Mordent left the bar buoyed by laughter.

Outside he leant against bare brick and dialled Astrid's number. She didn't answer. He couldn't blame her. There was one question he needed answering: how had she known about the bubblewrap sumo? Had someone told her, knowing that she would pass the information on? It all seemed contrived, but that was life in a nutshell. It wasn't only in books and movies that reality could be coerced into circumstances like a dog rounding sheep in a pen. Real life was equally pliable if someone wanted it to be. He opened his mouth and let out a low *baa*.

25
Baiting The Manticore

Morning didn't bring the heavy plod of police or a battering ram to Mordent's door. He slept clean and dreamless, waking without the alcoholic haze he had favoured the past few days and felt all the better for it. Sun created a white square on his ceiling, a boxing ring. As he watched, light cast the presence of two planes across the surface. Shadow boxers.

He guessed Marten's feint with the sperm had succeeded. Mordent's remaining time was determinate upon the second sample being analysed. He expected a chat with Kovacs would occur before nightfall. They had to find him before then.

His second appointment at the Fear Institute was fixed for that morning. In the corner of his room sat the roll of bubblewrap he had bought. Ironically, it was the only product of its type he had ever purchased. Instructions to those who *assisted* him had meant they had supplied the material. He took it with him to the car, not wanting it to be found in his apartment. It could be classified as a murder weapon.

On the route to the Institute he stopped off at Bukowski's for breakfast: thick slices of ham on toast, a strong black cup of coffee. He left the bubblewrap under the window seat, a little reluctantly. No doubt someone would find a use for it.

At the door of the Fear Institute he melded his mind to that of Raymond Greener. The same skinny man led him down the same hallway, Mordent imagining he had to sidestep cracks in the floorboards. Entering Copernicus Fear's office he saw the swivel chair was once again facing the opposite direction. He approached it, waiting for it to swing around, when the door closed behind him and Copernicus shouted *boo!*

Mordent jumped, turned. Copernicus leant his ancient frame against the wall, chuckling softly.

'Forgive me,' he said, 'but I always do this on the second visit. If no one jumps then they're not really scared of anything. Give me a hand will you. I'll never get back over there alone.'

Mordent stuck out his arm and Copernicus took it. He led him across to the chair as though he were carrying wood for a fire. There wasn't much to the man. Again, when he sank into the leather he seemed as though he were consumed by it.

Mordent returned to the other side of the desk, sat.

'I left you a challenge the last time we spoke. Did you purchase the bubblewrap?'

'I did.'

'And you kept it by you? Somewhere in your home where it would have been visible?'

'I did.'

'And how did you feel about that?'

'I had to skirt around it. I couldn't look at it directly. I couldn't stop myself from imagining the noise if the bubbles were to pop.'

'I see.' Copernicus pyramided his fingers. He closed his eyes for a moment. Mordent wondered if he had fallen asleep.

'Can I just ask,' Mordent said, 'is this the way you tackle all fears? Let me take something common for example, say a fear of rats or snakes. Would you advise the client to purchase these prior to the second consultation?'

Copernicus opened one eyelid. 'I am extraordinarily busy, sir. Can we stick to the matter in hand?'

'I *was* awaiting your reply.'

'And *I* was thinking.' Humour seemed to have left the building. 'The best way to alleviate your fear is to confront it. If the presence of the bubblewrap made you uneasy, then imagine your apartment filled with the stuff! Imagine yourself wrapped in it. My suggestion is to do just that. Roll on the floor in it. Eventually the fear will dissipate: what was unusual will become commonplace. If that fails, we resort to hypnotherapy.'

Mordent turned this over. 'It sounds to me as though you want to exacerbate the fear before you treat it?'

'And to a layman it might appear that way. Trust me, our methods are proven.'

'Do you have letters of recommendation from previous clients?'

'Do we?' Copernicus queried himself. 'I suppose we do. I don't believe we make those public.'

'So my next step would be to buy more bubblewrap? Furnish my apartment with it, dress in it, and then come back to you when I'm a quivering wreck?'

If Copernicus could have stood then he might have done. 'Don't be a dramatist! Dramatising your fear exacerbates it. Don't think it big, make it small. It's all in your mind – there's no rational explanation for what you have. Get control of yourself and control will get control of you.'

Mordent almost stood, but Copernicus settled, like a balloon slowly deflating, becoming smaller in the chair.

'Let me tell you,' he said, 'about the manticore. Do you know what that is?'

'It sounds like a mythical beast to me.'

'It was. Or is? I guess it all depends on whether anyone believes in it or not. But that's getting into semantics. The manticore is a legendary Persian creature similar to the Egyptian sphinx. It has the body of a red lion, a human head with three rows of sharp teeth, the wings of a bat and the tail of a scorpion. Legend has it that it can shoot poisoned spines to paralyse or kill its victims. It eats people whole leaving nothing behind.'

Mordent slouched. 'It sounds like something you wouldn't want to meet in a dark alley.'

Copernicus nodded. 'Terrifying, isn't it? Terrifying, and - as far as we know - non-existent. But let me tell you something Mr Greener, it is a struggle for me to even describe it in conversation. I - you see - am genuinely terrified of the manticore, and have been for most of my life; ever since I saw an artist's impression of the creature in an encyclopaedia when I was very young. I think it is the human face that underlies that fear, the idea of something normal within something abnormal, but either way I can't bear to look at a picture of one, and if I ever saw one then I would be the first to jettison my bowels.'

'I seem to remember,' Mordent said, 'that at our first meeting you had a phobia of being ignored. Do you change your phobias dependent on your clients?'

'Not at all. I was correct in stating I had a phobia of being ignored. In point of fact, part of that related to my fear of the manticore as no one would believe me. And I have eradicated that phobia. No, I mention the manticore as an example of living with something quite ridiculous but still being dominated by it. If I didn't control my fear of the manticore then it would possess me. As it happens, I have not allowed that to happen. And whilst on the face of it no one would be concerned finding bubblewrap in an alley on a dark night, I acknowledge that for yourself, my fear of the manticore is just as ridiculous. Hence, listen to my words, buy the bubblewrap, confront your fear, and then make another appointment where we can take this further.'

Copernicus dug his legs into the floor and half-spun the chair. The movement wasn't quite as smooth as it had been on the first occasion. He presented a half-face to Mordent; a still from an Ingmar Bergman movie.

Mordent rose. 'I'll take your advice,' he said to the side of the face which bore a grimace. He wondered if the unseen side was smiling at the theatrics. 'Thank you for your time.'

The door opened behind him. Mordent wondered if it were operated by a switch or whether the assistant listened in to their conversations. Either way he was led back to the outside world via a cash register and once in the street with the door behind him he wondered if he had just exited a fantasy world.

Either way, he had an idea that might prove to Benedict Holmsworth's satisfaction.

26
If This Were A Race Then The Past Just Caught Up

Mordent had switched off his cell before entering the Fear Institute, not wanting to be bothered by other concerns. Back in his car, sunshine turning his windscreen to Saran wrap, he checked for missed messages and found one from Emmeline Edwards. He returned her call.

'Emmeline? Mordent.'

'Due to the wonders of modern technology Mr Mordent I knew it was you before you did.'

He laughed. 'You got some information for me?'

'Certainly. But not anything I can tell you over the phone. I'm not even sure I should be seen in your company.'

'Oh?'

'Let's just say your position might be compromised.'

'I'm aware of that. Where did you want to meet? The tea room?'

'No, not there. I like to mix it up a bit. Can you meet me in an hour at Prospect Park?'

'Of course.'

'By the little bridge. And don't forget the potato salad!'

'Potato salad?'

'You'll either understand or you won't. See you there.'

Mordent killed the call, thought, then dialled it again.

'One more thing,' he said, before she had chance to speak. 'If you get the time, check out a guy named Ezra George. He'll be old. That's all I know about him.'

He killed it a second time before she could object.

Starting his engine he could only think of potato salad. Unsure whether she was kidding he drove towards Prospect Park looking for a delicatessen. A couple of blocks away he pulled up outside *Smidt's* and bought a tub. The guy with glasses behind the counter smiled.

'You taking that to Prospect Park?'

'How'd you guess?'

'Where did you think I got the name of the deli?'

Mordent shook his head. He was in no mood for riddles. As he left the joint he was sure the owner whispered *wonderman*.

The park was large, over five hundred acres, but Mordent was familiar with the layout. Under coercion, he could even name where a particular body was buried. When Emmeline had mentioned the *little bridge* he hadn't thought to question it. By the time he reached her he was sweating profusely, the sun violent on the day, yet couldn't remove his jacket for fear of revealing his piece. He handed over the potato salad. She was dressed the colour of their shed skins.

'Very droll, I'm sure,' she said. 'Did you get one of those plastic forks?'

Mordent sighed and shook his head. 'What is it with the potato salad?'

'I said if you don't know then don't ask.'

He shrugged. 'Forget it. I'm guessing that's the least of my worries.'

She nodded. A smile tried to escape her face but was reined in. 'You know things aren't looking good for you,' she said.

'I know someone's setting me up. How did you get to hear about that?'

She sighed. 'Part of the deal is you can't question my methods. You wouldn't like our information exchange going the other way. Treat other people as you would like them to treat you. Etc.'

Mordent grunted.

'Shall I continue?'

He nodded.

'You are a little schoolboy today, aren't you?' The smile broke through.

'It's this heat. Feels like I'm in a pressure cooker.'

'Have you ever cooked with a pressure cooker?'

He shook his head.

'So ditch the comparison. Anyway...I thought I should advise you that you're wanted by the police in connection with the three bubblewrap deaths. I'm not here to give you a head start, more a thumbs up. I don't believe you did it, but then what do I know? That's why we're meeting in an open space.'

'You can't seriously think I'd do anything like that?'

'With bubblewrap, no; but I'm damn sure you must have killed before.'

The look she gave went straight through his head and into the fabric of the bridge.

'And I'm not talking about lawful police killings,' she added.

'I've done nothing that can be proven either way.'

'And that's all that concerns me,' she said. 'I'm here for a specific business arrangement, but - and it is a *but* - should you be formally charged at any point in the investigation then my services are lost.'

Mordent nodded. 'Understood.'

He eyed the potato salad she had placed on the bridge, imagining the sour cream and mayo almost boiling in the tub.

Then he said: 'Three deaths?'

'There was another last night, Anna Kaplinsky. Is that your missing puzzle piece?'

He tried not to bat an eyelid; batted both.

'Are you serious?'

'Do I look like I'm joking?'

He rested both arms on the bridge. Tiny stone particles lodged in the fabric of his jacket, together with moss specks.

'Someone's got it in for me.'

'Any ideas who it could be?'

Mordent shook his head. 'Do you know why they've linked these to me?'

'I don't know the details, but I'm aware you were implicated with the first two and I was told the spec is the same for the recent death.'

Mordent nodded. 'It's better that you don't know,' he said. 'I'm just wondering if there's someway I can engage your services to find information the police won't be looking for. I could be incarcerated before the end of the day.'

Emmeline looked around the park, her eyes a surveillance camera. 'You pay me, I help,' she said.

'Let me think it through.' Truth was, he didn't know what to do, what to say. He let his eyes linger on her a moment, realised he was savouring everything, even the heat - now - even the sweat as it coursed into his arse crack. There were worms coming home to roost. He realised that depending on Anna's time of death it was quite likely she would have traces of his sperm in her mouth. A net was closing in. The blanket of noir would hang heavy on his shoulders as he was bustled into a police vehicle. In the dock, criminals would come out of the woodwork to testify like weevils shaken out of sea biscuits.

He felt woozy, leant harder against the bridge.

And all of this at a time where he was getting to know Berenice.

He sighed. 'I'll contact you if I get an idea on a lead. For the moment, zilch.'

'There *was* another thing. You asked me about Ezra George.'

'Oh yeh. That's something else entirely.'

'You want me to follow that up? You haven't given me a lot to go on.'

'He's likely to be local. I can't add more to it than that.'

'Not the singer then?'

'The singer?'

'George Ezra. A British boy.'

Mordent's knowledge of popular music ended with Thelonious Monk. He shook his head.

Emmeline smiled. She opened the brown clutch bag she had been holding and wrote out an invoice. 'That's for today. Bank transfer as usual.'

Mordent nodded. 'You're a good woman Emmeline.'

She laughed. 'You're getting nostalgic for a female because you're thinking you might not see one for a while. Let's try and keep you out of jail, right?'

He nodded. A moment was flung between them where they might have shaken hands or even hugged, but then it passed and they went their separate ways.

'Anna Kaplinksy,' muttered Mordent. 'I should have left her alone.'

29
Going Over To The Other Side

Mordent had booked himself into a hotel room following more drinks at Morgan's Bar. His apartment was no doubt being watched - either by the police or the real killer - and he needed at least one sleep before facing Kovacs and a barrage of uncomfortable questions.

In the lobby of the hotel he had stood at reception whilst the night clerk raised themselves from a poorly-lit anteroom, rubbing their eyes behind spectacle lenses at the post-midnight hour. Behind him another door bore the following message taped across at head height:

Fire door
please
keep
shut

Mordent couldn't help but notice that the word *elks* could be read downwards within the wording, like an acrostic poem. He wondered, in a semi-drunken haze, whether the door would open to a room stuffed with elks, or - indeed - stuffed with stuffed elks. This led him onto taxidermy, and Berenice, and melancholy enveloped him in an equally alcoholic embrace. The night clerk didn't appear to notice this, and barely exchanging a word handed him the key to his room.

Within a handful of minutes Mordent was fast asleep.

He woke clear headed, his unusual surroundings forcing acknowledgement of his situation. With that clarity he noticed the paper peeling away from the wall with a yellowish-tinge to the plaster beneath and remembered reading somewhere that Napoleon was killed by his wallpaper. In one corner of the ceiling plasterboard had dropped and cracked. Mould grew a forest scene under the windowsill. When he stumbled to the bathroom there was a distinct lack of hot water, and what liquid did emerge was rusty brown.

Still, he had been in worse places.

Pulling on his clothes he regretted not returning to his apartment for fresh underwear. He was sure he was going to need it.

Out on the street the skies were as clear as he wished his conscience could be. The intimation of another blisteringly hot day was already on the horizon. It could be smelt. Without a backwards glance at the hotel he headed over to Morgan's Bar and slipped into his vehicle, the interior already resembling a greenhouse. Driving over to Bukowski's he had a plate of meat and bread alongside a cool glass of milk. It wasn't quite a last supper, nor the final meal of a condemned man, but it filled his belly and he felt ready to take on Kovacs.

At the precinct he had no access to the parking lot.

An officer he didn't recognise, but who clearly knew him, waved his vehicle to the sidewalk. Marsham stepped out of the main entrance as though he had been waiting there for that very purpose.

'I'll take over,' he said.

The other officer took the car keys that dangled from Mordent's fingers and drove the vehicle around the block. Mordent's gun was in the glove compartment but he hadn't killed anyone with it. As far as he knew there was no bubblewrap within the vehicle.

Marsham pulled him to one side, spoke direct into his ear, having to bend himself a third to do so.

'Kovacs is ready to press a charge based on the evidence we hold. I don't need to tell you to stay schtum over anything that might implicate you further. Currently you're assisting us with our enquiries. Given the information you know about everyone - including me - I take it you wouldn't even consider any plea bargains if it came to that. There's a lot of worried old faces in there right now.'

Mordent took a step back. 'You're right. You don't need to tell me anything.'

He walked into the station solo. Bartholomew wasn't the man at the desk so Mordent couldn't go through his usual *wife and kids* spiel. The absence of familiarity at his arrival unnerved him, as though he were indeed a criminal in a parallel universe.

'I've heard you guys are looking for me.'

He gave out his name and address. Desk Guy called up and Kovacs came down. He watched as Mordent emptied his pockets and then arranged for him to be lead to an interview room. Kovacs did all this without any indication he had previously met him. He was professional to the last, and Mordent wondered whether a part of Kovacs didn't want to claim Mordent as a murderer. Whether he needed their symbiotic idiotic relationship like a remora needed a shark.

Which of them was which animal might be the starting point for an argument, but he wasn't in the mood for one.

He sat at a nondescript table. By the door, an officer was impassive. Mordent had been on the other side of the table on many occasions. In the very distant past he had committed quite a few violent acts there. Whilst he was often nostalgic for those pre-modern days he was glad that Kovacs would do it by the book rather than literally throwing the book *at* him. And when he considered that he was - in fact - innocent, then it was clear he had nothing to fear.

Yet a nervous sensation ran up and down his spine like the tingler in the Vincent Price movie. There was a definite threat that he couldn't just run ragged over. And a bribe was most certainly out of the question.

The door opened and Kovacs stepped through. It looked like he wore a new suit. It *always* looked like he wore a new suit. Mordent was sure it was the same suit. That was Kovacs all over. Kovacs was always a man who looked like he wore a new suit.

In contrast, Mordent might as well have slept in his. He frequently did.

Kovacs said something to the officer at the door who nodded and went.

That left the two of them.

Remora and shark.

Shark and remora.

Neither of them wanted to speak first.

Kovacs leant with his back to the door, he didn't move across to the table.

Mordent wondered if he was expected to lunge at him, physically or verbally; whether Kovacs had planned an escape route.

Then there was the matter of the absence of the other officer. Perhaps Kovacs wasn't going by the book after all.

Two, three minutes elapsed.

If there had been a clock in the room the only sound would have been its mechanism.

If Mordent had a pin in his pocket he would have let it drop.

They both waited, patiently, in the expectation that the other knew why they were waiting.

Then Kovacs said: 'Much as I would rather believe otherwise, we both know you didn't kill those women. Would you mind telling me what this is all about?'

Mordent realised his mouth was hanging open. He closed it. It was as though he had discovered Kovacs was a beetle or a medieval knight and that under the carapace or metallic suit something fleshy lived.

'Are you not going to charge me? Interview me?'

'I'll do both in good time. The interview is essential. Charging you will be important to send out the message that we're serious. But then you'll be bailed. Locking you up would only lead to more complaints about prison food. You're more useful to me on the outside.'

'To do what?'

'To catch the killer. That's what we both want, isn't it?'

Kovacs folded his hands before him. He remained standing.

'How do you know it isn't me?'

'Because as much as I want to believe it, you're not really that stupid.'

'Everyone else thinks you're out to get me.'

'That's because as much as you want to believe it, I'm not really that stupid.'

'Misdirection?'

'Misdirection.'

Kovacs walked towards the table, leant on it with both fists, suddenly the dominant monkey in the troupe.

'Now tell me,' he said, 'what bubblewrap has to do with any of this.'

30
You Can't Pogo To Disco

Back in the 70s, when music was fluid and Mordent was an officer of the law, when he could say *may the force be with you* on the right side of irony, when he could haul someone into an alley for a beating and it didn't matter if they were black or white, when officers collected and traded baseball cards they'd seized from young offenders, when the city was a band of disparate criminals and the lines between good and bad were blurred, when the vestiges of noir's mantle still clung grubby to the polluted atmosphere, when pimps and bums and whores and cops could mingle in any drinking establishment and not just Morgan's Bar, when the river was as full of bodies as it was of fish, and when the future seemed to be the present which was just a reflection of the past, Mordent was sometimes called out to skirmishes at music venues.

These weren't the jazz clubs he was familiar with, where men in black polo neck sweaters languidly drank shorts, their toes tapping in time to the score, the atmosphere thick with smoke from imported French cigarettes, and the sounds of brass instruments swollen with honey rather than the rat-ta-tat-tat of their misuse in marching bands, but *new* music venues where thc demarcation between sounds were more radically drawn, and the twin forces of punk and disco whirlwound their way through the city's youth like drugs being flushed down a toilet.

The fights at the punk clubs reflected the music: short, violent, punctuated with shouts and intimidating body-postures. Whilst those on the disco circuit were - if nowadays Mordent could even be permitted to think of such a term - gayer: shoves, pushes, prolonged and bitchy. In these latter fights there was the likelihood of a knife being produced. At the punk clubs it was all fists and feet.

Mordent wasn't drawn to either genre, but he could see the visceral appeal with punk, the intelligence hiding behind the thuggery. Disco was pure infatuation. Where punk offered confrontation, disco offered escapism. Where punks jumped up and down, like protestors, disco divas swirled and twirled like dervishes. If anything was certain, it was that you couldn't pogo to disco. For him, that summed up the difference, delineated the two groups into their camps. And whenever he needed someone on his side, whenever he had to be sure of someone, if ever - in the midst of separating a fight he saw a kindred spirit who might, in the fullness of time, become a useful associate - it was in the punk clubs that those targets were obvious. They wouldn't make informers, but if handled correctly they could be persuaded to help so long as it matched their ideals.

As Mordent rose through the ranks he utilised the services of some of those punks who flanked him as shadows. Should the mayor get tetchy, a hint of violence might change his mind; should a gangster apply pressure, Mordent applied it back. He was young and mean and no longer green and saw fit to reward those who helped him and dispose of those who didn't. Yet on the surface those edges whilst not obviously polished were at least honed. He gained a reputation as a rough diamond, earned respect from his superiors and criminals alike, without any one person investigating the mechanism that propelled him to the top. It was only when Kovacs arrived, at a coincidental period of management change, when health and safety and a wish to be seen to do things *properly* in addition to *well* altered the political climate, that Mordent began to get eased aside, his disreputable associates were disbanded, and eventually - disillusioned - he offered himself up for early retirement.

If Mordent was punk, Kovacs wasn't disco. If anything, Kovacs was all four members of Kraftwerk with their hands over their ears trying to eliminate Einstürzende Neubauten.

Yet: the way Kovacs spoke to Mordent in the interview room before the official interview - that was disco. And in the surprising disobedience to the ramifications of the system: that was punk.

Thereafter Mordent was carried through the system conveyor-belt style, like a particle in the food chain, before being dumped back on the street in his newly-cleaned vehicle like excrement on a silver platter. He had been charged and bailed without a dime being spent but only he and Kovacs knew that he was a free man.

His gun remained in the glove compartment.

Kovacs wasn't as stupid as Mordent liked to think.

31
Two Steps Forwards, One Step Back

Mordent returned to his office. Humidity was building in the city like a tower about to topple. The air was thick with it, and as he walked along the corridor to his office moisture clung to him as if he were strolling through a slightly defective carwash. Even the secretarial temps walking to and from the agency further down the hall had snail-trail traces of perspiration that clung to hairs he hadn't previously noticed above their upper lips.

His appreciation of the minutiae of life which had presaged his thoughts of arrest had started to annoy him. He could feel his usual curmudgeonly manner returning just as rain and darkness would shortly engulf the city. He welcomed it. That familiar overcoat was comfortable. He craved it.

Opening his desk drawer he looked at the slip of paper he had written a few days earlier. Then made an amendment.

Astrid
~~Simona~~
~~Juliette Darnier~~
~~Anna~~
~~Lola White~~

The list couldn't be narrowed further. He wondered again who had notified Astrid about the sumo club and whether they had done so in order to entice him there. He had no doubts about Astrid's allegiance. Needing to contact her he looked at his cell. No doubt Kovacs could obtain details of his records if he had to which would relate to both pre- and post-arrest calls. Whilst he had left out details as to the exact nature of the bubblewrap connection when Kovacs had questioned him, not wanting to implicate Astrid, he knew that if necessary her involvement couldn't be ignored. Whilst he hoped to draw the line at visiting her, a phone call or two couldn't harm.

True to her last word, however, she didn't answer. Mordent looked out of the window as his cell rang. The view an accompaniment to the tone.

Across the way, leaning against the opposite building, stood a man Mordent felt sure he recognised. Then memory kicked in. He was one of the thugs who had beaten him in the alleyway. The man's face wasn't familiar, but his stance. Mordent was convinced he remembered it silhouetted against the night. He stepped back a moment as the man looked up. Then, without further thought, he killed the ringing cell and took the steps two at a time down through the heart of the building and burst out through the double doors onto the street.

Traffic separated them. Obviously placed to check his whereabouts but unskilled in the art of surveillance the man looked Mordent direct in the face with recognition before realising *he* was recognised. He took off, a swift walk at first, breaking into a run when looking back and realising Mordent had followed. Their progress mimicked that of two children racing each other along the opposite sides of a riverbank, the fast-moving traffic between them preventing Mordent crossing to the other side.

Mordent didn't give the guy much credit. Numerous streets led off from the main thoroughfare but he continued to run parallel. If there was only a break in the traffic...

It came.

Mordent ducked into the middle of the street with a car width to spare. Horns serenaded him with all the force of Cupid's trumpet. A wing mirror tugged half-heartedly at his jacket pocket, but just missed like an angler pulling too soon on his rod. Yet he was only midway, and now he stood in the centre of the traffic, with no means to cross the final stretch, he realised his move had been foolish. He couldn't run down the centre without seriously endangering his life and the way forwards was blocked by the stream.

He watched as the man finally turned a corner, and whilst a gap in the traffic then afforded Mordent safe harbour to the sidewalk by the time he had reached that turn the man wasn't in sight.

He stopped, bent with his hands on his thighs, drew in a couple of breaths. Wondered about the connections.

A couple of hundred yards up the road he saw a phone booth. He started walking towards it. Astrid might not pick up his call if she saw it came from his cell, but perhaps she would answer if the number couldn't be identified. Whilst he was on the street, he might as well make that call.

The inside of the booth smelt of stale cigarette smoke. Where once a directory had been fixed there now hung a short piece of what resembled metal rope. Thankfully the box hadn't been pissed in, recently. Thumbing up Astrid on his cell Mordent copied over the numbers and dialled.

'Hello? Planet Wok. Can I take your order please?'

He hung up and tried again.

'Hello?'

'Astrid, it's Mordent. Don't hang up.'

'Where are you calling from?'

'Just a street phone booth. Listen, I only need one piece of information. You were the one who mentioned the bubblewrap sumo club. Where did you hear about that?'

She sighed. 'It was another client. I can't remember how the discussion came about. I only saw him the once. An old guy.'

'What was his name?'

'You know I can't give you that. Client confidentiality.'

'Astrid. Currently three women are dead, two of whom I saw briefly as a client. If that client is any way linked to this then he already knows you. That means you are also at risk. Someone wants to nail me and I need to know why. Can't you simply give me the name?'

There was a long pause. 'Would you have wanted me to give out *your* name?'

'We've gone beyond that. I'm on charge for those murders. I don't want to involve you with the police but I need to clear my name. Either way, you'd have to give up the name of the guy to me or the police. Which would you choose?'

Another pause. 'I really want to help.' He heard something in the background which he couldn't quite determine, then realised she was flicking through some paper. 'Let me check my bookings.'

Mordent hung on the line. Outside the booth a kid skateboarded on the sidewalk, the wheels emulating the rolling of thunder. He noticed the sky had darkened considerably whilst he was on the phone, as though the booth itself were some kind of time travel device, and as he noticed this – as if on cue – fat drops hit the windows as though capsules fired from a paint gun. The glass sides suddenly flowed with water, melting - in visual effect - as the rain came hard and fast. The rectangle of the booth resonated like a child's rattle, and he could barely hear Astrid speak.

'What was that?'

Muffled.

'I can't hear it. What was it?'

Muffled.

'Again?'

Abruptly the rain stopped just as suddenly as it started and within the clarity Astrid's voice bellowed with almost religious fervour:

'Ezra George! I said the punter's name was Ezra George.'

Mordent watched as the skateboarder passed in the opposite direction, no longer smooth and soaked to the skin.

'Are you still there?'

Mordent spoke slowly. 'I'm still here. Listen, could you go away for a few days. It's quite possible your life could be in danger.'

'I can't take my children out of school.'

'I'm serious.'

'I'll have to discuss it with my husband.'

'There's been three deaths, Astrid, all bubblewrap connected. Most recent is Anna Kaplinsky - she was the girl who originally put me onto you. I'm certain Ezra George is at the heart of this, although I have no idea why. The deaths are being pinned on me and you are the last possible victim. I don't want to lose you.'

'I'll see what I can do.'

'Please. And let me know, either way.'

Mordent hung up. He leant against the side of the booth. There was a movie once, he recalled, where the entirety of the film played out within a phone booth. He couldn't remember if it was a good movie or a bad movie. What he would give, though, for the rest of this case to play out whilst he remained in the booth. There was security to be had within the confined space. Outside the booth there was too much world to handle.

32
Too Much Water Too Close To Home

Back in his office the weather was schizophrenic, throwing heavy rain at his windows one moment then evaporating it swiftly the next. The weather reflected his turmoil. Having established it was apparent he was being followed he wondered whether Berenice could also be a possible victim. He hadn't considered it within the booth, where Astrid's safety seemed paramount, but on the walk back it seemed plausible. Something else that seemed plausible, that nagged him defiantly, was whether Berenice had anything to do with it. The coincidence of her arrival - out of the blue - was suspicious. Other than an old photograph of him standing with her mother and a slight family resemblance there was nothing to link the two of them other than wishful thinking.

Had he entered their relationship too buoyantly? Even if the photo was as genuine as it appeared to be, that didn't mean she wouldn't hold a grudge. Was her performance an act? Would she know the name Ezra George if he chucked it at her?

But if she were genuine and did need to go into hiding then he would need to reveal his fetish. Was that the first of many awkward parent/child dilemmas? Kovacs had said he would keep the charge out of the papers for now, but also they had to ensure the information about his arrest would reach the killer. Whereas he might fill Berenice in on the deal he had struck, it would be difficult to do so without stating *why* it was thought he was involved.

He never expected sex to be such a thorny issue.

Mordent wanted it all black and white, with simple clear cut angles that noir might afford. Shadows were acceptable in the genre - were, in fact, a necessity - but even those had sharp delineations and existed for effect. With the current case - a situation he wasn't even being paid to investigate - the waters were murky. Looking in one direction only soiled the other.

On a list of longing he needed dames in monochrome skirts leaning on darkened banisters in crowded hallways, curls of greyish smoke rising from elongated cigarette holders, their presence individual amongst the multitudes, their gaze matching his; he wanted villains shrouded under hats, their features indistinct, guns held tight in fists and blazing, sparking light in strobe effect, watching the soft-slump of a body with a certain satisfied glee; he wanted cities devoid of colour, single of purpose, wet streets reflecting buildings as though filmed through the mottled glass of a Man Ray movie, deliberate distortion; he needed himself, sure of thought, right and wrong on his side, edging one step at a time into a blackness which revealed itself as he discovered it, as though illumined by a torch beam in sharp focus. He needed the dame falling into his embrace as the villain fell to the floor. He needed the security of noir, the comforting complicity of blurred lines. He didn't want real life dispersed before him like a shotgun blast to the stomach. He didn't need to live that kind of life in Technicolor.

He picked up the phone.

'Berenice?'

'Dad?'

'Would you like to go out for a meal this evening?'

'Sure.'

'What do you like to eat?'

'Anything.'

He thought for a moment. 'Do you like curry?'

'I would eat my own feet curried.'

'That's my girl.' He gave her an address. 'Seven o'clock?'

'See you then.'

He paused. Dialled another number.

'Kovacs.'

'It's Mordent. Look, I held something back. There's a woman involved that you need to protect. I've filled her in but she won't get out of town. There's kids involved; her kids I mean. If you guarantee to be discrete I'll give you the address. She's the final connection between me and bubblewrap.'

'Give me the details.'

Mordent handed them over. Two kinds of guilt seared him as he spoke her name.

'There's another thing. Something I thought was unconnected. Guy called Ezra George. I know nothing about him. Old guy who knew of the sumo club and who might have led me there. Can you look into that?'

Mordent could almost hear the clicking of Kovac's brain, the simplicity of a metal ball rolling down a preordained juvenile track. 'That name sounds familiar. Leave it with me. Anything else you *forgot*?'

'Cut the sarcasm. I can't remember everything.'

Mordent hung up knowing that he owed Kovacs big time. Back in *his* day the evidence held on him would be good enough to convict. It wouldn't have mattered if he were guilty or not. But whilst Kovacs was keen to keep the conviction figures high he wanted to do it cleanly. The fact that he had increased those figures was a sure-fire testament to his patience, and - Mordent ruefully admitted - probably a good thing.

He decided to do a little investigation of his own and powered up his PC. The name Ezra George got almost thirty-nine million hits from his search engine but as far as he could fathom all of them were related to the popular musician with a very similar name whom Emmeline had mentioned. He trawled through it all the same, listening to some of the music as he did so. It wasn't a bad sound. But whilst at the end of it he might have heard the musician's entire oeuvre he was still no closer to finding the identity of the thug he was looking for. He considered his word choice, but the tag nailed it. Despite his age the guy had three deaths connected to him. Mordent just had to work out what beef he held.

For the connection was there. It had to be. Once that was established he could work backwards from it. Or forwards. Or sideways if necessary. It was better than twiddling his thumbs.

And whilst at his age he would be further pushing it to relieve his tension he couldn't risk visiting a massage parlour anytime soon.

He tapped his fingers against his desk. Took out the jumble of cards that he sometimes used to play patience during quiet moments and laid them out. Then he collected them again and returned them to the drawer. He was in limbo. Like a character halfway through a novel where all the scenarios had been established and the second half needed to be played out. There would be a crease exactly midway through the spine, illustrated by a white line where the bend had scored the image. Once he was over the hump the resolution would follow fast and sure.

In deference to the concept he reached behind himself, up and under his shirt, and felt his own spine. True enough there was a ridge. He realised how ridiculous he was being, how boredom was forcing him to the edge. Then he stood and looked out of the window again.

No goons waited on street corners. He thought back to the girl in Morgan's Bar, the one he had encountered prior to his trashing in the alley. Had she given a name? It seemed like such a long time ago, but then her face swam into his vision and *Grace* popped into his head. Grace Snowball. It was nothing to go on. If only he hadn't been so churlish in giving out his own name.

He wondered if her surname might have been George and again searched on the Internet. Other than fashion jewellery designed and handmade in Baton Rouge, Louisana, the only other reference was for a Broadway actress who had died in the 60s. Like a post-modern artist Mordent had once again drawn a blank.

The trail - if it ever was warm - had gone cold. At some point he had been watched, traced to Astrid, the bubblewrap sumo theme implanted, and then had progressed naturally from there. He should have realised he was being followed, but had no expectation of it. Now that he did, perhaps he would be more vigilant.

He understood that he wanted to call Hubie. Emmeline was a perfect replacement but wouldn't do for the situation in which he now found himself: alone.

On a whim, and with time on his hands, he headed out to the cemetery.

33
Down Among The Dead Men

Mordent knew of at least two bodies in the cemetery who hadn't undergone a regular burial.

He also knew how long it took to dig a six foot hole under cover of darkness.

It wasn't beyond his understanding to know what a body smelt like after it had been in the ground for twenty-four hours after the coffin lid had been prised away and they were given company for the rest of eternity.

He wasn't happy with some of the things that he had done, but if he hadn't done some of those things then he would no longer be there.

And *being there* was his favourite state of being.

The weather had reverted to almost unbearable humidity. He left his jacket and holster in his vehicle and strolled in shirtsleeves across to Hubie's grave. A handful of flowers wilted over the edge of a ceramic bowl, their position the posture of mourners, or maybe of drunks being sick the morning after the night before. The headstone was yet to be installed, and for the moment a short wooden cross marked Hubie's final resting place.

Mordent crouched, realising as he did so that he was only there out of boredom and not even a sense of duty.

The soil was a lighter brown than the surrounding area, the dug earth baked dry in sunlight. He raked his fingers through it, then rubbed his palms together. The heat gave it warmth. He wondered how deep he would need to push his hands into the soil for it to become cool. He couldn't imagine that it was a pressure cooker down there.

Just as at the funeral, he opened his mouth but no words came. He wondered what it was that he missed. The casual camaraderie, occasional bickering, information exchange? He was reluctant to consider a male bonding scenario, didn't want to be held by such a stereotype. Truth was, he couldn't discuss his current situation with anyone and he needed an outlet. His usual array of confidants - Marsham, Astrid, Hubie, even Martens - were now compromised. And their replacements - Berenice, Emmeline - were inappropriate.

He didn't consider himself old. And Hubie had been a few years younger. His death was hardly natural, but it crossed Mordent's mind that he would continue to lose people to the grave the older he journeyed. In days gone by he hadn't encountered many a natural death, they were just as unusual to him as violent deaths were to the general public. But the time would come where the road on which he ran would run out of tarmac, and those of his generation would stumble and fall until they were absorbed by the earth and all the nutrients it contained.

The difference would be as he fell Berenice would now pick up the baton. Mordent wasn't a fan of immortality being lived vicariously through children, but he supposed it was better than nothing.

In the end it would be all that he had.

He mumbled a few words Hubie's way, then stood. Around him the scene vibrated briefly through an onset of dizziness. He regarded the other graves, some unkempt. Alongside Hubie's he realised that what he had taken for grass were the remains of wreaths, some with legible writing on their white labels. He resisted the curiosity to read them. They weren't relevant. Wreaths were for the dead, not the living. Out of the corner of his eye, however, he caught movement behind a nearby tree. He paused, dared a second look. Nothing visible. Again he crouched, ostensibly to look at those wreaths after all, then swung his neck suddenly and saw the surprised face of the second goon who had decked him in the alley. The one with the gravel-voice. Professional, they were not.

For the second time that day Mordent had someone on the run.

The main car lot was some way from Hubie's grave. Only funeral corteges were allowed on the route and Mordent had to assume the guy was parked close to his own vehicle. In the near distance a line of black cars wound its way through the cemetery like ants, the coffin a metaphorical leaf held aloft. The guy saw the procession, and with respect began to skirt it, despite making his exit difficult. With less respect Mordent saw him leap a handful of graves like a steeplechaser. He followed a hundred yards behind, gaining a few yards here, losing some there. The heat in his lungs almost unbearable: a cigarette burn.

The scorched ground was slippery without traction. Mordent's feet went from under him almost exactly as it happened to Gravel. His head hit soil, inches from a gravestone. Scrambling up he watched Gravel do the same, as though they were linked through a puppeteer's rods.

He imagined summoning the forces of good to fight evil, a hundred arms ascending from the ground, grabbing at Gravel's ankles. But this was no more than fancy, and as Gravel reached his vehicle Mordent was no further than the point at which his rival had fallen.

In days gone by there would have been frantic moments whilst the pursued scrabbled with their car keys, attempting to open a door suddenly unyielding as though it were on the side of the pursuer, but in modern times and at great distance Gravel had unlocked the doors electronically, the vehicle assuming the role of a getaway driver without the driver. Mordent rested, palms on his thighs, as Gravel reversed out of the cemetery driveway, ironically scattering gravel as he did so. It was then that he saw the card.

It was a normal white business card with a rose wound around a microphone in the top right corner.

Grace Frost
Professional singer

There was a number printed below the words.

It was clear - fortuitously - that the card had dropped from Gravel's pocket as he fell, and remembering the puppeteer motif, Mordent retraced his steps to where he himself had slipped and picked up his car keys from the grass.

There was a lot to be said for serendipity.

34
She Was Only A Bird In A Gilded Cage

Emmeline came through for him.

'I shouldn't do this,' she said, over the phone. 'I told you if you were charged I couldn't be involved.'

Mordent had to respect that whilst beige might be her chosen colour it didn't extend to her personality. She was malleable.

'I'm trying to save my skin,' he said. His arrangement with Kovacs remained a secret. No one could be trusted.

'What is it you want me to do again?'

'I need you to make a call for me. Enquire about booking a singer for a wedding, bar mitzvah, birthday party, whatever you fancy. The woman will probably give you a price. Ask if you can meet in person, or see her perform. Hopefully she'll give you a location. Then report back to me.'

'Would you like me to check out her name, too?'

'You're a beauty. Of course I would. I didn't want to impose, under the circumstances.'

'I should be careful, dealing with a wanted man.'

'You and I both know that's hooey.'

'Nevertheless.' The single word hung in the air for a moment. 'I'll see what I can do.'

Mordent gave her the details and she hung up. He had returned to his office. The heat of the day had once again given way to thunderous applause. He wished he might invest in an office humidifier. Sitting in shirtsleeves he wanted to strip to the waist, and then some. Maybe he might then surprise the temps who click-clacked down the hallway.

His phone rang.

'So I spoke to her. She wanted to know how I got her number and I said a friend of a friend had given me her card. She has a regular spot at The Gold Angel, seven-thirty to nine, weekends. That includes today. I said I'd drop by and hear her sing and take it from there.'

'Did she sound suspicious? Anything else to report?'

'Nothing. Well, she wanted to take my number. It might well have appeared on her phone. I fluffed it, mixed up a couple of digits so if she had seen it she wouldn't think I was lying and if she didn't then she won't be able to reach me. Did I do good?'

'Just dandy. You got anything else on her?'

'She maintains a webpage with booking information. It's basic, one page only. I'll need to put out feelers with my contacts to see if there's anything more. It'll cost, of course, but take the phone call on the house.'

'That's kind of you.'

'That's not business. That's what it is. As I said, I don't want to be seen to do business with you whilst you're on charge.'

'So what did we just do?'

'I simply enquired about your forthcoming nuptial arrangements, as a friend.'

'Trying to marry me off?'

'No one would go that far.'

Mordent took it as a compliment. They exchanged a few pleasantries and hung up.

The Gold Angel was a high class dive downtown. Mordent didn't know it that well, hadn't frequented it much. He considered it a dive because it liked to think it was. In reality it was a modern establishment with retro trappings. It wouldn't have been out of place in a David Lynch movie. But it was all artifice, no heritage. Cruise ship crooners sank their careers there. Small time gangsters believed they were big. It wasn't a melting pot more of a stagnant pool. If Grace were performing there then he pitied her, even if her conversation with him had led to the fracas in the alley. Even if her relationship with George had put him on the line.

He called Berenice and rearranged their curry to whatever food The Gold Angel might serve. Because she had decided to work late she asked if he could collect her from the taxidermists. That wasn't a problem. To kill time Mordent drove slowly past Astrid's address. Her line of brownstones were flanked with trees and sure enough leaning against one of them holding a newspaper and a coffee was a police officer he didn't recognise but who was instantly recognised *as* a police officer. Mordent guessed recognition wasn't important. If it kept George or his ineffectual hoods away from her then that was all that mattered. He just hoped it wouldn't put off her regular clients.

He pulled up outside *Get Stuffed!* just before 6.30. The lights were on but the *closed* sign faced the street. On the front of the sign a nondescript animal lay on its back with its legs in the air. It seemed hand-drawn. He knocked a couple of times and Damian appeared, nodded, and let him in. Out of curiosity Mordent looked at the reverse of the sign, the same animal was now prancing with its hands on its tummy and its snout in the air over the *Open* lettering. It was something he hadn't noticed on his first visit.

'She's out back. I'll just go get her.'

Damian disappeared into the rear of the shop leaving Mordent with the critters. The low-lying sun cast a golden glow that seeped into the store and gave the specimens an even greater semblance of life. Imbued with the sun they attained a homely appearance which was simultaneously welcoming yet disconcerting. A macaw in a gilded cage spread its wings to the extent of the bars. Mordent realised that even dead the animals were contained. After a while he realised Damian had returned to the main storefront and was standing still, watching him.

'She won't be a moment.'

Mordent wondered if he had to practice the stance of an exhibit.

Then he continued: 'I've been working on your project. Certain details will be complicated of course, but it's an intriguing proposal. Where did you get the idea?'

Mordent was about to respond when Berenice entered. She looked radiant and for a moment he couldn't imagine she was his daughter. The lack of an innate sexual pulse however, confirmed that she was.

'I'm ready,' she said. She wore a fifties twirled dress in sunshine yellow and white heels with a pale cream cardigan over her shoulders. 'Are we going anywhere nice?'

'The Gold Angel. Do you know it?'

She shook her head.

'That's a good thing.'

'Is it like the Blue Angel? The Dietrich movie?'

'It probably purports to be. I've got to check out something there. Is that ok?'

'Oh! Exciting. I'll be your cover?'

'Of a kind.' Mordent then wondered if he might

get her into difficulties. He hadn't had to look out for someone before. 'Just follow my lead, don't speak unless you're spoken to. At the very least we'll have a meal, listen to a nondescript singer, and get out of there.'

She made a crook of her arm. 'Shall we?'

He played the game. 'Let's.' Then realised the role reversal. He wasn't good with form and function. They exited to the street.

Night came early to the city. Skyscrapers snagged the dark curtain and pulled it down to the streets like the curve of a toreador's cape or a magician's misdirection. Stars were absent across eighty per cent of the sky, light pollution smudging their glow, negating their million or billion year journey. Mordent imagined it would be like a singer out of state arriving to an empty stage, or a mime artist performing to a blind audience. On occasion when he had left the environs he had been surprised at the amount of starlight in the sky. Yet those pinpricks signalled a vastness he had been anxious to avoid.

Noir wasn't about starlight. Noir was the straightforward delineation between streets and the sky. Noir kept it simple and personal. Noir was for him.

He gunned the engine to The Gold Angel. Berenice was quiet. She sat with her hands in her lap looking out at the night as if it were the first she had seen of it. He glanced across to her.

'Everything ok?'

She nodded. 'Just silly stuff. When I took your arm back there I couldn't help but notice you're wearing a gun.'

Mordent shrugged. 'Just a tool of the trade.'

'Have you ever shot anyone?'

'Yes.'

'You didn't have to think about it.'

'You don't have to think about it if you've shot someone. It's just there.'

'Does it trouble you?'

'Only on nights where I don't sleep.'

'You get many of those?'

'Not as many as I used to.'

She nodded. 'You know, when I work with the animals I sometimes wonder how they came to us. Whether they were killed humanely, whether they had any last thoughts, regrets. I guess it's silly to imagine an animal having regrets, having things they always wanted to do but never could. And there I am, putting them in ridiculous poses, selling them as artefacts.'

'But it doesn't bother you?'

She smiled. 'Only on nights where I don't sleep.'

'And are there many of those?'

She squeezed his arm. 'Not now.'

There was a car lot on the opposite side of The Gold Angel. There was parking at the back too, but Mordent didn't want to cage his vehicle in case it was needed in a hurry. The front of the establishment glowed with gold paint. If it looked tacky at night then it would be shabby in the day time. Over the façade the statue of a winged girl stood on one leg. On closer inspection her other leg ended in a damaged plaster stump. Doormen flanked the entrance, thankfully not dressed in gold. Berenice's eyes widened.

'Here?'

'Here.'

'You sure know how to treat a girl.'

He smiled. She was a woman after his own heart who wasn't after his own heart. It was refreshing.

Mordent had booked ahead to secure a table. He had given the name of Raymond Greener just in case. He was guessing if the goons were around then they wouldn't try anything in a crowded place, possibly on home turf. It might be a gamble, but it was also his only lead. He briefed Berenice on this as they walked over to the entrance.

It was a simple matter to be led inside. Double doors opened onto a tiered area with plentiful tables covered in gold cloth. The maitre d' directed them to their seats in one corner with a good view of the stage. A comedian was warming up the next act. Mordent caught the end of one joke that didn't give rise to any laughter or applause. He glanced around at the clientele, didn't recognise anyone. Couples either single or conjoined sat in twos and fours. Unlike the epoch the club believed it emulated the atmosphere wasn't swathed in smoke. Modernity crumbled authenticity, thought Mordent. Complimentary wine arrived at their table which indicated the food prices were likely to be inflated. He glanced at Berenice and she smiled encouragingly back. It was clear that she enjoyed it.

They ordered some food whilst the comedian told jokes berating the audience which were only just on the right side of provoking a riot. Mordent warmed to him.

They ordered steak tartare and pomme frites. Mordent didn't hold much hope and when it arrived after only ten minutes his suspicions were confirmed. Berenice didn't seem to mind. They spoke freely and generally about nothing much at all, the way that old friends do. For a moment Mordent allowed the thought that he wasn't a PI, wasn't under charge, wasn't there to catch the singer, had never killed anyone or beaten anyone up, and was on the point of retirement which he could spend with Berenice popping round on Sundays to cook him dinner whilst he pulled vegetables and herbs out of a well-tended garden.

Reality nagged at the base of his neck with the sensation of a sniper's red dot illuminating his epidermis.

Somewhere, somehow, a trigger would be pulled.

Some day.

On stage the comedian concluded his set. Applause was brisk to warrant a quick departure from the stage. A compère in tails entered and pushed both hands downwards, as though plumping a pillow. Without further ado, he introduced Grace Frost.

Mordent hadn't considered the winter association between a *snowball* and *frost*, but when she glided on stage in a silver gown her movements were as fluid as an ice-skater's. She launched into *It Had To Be You*, the classic Isham Jones/Gus Kahn composition that Mordent remembered fondly sung by Dooley Wilson in *Casablanca* but also by Betty Hutton in *Incendiary Blonde*. It sent a shiver down his spine all the way to clichéville.

Berenice leant over: 'You can already tell this will be good.'

He nodded. A spotlight played on Grace's shifting dress, sequins firing reflected light like bullets from a shotgun. He hadn't expected it to be this good, whilst she might be down on her luck she knew what she was doing. Even so, there were a thousand singers in the city and getting good gigs was always going to be difficult. He noticed that whilst many of the diners seemed affected by her performance few of them looked up from their meals and the general hubbub of chatter hadn't decreased.

She finished the song to a smattering of applause and launched into *Fever*, another standard, a slow-burner. Mordent sopped up steak-juice with potato and relished the suddenly moreish taste as Grace moved effortlessly through the song. After a while he became aware of Berenice tugging on his jacket sleeve, whispering:

'She'll sing *Witchcraft* next. She certainly has you entranced.'

'She's good,' he said. He noticed Berenice had finished her meal. She poured them both a second glass of wine.

'It's her you've come to see, isn't it?'

He nodded.

'Can I ask why?'

He sighed. 'She might know someone who has it in for me.' He turned to face her, she deserved the truth. Or at least a sliver of it. 'Technically I'm under charge regarding three recent murders. The police are pretending to take it seriously. I prefer to do my own investigating, particularly when my neck is at stake. Grace might be involved. Don't look so worried. It'll work out just fine.'

Berenice regarded Grace with additional interest. 'She's quite attractive.'

'I suppose she is.'

'Well said in the knowledge that you knew it from the start.' She winked at him. 'Does she know you?'

'She'll recognise me if she sees me.'

'Is that going to be a problem?'

'I was planning on playing it by ear.'

Berenice wiped her mouth with a napkin. 'I'll talk to her.'

'You'll do nothing of the sort.'

'I will. And I'll stay out late and wear short skirts if I want to. And kiss boys. I think I'm old enough to make my own decisions.'

Mordent sat back, regarded this woman who was very obviously his daughter. Very obviously his.

'What were you thinking?'

'I'll see if I can speak to her backstage. How does that sound?'

Mordent thought it over. There might be a risk. He considered it worth taking.

'Fine. But before you go in call me on your cell and leave it open.'

She nodded. Then broke a wide smile as Grace segued from *That Ole Devil Called Love* into *Witchcraft*.

'Serendipity,' she said.

35
Behind The Scenes

Grace finished her set with *My Way*, a song Mordent didn't like at the best of times and which was only partially redeemed through her considerable talent. Some of the diners hadn't noticed it was her last song, and they seemed indifferent throughout; although he noticed that at least two tables were appreciative and Grace smiled towards both of them before she left the stage.

Berenice had stood a moment later. 'Wish me luck,' she said. He watched as she crossed the restaurant, her phone in her hand, then he answered her call and kept his cell to his ear as she dropped hers into a pocket. Muffled restaurant noises augmented those he could hear clearly in his other ear, as though he were listening to a faulty stereo. Truth be told he didn't expect to hear much, and was more concerned about springing to action should the link between them get broken.

Their waiter came over with the dessert menu. Mordent ordered coffees and asked if they could be given five minutes.

The clientele had slipped into two groups: those whose conversation grew slower and quieter throughout the meal and those whose had become bawdier. He considered the differences between the two, decided this was one of the divides within the human race who were at best a collection of similar monkeys grouped together through tribal coincidence and geographical location but who reverted to type once satiated and had no need to impress. He wondered which group he belonged to, but knew he was always the outsider and was happy to keep it that way.

A rock 'n' roll tribute act had replaced Grace on stage and as soon as they launched into *Rock Around The Clock* anything Mordent could have picked up from Berenice's cell was overshouted by the singer. The small dance floor in front of the stage became occupied by drunks who should have known better. The musicians should have known better too. They sounded like Bill Haley *on* a comet. He pressed his cell closer to his ear, ensuring that the line was still connected, feeling like a father watching his child make their way across the street, sensing time spooling out between them.

Five minutes passed.

The band were strangling *Chirpy Chirpy Cheep Cheep* – a song Mordent hadn't believed could have been worsened – when the waiter reappeared with a slip of paper on a silver tray. *Very 1940s.* Mordent picked it up but didn't have time to read it before the waiter said, 'Miss Frost requests your presence backstage. If you could follow me, Sir.'

He stuffed it into his pocket and stood. They eased their way through the tables via the dancefloor where Mordent got caught up in a conga inappropriate to the song, before appearing at the door of a dressing room which – despite the overall décor of the establishment – bore no gold star. Laughter could be heard from within and Mordent quit ideas about reaching for his gun.

The waiter knocked then left him to it, as though opening the door was below his station.

Mordent waited. He felt like an autograph hunter and to his surprise his heart tremored beneath his suit.

It was Berenice who let him in. Grace sat before a dressing table in front of a mirror surrounded with bulbs. Mordent's eyes adjusted to the glare like a deer caught in headlights. When he could see clearly he saw that she was smiling.

'We meet again, Stingray.'

Berenice rolled her eyes.

Mordent closed the door behind him. 'You sang well.'

'Thank you. I was telling your daughter here that it's a regular gig that pays well, despite the sometime indifference of the clientele.'

He nodded.

'I wasn't expecting to see you again,' she said. Mordent noticed a little nervousness creep into her voice. When she glanced towards Berenice it begged reassurance.

He wanted interrogation. He wanted banter. He wanted to pick her up and fuck her against the dressing table until the filaments of all the lightbulbs popped. He couldn't do any of these things in Berenice's presence.

He thought of asking her to wait outside. Thought again.

Grace tilted her head, an eyebrow raised. What had seemed like seconds was close to half a minute. 'You didn't just come here for my autograph,' she said.

He sighed. 'Ezra. I came to ask about Ezra George.'

'I don't know what to tell you.'

'How about the truth?'

'But what is truth? Isn't that just an agreement with the collective consciousness?'

'Then I want information.'

She put her hands in her lap. Her eyes were wide when she looked at him. 'I still don't know what to tell you.'

'Then let me tell you something. After our chat a couple of goons waylaid me in an alleyway and warned me to stay away from George. Did you know about that?'

'I didn't know about it but I knew about it.'

'That doesn't make sense.'

'I didn't know it had happened, but I knew it would happen. They didn't hurt you, I hope?'

Mordent shook his head. 'What is this nonsense? You knew about it before it happened?'

Berenice laid a hand on Grace's shoulder. 'He's in a spot,' she said. 'Why don't you just tell him what you told me?'

Mordent looked from one to the other.

Grace said: 'I've never met Ezra. I wasn't in a relationship with him. I don't only sing, I'm an actress. I was hired to feed you some lines. They were honest about it, said you would be *spoken* to afterwards. I didn't question it too deeply, why would I? I have to eat just the same as everyone else, and the snowballs were free.'

Mordent ran a hand through his hair. 'It wasn't all scripted, couldn't be. What did they want from me?'

'They wanted me to give you the name of Ezra and they sought confirmation of that girl's name from you.'

'Lola? Lola White?'

'That's right.'

'This Ezra is setting me up for a fall. But why would he want to give me his name?'

'Maybe it's not Ezra,' said Berenice. 'Maybe Ezra is a front?'

Mordent thought it over. 'Ezra *could* be a front. No one knows much about him. Maybe they gave me his name to throw me off. But why would they ask about Lola?'

'They had the name,' Grace said. 'I just had to hear it from you.'

'Who is Lola?' Berenice asked.

Mordent shook his head. 'Just someone I knew. Don't worry about it. She's dead, in any event. Has been for a while.'

'Oh.'

There was more but Mordent wasn't going to give it. Ever. Not to her.

'I had a wire,' Grace continued, a little embarrassed. 'When I left the bar those goons you referred to took it off me and thanked me. That's the last I knew of anything.'

Mordent rubbed his chin. 'You do this often?'

She shook her head. 'I'm sorry if it got you into trouble. I did enjoy our chat.'

'So did I.'

The three of them stood like newbies in a ménage a trois, no one knowing who should make the first move.

'Perhaps we should be going,' suggested Berenice.

Mordent looked from one to the other. 'Can you wait for me outside? I ordered coffee.'

She bit back years of abandonment.

'Sure.'

Mordent let her out. Once the door clicked shut he walked over to Grace and gripped her chin between his fingers. She gasped. Her skin was soft. Mordent relaxed his grip.

'I don't know whether to hit you or kiss you.'

She bit her lip. 'Both.'

He shook his head. 'I'm no longer that kind of guy.'

He bent and kissed her. She tasted of cherry cola. Her fingers found the back of his neck and pressed him to her, tingles in his hair. Mordent moved his lips across her cheek then down to her throat, her make-up powdery against his tongue. He passed a hand over her right breast within her silken dress and she gasped, then gripped his wrist and gently pushed him away.

'Not here,' she said.

He stepped back. 'Anywhere?'

She nodded. He needed her.

She needed him. He nodded.

He needed to ditch Berenice.

'Gimme fifteen minutes,' he said. 'I'll see you out front.'

She stood and kissed him again. 'Fifteen minutes.'

Mordent closed the door, made his way back to the table. The band were murdering *Jailhouse Rock*. The crowd didn't care. Most people were dancing, the tables abandoned. Over in the corner Berenice was sipping coffee. Mordent remembered the piece of paper in his pocket, pulled it out. He didn't recognise the handwriting, but then he wouldn't.

Come over, it said. *I don't trust her.*

He wondered which of them had written it.

36
The Sack Race

Fifteen minutes later Mordent pulled up out front of The Gold Angel from the car park over the road. He had waited for a taxi to pick up Berenice after he had given an apology. Her meeting with Grace had left her with the latter's surname. Mordent hoped it wasn't the start of an argument. He couldn't be dealing with that.

Grace hadn't changed. She floated out the front of the establishment like the Silver Surfer. Mordent watched as she swung her legs into his vehicle, considered the metaphor. Perfume, recently applied, tickled the hairs in his nostrils. He didn't like the stuff, sniffed back a sneeze.

'Where are we going?'

Mordent considered his apartment. 'Your place?'

'Ok.'

There wasn't much of a decision to be made. Mordent took the address and they cruised out into late night traffic like a seagull entering the jet stream. Grace opened her handbag and pulled out a cigarette. 'Do you mind?'

Mordent shook his head. She could do anything when he was on a promise. He watched her light it then inhale. When she spoke her words floated on clouds.

'Can't do this in the club anymore, not even in my dressing room. It's crazy, gives my voice the edge.'

He noticed that her hand was shaking.

'How did they contact you?'

'They ran an ad in *Backstage*. I gave them a call.'

'They *auditioned* you?'

'I wouldn't say that. They didn't appear to know what they wanted. I got the impression not many people responded.'

'Didn't you think it odd?'

'Sure. But what isn't odd in this city? You get the chance of a little cash, a little work, you take it. I wasn't concerned it was legit. Maybe it was a test, would lead onto other things. But of course I've heard nothing since.'

She took a long drag on her smoke and wound down the window to exhale.

'So, what's it all about?'

'Lola White was a girl I knew when I was on the force. She was murdered. We never caught the killer.'

'She was a policewoman?'

Mordent laughed with some force. 'No.'

'Then she was your lover.'

'You could say that she was.'

'But then I know this. You told me that in the bar.' She shook her head. 'I'm always forgetting things.'

'I think you're asking again to find out the truth.'

'Maybe. So you're no longer in the force?'

'No. I left some time ago.'

'You want to search me for a wire?'

'Later.'

'What are you doing with me?'

'I would have thought that was obvious.'

'But why?' She flicked the cigarette onto the highway, it bounced, spat, and flared like volcanic ash down a mountainside. 'I'm all over the place at the moment.'

Mordent smiled. 'That's how magnetism works.'

She placed a hand on his thigh. 'I thought it was only like this in the movies.'

'And you *want* to be in the movies.'

She removed her hand. 'I do. I *did*. I'm too old for it now. I'll sing til the money runs out then I'll run.'

Mordent turned off the main highway. Their conversation became practical. Grace directed him down a couple of quiet streets until they pulled up beside a brownstone.

'You sure you want to come up?'

He nodded. 'Little would stop me now.'

She smiled. 'I've got syphilis.'

He roared: 'I bet you say that to all the boys.'

Mordent followed her into the apartment. The elevator was a cage that ascended the centre of the building. Enclosed with her he became aware of electricity in proximity. Through the silk dress she was like a dolphin under water. He put thoughts out of his head about bubblewrap and deaths. He hoped they hadn't been tailed.

They were silent as they rose. Not for the first time Mordent wondered what went through a woman's mind prior to sex, whether their expectations were the same as his. He realised he had been paying for it for some time. That started to bother him.

It had been too easy getting her in the sack.

He wondered about the note.

As she pushed her key into the lock he considered turning back. Didn't.

He couldn't stop thinking of Groucho Marx as they made love, all club and no member.

Afterwards she pulled the sheets up to her chin. Her make-up had been erased during the evolutionary struggle. The cosmetic sparkle had gone, replaced by a natural glow. But it couldn't hide the lines, the creep of age. She had been right, Mordent thought, she could no longer take acting seriously. The demands of the modern age appealed to an increasingly younger audience and therefore increasingly younger stars. Her light was about burnt out. He had just experienced a supernova, a stellar explosion which briefly outshone the entire galaxy, but one which would fade over the coming months. No wonder she had to pick up work as and when she needed it. No wonder she picked up men exactly the same way.

He allowed himself the luxury of being disparaging now he was sated, and despite himself he felt much tenderness towards her. No doubt she thought the same about him.

He was about to say *thanks* then realised it was a synonym for *how much do I owe you*. She pulled a hand out from underneath the blanket and reached for his. They connected.

'You can stay,' she said.

His eyes were already closing.

37
Another Memory: A Dream

Lola lifted her head from his lap.

She smiled.

'My turn.'

She turned around. Her ass was a moon, a perfect sphere. She edged backwards until she was inches from his face. His flaccid penis was brushed by her cool breasts. The urge had dissipated with the expulsion, but Mordent was in love. He reached out for a toy and parted her labia with his fingers, inserted the object with quiet precision. She gasped at each ridge, snaked a hand underneath and gripped the end, held it. Mordent wetted his finger, ran a circle around her anus. She jolted the dildo inside herself, a sporadic rhythm, as he pushed and prodded and finally gained entrance, heat evident on the tip. Despite himself he stirred against her, between her. She moved further back. He bent forwards, extended his tongue. As it wriggled against her she bucked and moaned, expleted. Suddenly sitting backwards she crushed his face into her softness, trapped his tongue. Each rib of the dildo knocked her pelvic bone as she worked faster and faster, as he struggled for breath. He kept the motion, kept it going, pushed thoughts of mortality out of his head as the crush in his chest eased to unbearable. Then just as quickly she was off, shaking, gripping her hand between her thighs. She removed the toy slowly, a glistening icon.

They held each other tight.

'That was intense.' She was all smiles. In their post-coital moments she often seemed much younger than the *much younger* she already was. Mordent felt overwhelming affection for her.

He brushed a strand of hair away from the side of her face and after the movement it fell back again. The motion was a simile for their relationship.

'I love you,' he said.

She didn't hide the frown. 'That's not really what we're about.'

'I just thought I would say it.'

'Don't. Don't spoil it.'

They untangled. She rolled onto her side and after a while what Mordent thought was crying turned out to be a noise in her sleep.

He sighed; he slept.

When he woke they were eating bauxite under the viaduct. Her teeth were yellow and she appeared wasted; sodium painted. Around them couples copulated with abandon, a silent disgrace. Mordent rose to his feet then realised he was already standing. He looked down on Lola from a great height, an increasingly spiralled height. He experienced vertigo as the ledge on which he was perched retracted into the mountainside as the mountain itself pushed higher and higher towards the sky.

Until Lola was no more than a white figure sitting beside an ice cream van. A speck of pure in a tarnished world.

Until his feet were balanced on the width of a ski and the drop was a thousand foot to tree canopies.

He knew he was dreaming, but couldn't

extrapolate the dream from memory. Was he dreaming a memory of a dream or was the dream inside the dream just a dream. He couldn't move on the ledge – paralysed with fear without the fear. Something advised him to fall – a not unintelligible voice. He knew he would soar with abandon, landing on his feet before Lola just in time to catch a drop of ice cream as it slid down the cone onto her fingers. But it wasn't a time for heroics. Overhead, clouds clouded with darkness. The rich verdant foliage became shadowed with noir, the forest landscape changing like a girl becoming melancholic with age. The trees folded in on themselves, were compressed into steel, their structures transformed into skyscrapers, and Mordent became a free climber, a human King Kong scaling a pylon, the sky wet tarpaulin almost within reach, dripping black tears onto his worn black clothes.

He clung: intense and terrified.

Letting go nothing happened. There was no gravity. He floated. Making swimming movements he checked out the terrain. He imagined this was what scuba diving was like. A bug, a water skater, clinging to a malleable surface, looking down at the depths below, a slow drop. He bobbed towards the blackness of the sky.

The dream was a metaphor, right? he told himself. His subconscious mind coded when it would be so much easier spelling it out. But that was how the subconscious worked. It was an informer, but one that needed leaning on, one where you had to apply some pressure. And what happened when you lost everything was that you had to start again. You had to start all over again. That was how the subconscious worked. It didn't retain anything; it retained everything. You just needed to know the code.

He rose out of the dream as though the world had been inverted and he were holding a lifebuoy; it tugged him sky/downwards. As he *rose* aspects of his life gurned at him, soluble memories. Fleeting, distorted glimpses of the numinous. Lola came into view and she was indeed holding an ice cream cone. He stuck out his tongue but sailed passed her. The world inverted again and he floated above her bed and then he was above Grace's bed and then he was in bed, with her, jolting awake, a bead of sweat on his upper lip licked off leaving the trace of salt on his tongue.

38
Dot To Dot

Mordent eased himself from under the covers. Grace remained motionless, caught like an exhausted fly in a spider's dream. He pulled on his clothes, stuck his head around the adjoining bathroom door and squeezed some toothpaste onto a finger which he then ran around the inside of his mouth.

He thought about leaving a note. Didn't. There was more time he wanted to spend with Grace, but he needed a clear head for now. Just because she slept with him didn't mean she was on his side, however much he wish-fulfilled it.

He took the stairs instead of the elevator, there was something about being caged solo that was abhorrent. By the time he reached the ground his cell was ringing and when he answered he found himself talking to Kovacs.

'Mordent.'

'Yeh?'

'We had a man watching you, but you gave him the slip.'

'I didn't realise you had someone on me.'

'That was the point.'

'Then I hardly gave him the slip. He must have fallen all by himself.'

'Where are you now?'

'Safe and sound, returning to my office. All ok?'

'For now. No more murders and we're keeping an eye on your bubblewrap sweetheart.'

Mordent leant against his vehicle. Kovacs was enjoying it too much.

'There's something, though. The name you gave me? Ezra George? I knew it sounded familiar. There was a case a long while back, whilst you were on the force. We both worked it. Situation appeared to be suicide but turned out to be murder and the murderer went back and killed a possible witness. That witness's name was Lola White. Recall her?'

Mordent couldn't deny that he did.

'George was the girl's grandfather. On the paternal side. He was her legal guardian - or rather he had been when she was underage. He had a beef with us that we should have offered witness protection. That complaint didn't get to the rank and file and was resolved internally. But it must have been mentioned to me in passing as I've remembered it.'

Mordent couldn't deny the power of Kovacs' memory. He continued:

'The case was never closed. It's unlikely it ever will be. Chances were the original murder was a drug-related killing and this Lola got caught in the crossfire. The immediate connection isn't obvious. But what you think might be clear is that this Ezra George held *us* responsible, perhaps specifically you and me because we were involved with the case. If so, maybe you were the easier target.'

'You don't think you need to be worried yourself?'

'Unlikely.'

'Because...?'

'Because you know why. Listen Mordent, Lola's effects were recently released to her family. The force has been going through the archives, getting rid of some stuff to make space for others. Her effects were dead wood. Amongst them was a diary. Now, I know no more than one thing: the contents of that diary were marked irrelevant as they didn't progress the case. You know who signed off on that?'

Mordent knew, but Kovacs had to tell him, to join the dots.

'Who?'

'You. You signed it off. You declared it irrelevant. That diary – returned to Lola's family – didn't hold a key to the case, did it? But it did hold something else. It held the key to you.'

'That's some surmising.'

'I had to think about it, rack my brain. If there was a vendetta, why start now? Why not years ago? Why not me? The return of personal effects had to hold the clue, to have initiated it. So why didn't the diary form part of the investigation? Because it *was* a diary. And what information do diaries normally contain? I'll tell you. They contain information that the diarist wants no one else to read. Ever. Why didn't you want the diary part of the investigation? Because you're mentioned in it. Has to be. Logic. That's how I work and now you'll tell me I'm wrong but we know that I'm right. Tell me I'm wrong.'

'You're not wrong.'

Kovacs almost sounded disappointed. There was a pause. 'I'm assuming you weren't withholding anything that might have resolved the case.'

'No.'

'And so the information was personal. You had an affair with her.'

'I think the word *affair* only pertains if we were in other relationships at the time.'

'Point taken. So you were in a relationship with her.'

'Yes.'

'It would have been – I imagine, especially aware of the age difference – quite a volatile relationship.'

'Sexually volatile, if that's what you mean.' Mordent couldn't help relish any aspect of discomfort he might switch from himself to Kovacs.

'I see. Stuff that she wouldn't want her family to become aware of.'

'Depends on her family.'

'We'll take it as red that there were things in that diary they wouldn't want to know.'

'Are you saying this George guy is killing prostitutes just to blame deaths on me because I fucked his precious granddaughter up the ass? Seems rather far-fetched.'

'I'm saying that it might be the case they believed you had her killed. That they thought it might have been tied up into the ongoing police investigation for convenience. That it was never investigated fully because of that assumption. Might that be something to kill for?'

A dead cold weight shifted in Mordent's chest; a pressing certainty that by the end of the investigation he might be in jail.

'Is that what you think?'

Kovacs took his time. 'About their motives or whether I believe you killed the girl.'

'Either. Or.'

'I think we would have had the biggest lead on this case so far.'

'That's cryptic. It's unlike you to be cryptic. You're holding something back. What's with the *had*?'

Mordent could hear Kovacs' sigh. Evidently he wanted to play the conversation out for as long as possible.

'The girl's grandfather, Ezra George. He died a few weeks ago. Natural causes.'

Mordent bit his lip. 'So George dies. His belongings get passed into another's hands. That's the person we need.'

'It's a line of enquiry we're currently looking into.'

'There's something doesn't add up. I can't put my finger on it.'

'When you do, call me.'

'Yeh, right. You didn't answer my other point.'

'Which was?'

'Whether I was now implicated in Lola's death.'

'Oh that. I don't see that being an issue.'

Mordent grimaced. 'The more you talk to me the more you'll morph into me. Insincerity doesn't suit you.'

'But it does make you squirm a bit. That's one of the pleasures of this job.'

'Go hang yourself.'

Mordent ended the call. He ran his fingers over the smooth surface of his cell, wondered what bugged the back of his mind.

He'd thought of the dot to dot analogy during the call. Everyone knew it. You had a blank page with numbered dots and you followed the numbers one by one until you got a picture. If only crime cases developed numerically. The way he saw it you joined together what you knew and by the time you were finished you had mesh. You then had to highlight some of the dots to make the picture, but it all came down to guesswork. What usually happened is that way before you were finished someone came over and gave you the answer they'd found under other means. Joining things dot to dot was a fallacy with police work. Life just wasn't that easy.

Either way, he was missing a few dots.

Not only that, but someone had added a dot.

Astrid.

If George had recently availed himself of her services then he must have been the biggest stiff she ever had.

39
Chasing A Tail

He got into his vehicle. No more Mr Nice Guy. If he ever was.

He needed to speak to Astrid. Face to face. He was sure he would know if she was lying.

If she was lying he wasn't sure what he would do.

If she was lying he wondered if *he* would hide it.

Things were stacking up. Kovacs' logic made some sense. If Lola's diary contained details of their sexual activity then there *was* a link between what she had experimented with and her death. Namely, a drug called Flunitrazepam she used to literally knock herself out. She had been immobilized but lucid when her attacker had set her on fire. It was an horrific death. Mordent had taken some time to get over it. He could understand a family member wanting retribution. He could understand how he might be perceived to be in the front line.

And if he had found it difficult to imagine someone would kill just to frame him, on reflection it wasn't impossible. Prostitutes had a history of being subjected to violence. Serial killers from Jack the Ripper to Gary Ridgway, Robert Hanson to Robert Pickton had taken that opportunity. Some killers expressed the moral high ground either through religious or social justification, but it didn't help that sex workers became easy prey due to the nature of their work.

It also didn't help their cause that they often had to take clients to out of the way places where either of them were less likely to be disturbed, or that their employment often led a disappearance less-likely to be investigated than that of a law-abiding citizen. In the case of Joel Rifkin, who confessed to killing seventeen prostitutes in the New York area between 1989 and 1993 there hadn't been a missing persons report filed on any of the women during that time. And Mordent remembered a study where 68% of sex workers had stated they had been raped during the course of their work.

He wasn't entirely innocent himself, having had to kill a worker once who had turned a gun on him, but bottom line was that he respected a profession which met the nation's needs. It was certainly more honorable than a lawyer or a realtor or a politician.

Traffic was light around Grace's apartment. He made easy progress across the city. The heat of recent days had begun to dissipate but it still clung to the inside of his vehicle and he drove as if surrounded by warm putty. His car wasn't air-conditioned, he didn't have the money for that, and he considered suffering was as much a part of a PI's job as it was that of an artist. Still, on some days he needed a blast of air in the face.

He pulled onto Astrid's street just in time to see her enter a car outside her building. His eyes scanned left and right for the police officer posted to keep her safe, but the area was deserted. He couldn't catch the license plate at that distance. It might have been an unmarked police vehicle.

Mordent slowed to a crawl, edging up the street like a cat approaching a bird. He just hoped he wasn't a domestic cat, with no hope of a kill.

As her vehicle eased away from the kerb he kept a safe distance. They seemed to be in no hurry. Passing her apartment building there was still no sign of her guard. He had to make an assumption Kovacs was taking her to a safe location. Yet why hadn't he mentioned it on the telephone, unless he thought Mordent was in fact a menace? Or if something fishy was going on.

At the bottom of the street the car accelerated into mid-morning traffic. Mordent was held at the junction. He bided his time, but found his fingers tapping the steering wheel. With a break in the traffic he drove across two lanes just in time to beat a red and turn off the main drag in pursuit of the other vehicle. They took a left then another right. Mordent knew the area well enough to understand other routes were easier, more direct. Either the driver had noticed him and was trying to establish they were being followed, or Astrid was being disorientated. Either option wasn't good.

The vehicle ahead swung a sharp left, bumped up a kerb and cut across an area of parkland.

It was getting worse.

Mordent skirted the parkland, a parched green square, keeping his right eye on the vehicle. A woman with two children were separated by its passage, darting either side. Mordent couldn't hear the language which followed but guessed that it was choice. What was clear was that the driver didn't know the area, but Mordent did. By the time he had turned the third corner of the square the other vehicle had only just managed to get back on the road: trees, play equipment and wildlife having blocked its progress.

They were bumper to bumper. Mordent could see Astrid in the back seat. Beside her was another figure with one upfront. He wondered if they were George's goons, or Son-Of-George's goons, or Whoever-Happened-To-Employ-Them goons. He couldn't tell from the angle. The street was narrow. Mordent edged his vehicle forwards, nudged. The jolt was minor, an electric shock. They pulled ahead faster but the width of the road hampered progress, pursuit in slow motion. He nudged it again, secure in the knowledge the vehicle wouldn't suddenly overturn, was confined by brick buildings either side. They were closer than one vehicle towing another. And suddenly they were closer still.

The road widened. The car in front roared forwards and before Mordent had a chance to stomp the gas he was dragged along in its wake. A sharp left created a cacophony of twisted metal. Mordent lifted his feet from the controls. He was attached to their vehicle, bumpers merged like two teenagers locking braces. As the car ahead hit the main drag Mordent's wheels screamed sideways, pulled across the carriageway, swung out and butterfly kissed another car on his left-hand side. Car horns shouted like disturbed geese.

Up ahead a traffic light flipped to red. He was accelerated across the gap, the lead vehicle moving at speed as though they were a rod and he was a worm on a line being dangled in front of an advancing shoal of metal fish. Cross-traffic caught in cross fire, cross drivers leaning on those horns. Before the sanctuary of the other side Mordent saw one vehicle skid away from his passenger door in a toreador's turn; a ballet on wheels. He was reminded of JG Ballard's *Crash*, but felt no sexual thrill from the dance. Like a rider at a fairground he had little control of the route. His feet poised against the pedals in case of disconnection.

Another sharp left. His vehicle again swung out but the bumper held. He pushed hard on the brake twice – *pump pump* – straightened his vehicle in time for it to follow the other car down another narrow alleyway. The guy on the back seat turned his head and Mordent had a clear view of the goon at the cemetery.

Any doubts that it might be police were long gone, but at least no other parties had entered the fray. And he knew he was dealing with amateurs.

He grinned: a big peachy pineapple grin.

The guy looked away.

Mordent pushed his foot to the accelerator.

The alley was narrow and long. He knew where it would end. A patch of waste ground at the back of the business district which was once a car park and was now a piece of real estate going begging for development but which was subject to a preservation order because someone once famous had pissed there. Or something. Either way, it was open and empty, and with his foot on the gas Mordent propelled both cars towards it, slamming on his brakes just as the lead car emerged into that space.

The bumper tore off their vehicle as Mordent's ground to a halt, the force spinning them into an open space tufted with blistered grass, used syringes, and discarded contraception balloons. Their car performed a perfect arc before shuddering to a stop. They were now facing Mordent who blocked the only vehicular access to the space. Reacting quickly, both goons exited. Car doors opening like batwings. They stood, confused, glancing from one to the other and then at the narrow passage at the rear of the complex which pedestrians used to gain access to the main drag. As one, they ran for it.

Mordent gunned his engine, swerved around their vehicle, winked at Astrid who was stock still in the back seat, and then headed for both goons, who each leapt a block of concrete Mordent hadn't seen within the vegetation. His bumper - their bumper - slammed into the surface and buckled. Mordent jerked forwards, his forehead hitting the sun visor which had dropped during impact, a line of pain written across his skin which shot light out of his eyes that then circulated around his head; birdy-style. He reversed in a metal scrunch, the lip of their bumper caught over the concrete. Then cut his engine as the goons made the alleyway and confirmed their escape.

Swearing, he checked out of his vehicle, glanced at the bumper damage which seemed to be all theirs and none of his, then walked back to their vehicle where Astrid still sat. He entered through the open car door and sat beside her. When he closed the door the vibration was akin to wakening Sleeping Beauty with a metallic kiss. Astrid's eyes focused from a land far away. They were smeared with black mascara like the rings on a lemur, although the tears themselves had already dried in the heat.

'You ok?'

She leant into him. 'I was scared.'

More tears brimmed at the edge of her eyes, like a bath run to capacity. She blinked them back.

'I'm being foolish.'

He squeezed her affectionately. 'Not at all. What happened?'

'Guy buzzed my apartment, said he was from the police. I suspected you'd contacted them because I'd noticed someone outside the past couple of days. They couldn't have put their best operative on it, he might as well have had a neon sign over his head.' She allowed a smile. 'He asked me to come down because he had the postman with him who needed me to sign for something. Truth is, I was awaiting a parcel otherwise I'd have realised it was a ruse. So down I go. The cop I'd seen waiting was pushed behind me as I opened the door and I was pulled out. I think he was concussed, not dead. Then I was advised to enter their vehicle. At gun point. In those situations, I guess that's what you do.'

Mordent nodded. 'I saw you get into the car. Lucky I came along in time.'

'They didn't speak much, but it was clear they knew they were followed. I'd say they were amateurs.'

'That ties in with what I know.'

It was hot in the vehicle. Sweat pooled at the base of Mordent's buttocks.

'We need to get you somewhere safe.'

She nodded, defences weakened. When she spoke her voice cracked. 'Any idea why they didn't just kill me like all the others?'

Mordent shook his head. 'Not sure. I don't really know what's going on.' He paused. 'This George guy. You think you'd recognise him if you saw him again?'

'I think so.'

'How long ago was it?'

'A couple of weeks. I told you.'

Mordent nodded a second time. He decided to hold back on George's death. Astrid's head lay on his shoulder. He kissed her forehead. He hadn't realised how much she meant to him. Or maybe he did. Truth was, dames came and went but some were keepers. Slowly they disentangled until they were both outside the vehicle. Mordent walked back to his and extricated the bumpers.

'You think the police will be able to trace them from their vehicle?'

'Maybe. Unless it was rented under false ID. Who knows with these guys.'

He thought over the options. Wondered if it was better for himself to find a place for Astrid to hide. But then she had family.

'I can arrange a safe house for you. You sure your husband will be ok with that?'

'He knows my work, you know this.'

'Maybe he'll think of talking you out of it.'

She smiled. 'I love my job. He enjoys it too. I've never had a problem such as this before. It's a one-off, I'm sure.'

Mordent scratched his scalp. 'For how long, that's the issue.' He thought. 'When this George guy saw you, how did bubblewrap come up in conversation?'

She sighed. 'It was his first appointment. To be honest, we just spoke. I did wonder whether he would be able to complete. He wanted to discuss his needs. It wasn't much of a conversation. Looking back, it was a bit weird. He didn't *feel* like a client. There's shyness and there's those that hold back, you know. Anyway, at the end of the appointment he picked up his jacket and the flyer fell out. I couldn't help but see it. He said I could keep it.'

'You never showed me the flyer.'

'I don't know that I have it, but I remembered the details.'

Mordent nodded. His desire to trust Astrid screwed up his emotions. It felt like he was containing an explosion within his chest.

'Let me make a call,' he said, 'then we'll go back to your place and look for it.'

She nodded and he rang Kovacs whilst she kicked around the dust in the lot like an extra from Russ Meyer's *Faster, Pussycat! Kill! Kill!*. It wasn't a bad comparison to make.

40
Down To The Lake I Fear

Kovacs already knew of Astrid's disappearance. The jumped cop in her apartment building had been discovered by another tenant. He'd received a nasty bang to the back of the head but wasn't dead.

'We need to get her to a safe house, with her family. I'm heading back to her apartment. She can ID George if necessary. You got any photos of him?'

Kovacs hadn't, but was sure they could get some.

'These guys are amateurs,' Mordent said. 'If they wanted me caught in the net then why kidnap her? They don't know what they're doing. I get the feeling this is either bigger than we first thought, or so small that it can screwed up and inserted into your anus.'

Kovacs wasn't happy with the comparison.

Mordent hung up. They waited for the cop car Kovacs had promised would arrive. Davey was driving it with a colleague Mordent knew riding shotgun. Davey didn't speak much. He'd obviously had orders which disagreed with him. Once they were on the scene, Mordent drove back down the alley with Astrid beside him. He resisted the urge to touch her thigh through the material of the tight skirt that she wore.

It wasn't that Astrid was a timekeeper - that as soon as he touched her, a clock would start in her head just like that of a taxi driver – but that he knew it was inappropriate. The relationship you had with a woman of ill repute didn't coincide with that of a regular woman. No matter how close it sometimes felt. That was - Mordent ruefully understood - just part of the service.

Thankfully neither her husband nor children were about when they reached her apartment. The brownstones in this district always seemed freshly made, like new-baked bread. There was none of the tawdriness of Mordent's own apartment. A cop in the open doorway let them in. Mordent could feel Astrid bristling. Whilst her husband might be aware of her work he knew her neighbours weren't. He couldn't help but feel that in some way he had brought this on her head.

Kovacs was waiting, his features torn between a smile and a grimace. Astrid fumbled with her keys and let them in. Kovacs was discreet, told the other officers to wait downstairs. They stood in Astrid's living room and Mordent couldn't help but feel embarrassed. Kovacs was getting to know more about his private life than he ever would have wished.

He made an excuse about using the bathroom. If Kovacs noted he didn't need to ask the way then it didn't register. Whilst Kovacs did some preliminary questioning Mordent rooted about the bedroom. If there was a flyer then there might be fingerprints. Astrid's apartment had a separate bedroom from the one in which she shared with her husband, although she had previously said they sometimes had *fun* in there. He didn't doubt it. As he ploughed his way through an assortment of vibrators, dildos, plugs, masks, rope, chains, candles, pinwheels, two magic wands - one fairytale, one electric - costumery, wigs, gel, lube, beads, gloves, and some objects totally unidentifiable he saw in his mind's eye each of them in use. By the time he had finished he was almost shaking with frustration. His sex urge hadn't diminished since last night's excursion with Grace. If Kovacs hadn't been in the other room he would have taken it further.

He rummaged through her underwear drawer, not that he was expecting to find anything. Silk and satin slipped through his fingers.

He spent longer in there than was necessary.

When he returned Astrid passed over the flyer to Kovacs which he dropped into an evidence bag.

'It was with some paperwork,' she said.

Kovacs nodded to Mordent. 'Good call.'

Mordent nodded back, bemused.

Kovacs looked across to Astrid. 'Get a few things together, for yourself and your family. We'll take you into the precinct for a formal statement and to see if we can get a photofit of Ezra George and your assailants from you. Once that's done we can take you to the safe house. I anticipate closing this case quickly now we have something to go on. Thank you for your assistance.'

Astrid disappeared to fill a suitcase or two. Kovacs nodded to Mordent.

'I guess you're off the hook unless you hired those goons.'

'We both know that didn't happen. What do you think about Ezra George?'

'I think your girlfriend's telling the truth. That she saw an old guy, in any event, who claimed to be George. She's vague about when, but it has to be recent because that club has only just started with the bubblewrap – according to the investigation, they were on beans around the time of George's death. So it doesn't add up. Hopefully we can get something from the flyer, the car registration, and her ID-ing her kidnappers. In any ordinary investigation it would be enough. But considering you're involved I guess it's not that ordinary.'

Mordent decided not to make a fuss over the girlfriend word. Kovacs could have his fun, so long as he was assisting.

They kicked their heels a bit, waiting for Astrid's return.

Mordent began to wonder if Berenice were safe. Shook the thought out of his head where it lodged on the floor amongst all the other damaged thoughts he had ever had. He was knee deep.

Decisions: how could you predict the ways they would turn out? On the macro level it might be as big as whether he had stayed with Berenice's mother, on the micro level it was the butterfly effect. He hadn't breakfasted that morning...had it saved Astrid's life? As an investigator you were supposed to follow certain leads, make necessary connections, but this didn't take into account the wider world – a web of possibilities that existed as an outer bubble, a fragmentary paradise. What was that quote from *Alphaville*? Once we know the number one, we believe that we know the number two, because one plus one equals two. We forget that first we must know the meaning of plus. That was how Mordent felt: that he was always chasing the meaning of plus.

Astrid returned to the room and suddenly one plus one did equal two. She had changed and looked stunning. 'Well,' she said, 'where do we go from here?'

'Down to the lake I fear,' muttered Kovacs.

Neither of them understood the reference.

41
An Unpleasant Emotion Caused By The Threat Of Danger, Pain, Or Harm

Mordent resisted the urge to kiss Astrid's cheek as she ducked into the police vehicle. She seemed restored to her usual self, but he noted her glance up at her brownstone no doubt wondering about her neighbours. He assumed she'd be able to spin them a story if necessary. He'd always found her an exceedingly agreeable actress.

Kovacs confirmed they would drop the charges because of the incident. It wasn't the best situation, but the killer had been working to an alternative game plan. Those goons would report back to whoever they had to and it would be obvious that the police would consider Mordent in the clear. They would forge ahead on the angle they had. Mordent watched them leave with mixed emotions. They had more evidence, but it was nothing he could personally investigate. To keep his mind off things he decided to return to the other case he was working on. At least, the case he was being paid for.

He rang Benedict Holmsworth's number.

'Mr Mordent?'

'That's me. I've got a lead on the Institute of Fear, but I need a payment up front.'

'I think you'll find its The Fear Institute. If your powers of deduction falter at the first hurdle then I have some concern about pushing further expenses your way.'

'Listen, it's a doozy. You'll love it.'

'Perhaps you would care to fill me in on the details?'

'I can't do that. Well, I could. But I'd rather I didn't.'

'Because...?'

Holmsworth's accent was beginning to jar. Mordent wished he was in the position where he could pick clientele rather than the other way around.

'Because if I tell you what I need the money for then you won't pay it. You have to trust me with this one.'

'I'm not an easy target.' There was an edge to Holmsworth's voice. Mordent knew it was a fallacy to expect those with money to part with it easily. That was why they had the money in the first place.

'I understand this. Listen, you put me in a position of trust when you employed me. I'm explaining that in order to bust this organisation sky high I need the money to do it. You don't pay, then their operations continue and you don't get the result you employed me for. It's quite simple.'

If there was a clock in Holmsworth's head Mordent knew it would be ticking. He picked dirt out of his fingernails as he waited.

'How much do you need?'

Mordent told him. Then gave him his bank details. The money would come in useful.

He didn't have an appointment with the Fear Institute but he drove over anyway. Panic-mode would get things done.

His car hadn't suffered from that morning's collision. He had checked his own bumper and it was intact, other than scratches which reminded him of proverbial notches on bedposts. When he considered his own notches he realised he would have whittled down the bedpost to a burnt matchstick, the head teetering ungainly at the tip.

The city's inhabitants would consider the weather beautiful, but Mordent found the increasing relentless heat was starting to wear through his patina of noir; like a light shone direct on sunglasses. Whereas others viewed sunlight as a welcome source Mordent only saw the distress that it caused. You put anything under the spotlight and it showed the strain. Cracks were picked out on otherwise blemish-free buildings, their embedded dirt emphasised. Faces bore wrinkles, beads of sweat, cracked make-up, all the symptoms of age. Discarded clothing created white-flesh obscenities, ripples of cellulite, inappropriate gestures. Give him the night, cool and crisp, where realities blurred and everything wasn't under the microscope. Give him anonymity. Give him death.

He was beginning to stink under his jacket. Half-dead already.

Because it wasn't just sight which was affected by sunlight, but the olfactory sense. Within his vehicle body odour pooled in the air, a stale reminder of his animal self. Outside, tyre rubber mixed with melted bitumen: asphalt perfume. The smells of hot dog vendors sickened his stomach, split sausages spitting in the sun. Unnatural chemicals oversprayed by paranoid office workers funked around their torsos. Dog excrement steamed and baked.

He pulled up outside the Fear Institute. He realised not only had he missed breakfast, but lunch. His stomach growled, as irascible as himself. For a while he watched as nothing happened. The organisation didn't seem that popular. He wondered if it was losing business, whether in an age where everyone claimed they could help you with everything that there was no place for an aged eccentric. Perhaps Copernicus would have done better business on the East Coast. Here, in this city, most of the inhabitants were jaded or astute. Perhaps he would point out the hole in their business plan when he nailed them.

He pulled down the vehicle's sun visor, then slid a piece of plastic to one side to reveal the mirror. He ruffled his already ruffled hair. Decided that looking dishevelled came naturally. Noticed there was a thin red line where he had banged his forehead in the collision that morning, looking like the mark a child's hairband would leave if it had been kept in place overnight. He ran a finger along the groove, annoyed that Astrid hadn't mentioned it, aggrieved Kovacs had seen it. It might well be a scar of war, but it made him look like an idiot.

He removed his jacket, then his holster. Placed the gun in the glove compartment. Considered that the space would be more properly described as a gun compartment. Realised the only pair of gloves he ever wore were to conceal fingerprints if he were firing a gun. Wondered what Berenice might think of that. Wondered what Berenice might buy him for Christmas. Whether it would be gloves. Wondered how long it had been since anyone had bought him something for Christmas. Wondered what he would buy for her.

He shook his head. Christmas was a long way off. A meteor might hit and they could all be dead by then.

Wishful thinking.

He exited the vehicle and wandered across to the Institute's door. Banged on it rapidly, non-stop, until finally it was answered.

The look the skinny guy gave him was disdainful.

'Mr Greener. We do not accept impromptu appointments.'

Mordent shouldered into the doorway. 'I must see Mr Fear. It's very important.'

'I've just explained to you that it isn't possible.'

'Is he with another client? I must see him. I'm at my wits end.'

Mordent found hysteria didn't come naturally, but he milked what he had, decided persistence was key.

'As I've explained...'

Mordent tried to bolt through, was held back by a gentle pressure on his shoulder.

'You've made your point. I will see what I can do. Please, wait here.'

Mordent sat on a studded leather chair in the narrow hallway. If he was wearing shorts it would stick to his skin, leave a sliver of epidermis behind him as he rose. Yet the interior of the building was considerably cooler to the outside temperature and he luxuriated. Allowed himself the pleasure of closing his eyes. Inside his head, noir reigned.

He was almost asleep by the time he was beckoned.

'Mr Fear will see you now, despite the irregularity.'

Mordent rose slowly, wanting to frustrate the officiousness now he had got his way. Truth was, the mantle of sleep held him down, and as he slowly walked up the corridor it was as if he were becoming unstuck, his imagination spooled back from a potential dream he had been on the point of tipping into, a hand clasping the cliff face of reality.

He was disappointed when he was shown into Copernicus' office. The man sat facing him behind his desk. Steam from a cup of coffee spiralled skywards, a half-eaten bloomer sat on a plate held within ageing fingers.

'Sit down, sit down.'

Mordent didn't need to be told twice, and said so.

'It's a figure of speech.' Copernicus took a bite from his bloomer, a slip of ham pulled out from the bread and hung down over his chin like a lengthy tongue. Copernicus bit through it and it fell to the plate. 'Please excuse me. Some of us were having lunch.'

Mordent nodded, apologised. 'It's the bubblewrap,' he said.

'Of course it is. Did you do what I asked?'

'I bought several rolls. I laid it out on the floor of my apartment like carpet. I walked over it barefoot. I can't go back there again.'

'Nonsense. Do you feel any reduction in the frisson of fear?'

'None.'

Copernicus leant forwards, picked up the coffee cup and sipped from it as though it were liquid mercury. 'What do you feel?'

'Fear. I feel fear.'

'Stronger than before?'

'Definitely.'

'Well, as I said, we have to confront our fear in order to fight it. And we can only really fight it when our fear is heightened. That's when we make the most of our potential.'

Mordent shifted in his seat, attempted to look uncomfortable.

'You mentioned hypnotherapy.'

'Did I? I mean, I did. It's still too early for us to go down that route. Did Jones take your bank details on your first visit?'

'Yes, but...'

'Hypnotherapy is an expensive process which isn't to be taken lightly. We invest a lot of time with such clients. A lot of time.'

'Money is no issue Mr Fear.'

'I'm glad to hear it.' He coughed, violently, and spat a piece of bread into his coffee cup. 'For you, I mean. If you want to rid yourself of this phobia.'

'I do.'

'Then escalate the process. Do you know what fear is? I'll give you the dictionary definition.' He put down the cup, steepled his fingers. 'Fear is defined as an unpleasant emotion caused by the threat of danger, pain, or harm. I would quantify that definition and state that it is a *perceived* threat. Consider this: is bubblewrap a danger to you?'

Mordent decided to answer slowly, thoughtfully. 'No. Unless I became suffocated.'

'Might it cause pain?'

'Possibly.'

'Harm?'

'I guess unlikely.'

Copernicus threw his hands in the air. 'All of these are unlikely, but your irrational fear cannot help but consider them perceived threats, just as your rational mind attempts to negate them. Your responses became more rational the longer you considered it. We need to slow down your response time to eradicate the fear. Return to your apartment, take the bubblewrap to your bed, sleep within it. Come back to us only when you cannot stand it any more. At that moment you will be ready for the hypnotherapy.'

Mordent nodded, slowly. 'Are you not trying to exacerbate my fear?'

'Of course, I have just described doing so.'

'Do all your cures follow the same pattern, or can some be more readily overturned.'

Copernicus folded his arms. 'It would be unprofessional to discuss other clients.'

Mordent stood. He had done enough to satisfy himself that the Fear Institute was exactly what he thought it would be: a sham.

'Before you depart, what is that mark across your forehead?'

Mordent looked at Copernicus, a wry smile elongated his features.

'I banged my head against my sun visor.'

Copernicus nodded. 'I get a similar mark wearing a baseball cap. Jones will show you out.'

Mordent made his way back down the corridor, entering the blinding white light of the street felt like arriving on stage.

He just didn't know how to perform.

42
Change: The Illusion Of Progress

Mordent couldn't remember the last time he had a drink.

That was the problem.

He sat in Morgan's bar, gazing at the empty glass in front of him. The heat on the street couldn't penetrate the black painted walls. The sun was held at bay.

The glass bore wet stains down one side. Was it whisky or bourbon? He regarded them closely, the pattern resembled rice fields photographed from above in grainy black and white. Or was that simply a pattern he wanted to believe in? Wasn't it the case that his mind hoped to find patterns in everything?

That was police work. Not just dot to dot or putting a puzzle together or any of those old *old* clichés; but finding patterns where there were none. Genuine patterns, not pareidolia. That was what he was thinking.

Morgan was outside whispering distance. Mordent was aware of a gentle hubbub of conversation behind him. Words which were thrown but weren't meant to be caught.

He wondered if his seat were a swivel chair.

He wondered if he were in motion.

Drink: the PI's nemesis.

Yet he knew that was a caricature to be avoided.

He turned the glass slowly, from side to side. The rice fields changed to photographic negatives to opaque districts. He hadn't spoken for a couple of hours. His tongue felt heavy in his head, like rolled-up carpet. A cartoon tongue.

He couldn't quite remember when he had begun drinking.

It was all a blur.

He remembered an occasion where he had met Hubie in the bar. Hubie had poured out his heart just as Morgan had poured out the drinks. It was an uncomfortable conversation, one Mordent had rare experience with. Ultimately the resultant investigation led to Hubie's death. Perhaps Mordent should have left well alone, or perhaps the cards were stacked to begin with. Perhaps they were always stacked, or perhaps there were no cards at all. Some days, both options were likely.

Mordent noticed his face reflected in the glass, sideshow mirror-style. It must have always been visible, but he had only seen the stained patterns. Focussing his gaze revealed his face, distorted and sallow. Perhaps that was all he needed to do with the bubblewrap case, refocus his thinking. Perhaps the answer to be had was there all along.

But these were drunken musings: thoughts that made sense at the time but made nonsense come daylight. He once knew of a writer who kept a notebook by their bed to write down ideas in the night. What seemed blisteringly good at 3am was often trite in daylight. Again, the mantle of noir - the aspect of the dark – coloured experience. It proved that night and day were truly different worlds.

Mordent imagined a world in reverse. A world in which most of the population worked throughout the night, took twilight vacations, went to the beach under moonlight, lived the majority of their lives in darkness, only to sleep come sun-up, leaving the daylight for mobsters and criminals, for prostitution and alcohol. They would have to create a new word for the genre that he loved to his heart. Noir wouldn't make sense. Its cramped darkness, shadows, angular lines wouldn't sit with a blue sky world. What was the opposite of noir? He considered *blanche,* wondered about the fit, wondered whether it held the same depth, if it would catch on with the population or its feeders of criminal material: the novelists, filmmakers, those who would need to embrace blanche. He got so worked up with the idea that he forgot about the patterns on his glass or that he was even sitting in the bar. He had a transcendental meditative experience.

And then the fantasy crumbled, the intricate world of *blanche* so carefully assembled in his mind became no more than a 3am story, its foundations ruined before they were built, it's existence no more than a pathetic fallacy.

He caught Morgan's eye and beckoned him over for a refill. Politics often used the notion of *change* as a way to convince the public things were happening. Mordent had heard *change* described as *the illusion of progress.* He liked the metaphor, but it sat just as well with him as it did with the politicians. Getting drunk in Morgan's Bar might affect his view of reality, but that illusion would be burnt off come morning.

He drank the remainder of his final drink slowly, fought with his lucid mind to come to terms with the extent of the investigation, then slid off the bar stool like an evolutionary form returning to the slushpile.

Morgan had pre-booked him a taxi.

Mordent knew that it had to be bad.

43
Blanche

Mordent woke with his head the shape of a Buick. Its engine throbbed although it wasn't firing on all cylinders. He rubbed his eyes, felt the sluice of vitreous humour that slipped with the movement. Or was it aqueous humour? Either way, he didn't find much humour in it.

He stood, scratched, yawned. Sunlight streamed through his threadbare curtains casting reverse shadowplay figures on the wall above his bed. He smiled. He loved the scorch of the sun, the yellow night. Such circumstances made it easier to catch criminals who were otherwise obscured by the noir of the day, where black and white silhouetted everyone from office workers to shop workers to pedestrians to tourists and replicated them through shadow to become extras in their own lives. At least in the glare of the sun it was harder to hide. This was why PIs such as himself loved to work at night.

This was why he slept during the daytime, when it was cooler, when darkness shrouded his eyelids and unlike the majority of the city's occupants he found it easier to rest. Not for him the tunnelled rat-race, the blinkered existence that daytime afforded. Where others slept, their blindfolds blotting out the sun, he was abroad in the city, checking out the wide deserted streets for felons, making a note on everything spread out during the heat of the night.

He showered. The water jetting with force onto his face, feeling it trickle down his body with the intimacy he would have loved from a woman. His working hours didn't suit when it came to relationship building. No female worth her salt wanted her skin aged by the glare of the sun, so he was left to peruse the prostitutes who favoured the brightness as a means to accentuate their wares. In contrast, no one wanted a whore they could only see during the half-light of the day.

Blanche. The literary term suited him. The rays of the sun illuminated his profession, carried with them the clarity that his work required. How did the phrase go? *When it was all light, it was all right.* That sign had been pinned over his desk when he was in the force, and the only reason he hadn't taken it with him when he left was because it would have been theft. Stealing was something that Mordent didn't do.

He towelled himself dry, considered the case he was working on in front of breakfast: ham and eggs sunny side up. He had been employed to investigate a company known as The Fear Institute. Working at night suited the nature of the investigation. Human's primal fears came from opacity, from the limitless horizon. What could be more terrifying than seeing what was directly in front of your face? The organisation played on those fears, forced confrontation. They suggested their clients sleep during the day where dark was snug, and embrace sunlight as though it were not an illuminating monstrosity. Mordent had tailed one of those clients, found them stumbling in the vastness of hitherto concealed streets, their fingernails clenched tight in their palms, their eyes bleached with seeing, a face aghast at the limitless view.

It was then that Mordent realised the Institute's aim was far from eliminating fear, but sought to perpetuate it as part of the *cure,* enabling their clients to become dependent, enabling money to roll in the coffers. Whatever *coffers* actually were. He made a mental note to find out.

Like a sunspot he burst onto the street. Most residents had retired to their homes for the night. He loved the wide-open spaces, the empty highways save for a handful of cars filled with goons no doubt up to no good. Automatically he registered number plates only partially obscured by the solar glare, it was wise to know who might be about. In the day time, when darkness shrouded the populace, it was difficult to be picked out of the crowd, but in the glorious night he was just as easily a target as were crime's perpetrators. Even so, he loved the blanche overtones, the all-encompassing world. Glancing from left to right, almost giddy with possibility after shedding the day's mantle, he almost felt like breaking out in song.

Mordent woke in a sweat. Light streamed through his thin curtains, gave them a glow like a well-showered woman. He scrabbled for his watch. It was eight in the morning. Standing, then hobbling on Bambi feet towards the window, his heart pitched like a sailing ship in high winds. He opened the curtains, became flooded by sunlight like the vampires at the end of Bigelow's *Near Dark* or as if spotlit by a police helicopter. His eyes struggled to focus, his worse fears dreamily realised; then he saw life on the street below: the usual cacophony of vehicles and pedestrians, metal and meat. Sighing, he shook his head vigorously as though to dislodge the effects of the dream. He imagined aspects of it falling to the carpet, scrabbling away to dark corners, under the bed, inside the wardrobe. His head throbbed with the hangover. He wished he were dream himself.

He sat back on the bed. Scratched. Realised he was emulating that *blanche* world. The word sat disagreeable in his mind, the antithesis of everything he loved. Yet, as he mused about the inflammatory nature of the subconscious, he saw the grain of truth roll out of the dream machine. The Fear Institute was indeed perpetuating fear in order to sustain its own activities. And if it believed it might freak Mordent out with excessive bubblewrap, might it also be the case that a heart attack could be induced through exposure to hordes of rats: neither murder nor manslaughter, perhaps, but enough to tip Benedict Holmsworth Snr over the edge.

He knew this nugget had been in his mind all along, didn't quite thank the dream for bringing it forwards.

He closed his eyes. Losing one sense heightened the others. His hangover made his head feel like an inflated balloon, puffed to bursting point. The line across his forehead where the sun visor had hit was a fishing line pulled taut. His tongue was a furred carpet where dreams had been discarded. If he stretched his imagination far enough he might almost taste them.

Resisting the urge to take a shower he got back under the bedcovers. He didn't want a return to blanche - was sure he couldn't effect it even if he did - but the hangover would have to go somewhere before he was welcomed into the day.

44
Collecting Calls

He was woken by the sound of his cell, the vibration resembling leprechauns river-dancing on his side table.

His right arm folded itself out of the bed covers with the mechanical movement of an angular lamp. The rectangular device fit within his grip like operating a successful claw grabber machine. By the time it reached his ear his metaphors were exhausted. His slit-eyes saw it was Marsham and he decided to accept the call.

'Yeah?'

'Don't be so enthusiastic. It's me, Marsham.'

'I know who it is. What do you want?'

'You sound like a bear that got out of the wrong side of the bed this morning.'

'That's because I'm *still* in bed.'

'Alone, I trust?'

Mordent could detect a smile in Marsham's voice. The way he was feeling, alone was best.

'Just cut to the chase.'

'Kovacs asked me to fill you in. I'm presuming he means with information. The girl, Astrid, and her family are safe in the safe house. You could say they're as safe as houses.'

'Humour doesn't come naturally to you Marsham.'

'I do my best.' There was a pause. 'Anyway, she gave a statement to Kovacs and by his reckoning this

Ezra George who visited her was already dead. I guess he's the biggest stiff she ever had.'

'I've already done that joke. And we've just discussed humour. Tell me more.'

'Kovacs has arranged for the body buried as George to be exhumed. Just to be on the safe side. He appeared to have no living relatives, so your idea of that girl Lola's personal belongings being passed onto a potential killer seem unfounded. We've also searched George's last known abode and there's no sign of habitation since his funeral nor is there any information about the girl. The house looks just like a dead man would leave it. Empty. Yet full. You know what I mean?'

'You're still not going to get a gig at Carnegie Hall. Go on.'

'They've dropped the charges against you. I'm sure you're aware of that. Kovacs kicked up big that he was in with you on that one. Seemed like he'd cracked for once, shown a bit of human under the robot skin. I think he realises that the few of us remaining in the office who remember you still hold you in respect. Maybe he wants some fame by association. Either way you're cleared. Not that I ever doubted it, of course.'

'Of course. Although you were quick to disassociate yourself.'

'Survival of the fittest, buddy. Survival of the fittest. Still, it seems you're not lying down near the waterhole yet.'

'You got anything else for me?'

'Not a lot. I'd suggest you lay off the prostitutes for a while. That's the only advice I could give.'

'As though you haven't paid for it yourself.'

'Don't need to mate. I've got a harem back at the ranch.'

'That's what they all say.'

'So what exactly is it with the bubblewrap...?'

Mordent didn't give him the satisfaction of an answer. He lay back on the bed, head in his hands. The trouble with guilty secrets is that once they were exposed you were only left with the guilt. Not at the act itself, although sometimes the frisson of guilt added a little something to it at the time, but the embarrassment that it was out in the open. He didn't want to get ribbed for it from now til the end of time. He decided he'd have to bluff it out, allow no jibes. He could bully his way through until it was forgotten.

He turned his cell around in his hands. He was due an upgrade but technology had begun to advance away from him. His ex-wife, Maria, had previously dealt with such things - in the short space that she was actually around. The last he saw of her he was lying in a hospital bed covered in bruises. Her exit hadn't suggested she wanted a return match, but sometimes you just needed somebody. He wondered what she would think about Berenice, wondered if he wanted them to meet. Perhaps it would overcomplicate matters, but suddenly the idea of family bred more ideas of family. He called her number up on the display. Thought for a moment. Cancelled it.

Life was complicated enough.

Instead he scrolled through his text messages, opened a blank one, and sent this to Berenice:

Hey. Sorry to ditch you last night, but you were a great help. How's it going with my project? I have the funding. x

He didn't expect an immediate response.

Didn't receive one.

The case rolled around in his head like two dice in a shaker. Mordent wasn't a gambler - he couldn't have all the vices - but he knew when something didn't add up. The key was now held in a dead man's fist. And there was one person who knew the dead better than anyone else. He decided to place a call to Martens. Ordinarily he would have dialled direct, but Martens might not take the call if he hadn't heard Mordent was in the clear. He got himself routed via the hospital. Gave them a sob story they couldn't refuse.

'Morgue.'

'Martens. It's Mordent.'

'I thought we were quits.'

'You haven't heard? I'm in the clear. No more Kovacs' bad boy. There'll be no audit trail from you to me.'

'Sounds too good to be true.'

'Doesn't everything?'

'So what brings you to my neck of the woods. I've no more cadavers suffocated by bubblewrap. You calling about something new?'

'Same case, different body. Kovacs is exhuming a guy by the name of Ezra George. Is that coming your way?'

'Wait. I'll check.'

Martens disappeared. Mordent could hear footsteps echoing as if down a long corridor. He imagined it was the sound that would call to you from Death's waiting room.

'It's all booked in. That exhumation paperwork can take a while to get through but Kovacs has rushed it somehow. It's not for me, though. Clements is doing that one. You won't know him. He's new to this office but not new to the job. Works alternate shifts. I might be able to get you the result but can't guarantee it. Examination is scheduled for this afternoon.'

'Ok. Tell me something. If someone dies of natural causes what evidence is required of their identity before they're buried?'

'Thought you would know that one. They're usually identified by a nearest relative.'

'And if there's no relative?'

'Then DNA or fingerprinting might establish identity. Even so there's still people nowadays who are unidentified. It might delay a burial but it won't prevent one.'

'The guy Kovacs is exhuming. What if the body isn't who it was thought to be?'

'Then someone's cocked up or we've had false information. What are you thinking?'

'I'm not sure. Just that this case is fishier than a fish farm.'

'I've seen fishier.'

'I bet you have, working at the business end.'

'I thought we were cutting those jokes out.'

'And spoil our fun?'

'There is that. Listen, I've got one for you. There's two female cleaners working in the mortuary when they see a corpse with a massive erection. 'I'm having some of that', one of them says. So she rides it and when she's done she says, 'God that was incredible. The best sex I've ever had!' So the other cleaner looks at the satisfied expression on her face and says, 'I wish I could have a go. But it's my time of the month.' The other woman says, 'Go on, he's hardly likely to complain!' So the woman mounts him and after about ten minutes she hears moaning coming from the corpse. 'Jesus!' she says to her mate, 'he's still alive!' To which the corpse says: 'Alive? Another transfusion like that and I'll be back to work on Monday."

Mordent smiled but didn't show it. 'They don't get any better, Martens. But then I guess you're not the intellectual type. You wouldn't know Die Fledermaus from Die Fieldermouse.'

'Awww...go boil your head. It'll improve your looks.'

They exchanged a few more pleasantries before hanging up. Mordent checked his phone. Nothing from Berenice. Maybe she was mad at him. Maybe she had her hand up an animal's backside, working them like a puppet. He had no doubt they had fun and games at the taxidermists, no matter the amount of respect that might be shown on the surface. Especially as she seemed to be a chip off the old block.

He rose from the bed. Had that shower. There was little use in sitting around waiting for things to happen or for others to provide the answers. It was time to do what he was good at. To investigate, for once.

45
Unlawful Entry

A quick call to Jamieson provided him with George's former address. George once had money, that was clear. He lived outside the city and using internet maps Mordent could see that whilst there wasn't much land associated with the property it looked like it could have been plucked off an English country estate. White columns lined the front of the building with a Georgian triangular cornice over the doorway. Jamieson had told him the building was subject to probate waiting for family members to come out of the woodwork. Mordent thought of changing his surname to George.

It was a good couple of hours away including traffic. He pulled up outside Bukowski's and stocked up on sandwiches and coffee. In the trunk of his vehicle were gloves, a crowbar, flashlight and all the tools of the trade for a would-be burglar. Anything Kovacs hadn't found, he would find. If there was nothing to be found, he would find that too.

It had been a while since he'd had a long drive. He tuned in to his favourite jazz station and let the music carry him as traffic thinned then disappeared. In the city it was rare to get into fifth gear, often hard to get out of third. The car's engine appreciated the drive, like a cramped airline passenger finally stretching their legs. He cruised like a movie-star, imagined the backdrop in his rear view mirror to be stock footage superimposed on the screen, almost felt comfortable enough to take his eye off the road, as if the other traffic wasn't even moving.

He slapped his face, once, twice, then drank some of the coffee he'd ordered.

The roads became narrower, vegetation scrubbier. Occasionally he saw wildlife: birds alien to the city, or a glimpsed squirrel, drifting upwards in a tree. The security blanket of buildings unravelled. He felt open, intense. Approaching cars were so far in the distance they advanced like knights on horseback. He imagined darkness falling, their headlights becoming lances, as they directed themselves towards him then pulled away. He took another shot of coffee. He decided to drink less. He'd heard coffee could make you paranoid. He wondered what happened if you already were.

Despite the apparent uniqueness of the building Mordent passed several similar properties before arriving at George's address. There wasn't much of a driveway, just a patch of compacted soil between two sides of yellowing grass resembling an open cheese sandwich. Mordent parked by the side of the road. It was a quiet district. Quiet streets were harder to be inconspicuous within than busy roads, the best approach was to look as though you owned the place. He opened the car door and took the bag of tools out of the trunk. Strolling down the driveway he resisted the urge to whistle. No one whistled nowadays, that instrument was broken.

The main entrance was roughly a hundred yards from the road. A ragbag of trees, planted almost indiscriminately, broke through the lawn. Mordent didn't have names for vegetation. They didn't look healthy. As he approached the house he noticed the paint was peeling on those white columns. The house had been glamorised on the internet: the camera did lie. With cameras on his mind he kept an eye out for security devices but there was nothing apparent. Skirting the main entrance he headed round back. It was a long way round. He checked out windows along the way but it was clear there was no one inside. The absence of vehicles in the drive corroborated this. The building remained furnished. Vultures had yet to descend.

At the back door he forced the lock with the crowbar and slipped inside. Stale cooking smells hung in the air as though they'd been clipped to a washing line. An adjacent door led to a darkened cupboard containing several pairs of rubber boots. A heavy black jacket hung on a peg resembled the skin of a manatee. Gardening tools slumped in one corner, their handles intermixed like a game of Pick-Up-Sticks. Mordent took out his flashlight and shone it in the dark places. Insects scurried. There was nothing of interest.

He moved into the kitchen. Block-white cupboards would have gleamed when new, but displayed fingerprints in a forensics' dream. Mordent wondered if they had dusted here. Stacked pans lay on the draining board like a robot knight. He wondered what it was with the medieval metaphors. A couple of pans encrusted with old food lay in the sink, semi-submerged in foul-smelling water. The place held the look of somewhere left in a hurry, consistent with the sudden death of someone who had no family to clean up after them. Mordent thought it over, moved on.

A large spacious room opened up on the left-hand side with a gleaming ebony piano dominating the floor space. Mordent made a circuit, carpet plush against the soles of his shoes. Bookshelves lined the walls, the usual gamut of populist male fiction: James Patterson, John Grisham, Lee Child, Jeffrey Deaver. Mordent didn't care for them, but he flicked through a battered copy of the short stories of Cornell Woolrich and placed it in his bag. He opened the lid of the piano, put a finger down on one of the black notes: a resonant tone vibrated air particles. Closing the lid he moved on.

A second living space bore the signs of having dominated George's existence. A threadbare corduroy armchair faced a widescreen wall-mounted television. A glass coffee table suspended a mug, whose contents were also suspended; a filmy residue topped in floating blue mold. Two writing desks flanked the television. Kovacs men had had a good root around. Papers festooned the surrounding floor, drawers were open. Mordent flicked through some of the documents: the usual paperwork you might expect from an elderly gentleman. Bills, receipts, insurance policies...he took a good look at the latter. George's wealth was destined for good causes. The sale of the house would benefit a number of charities.

Perhaps there *were* no living dependents. Mordent's eyes were drawn to framed photographs on a sideboard. He had expected them, but they were still a surprise. Moving from his crouched position on the floor he walked towards them. There were six in total, half of which featured two people, and all of which featured the same one.

Lola White.

A couple were school photographs. Lola in a blazer and white shirt, tie loose, hair in pigtails. She couldn't have been older than twelve yet it was the Lola he had known. Her expression, the glint in her eye, the cheeky smirk of her lips: nothing had changed. In the second photograph she was older, but still had the pigtails and the cheek. Probably fourteen or fifteen. In the final solo outing she stood, full-length, against a white wall. It was the most recent image. He had never seen her handwriting, but diagonally across the bottom right hand corner she had written *To Grandpa George. Love Lola x.*

In the three remaining photographs she was a pre-teen five years and upwards playing with her grandfather in what Mordent recognised was the rear of the property. In one he stood behind her, pushing a swing. In another he was out of focus, standing to the side, watching her ride a red bicycle. In the last they both peeked out from a wooden Wendy House. In all the photos they were smiling and in all the photos the familial love showed in spades. Mordent realised his eyes were wet. Lola looked no different in any of the photos. The same blue eyes, the same pigtailed hair, the same cheeky expression. She was the perfect template for herself.

He rubbed his sleeve against his eyes. The clues had to be here. He ruffled through the sideboard drawers, through pieces of paper unidentifiable that should have been thrown out years ago. Moving out of the room he ascended the stairs, realising with each step that not only George but Lola would have lived here. She had never mentioned her parentage, perhaps that was understandable. At the top of the stairwell were four doors. One presumably was the bathroom, one would have been George's bedroom, the other unknown. But the fourth room still bore a name tag: *Lola*.

It had been stencilled using separate letters on the painted white of the door. Mordent knew this because each letter wasn't properly aligned with the other. He imagined Lola doing it, standing on a stool, whilst her grandfather watched. Her pigtails flicked behind her so they didn't get in the way of her pencils. Mordent didn't want to enter, didn't want to see her life as it had been before she met him, didn't want to imagine her as anything other than his compliant beautiful fuck-toy. Turning his back, he decided to try the other rooms first.

One, indeed, was the bathroom. A cream plastic mat was half-turned over in the bath, sucker pads skywards, as though an octopus steamrollered. The edges of the bathroom cabinet mirror were mottled with discoloration. The toilet had seen better days. Mordent suddenly had the urge to urinate, decided to sit rather than stand. When he flushed the sound ran like running water throughout the entire house.

The second door he tried was the spare room. Spare of anything. Uncarpeted, unfurnished; a box waiting to be filled. George's bedroom was clean, devoid of character. White linen lay flat on a seemingly freshly-made bed. Underwear drawers contained a mix of the old and the new, the worn and the faded. Mordent looked under the metal bedframe: zero. He returned to the hallway, entered Lola's room.

If this was the year 2097 Lola's domain would be an art installation titled *A Teenager's Life In The Latter Part Of The Twentieth Century*. Band posters were wallpaper; trinkets, bracelets, sundry jewellery hung from porcelain hands or pens upended in Coca-Cola glasses; character motif pants spilled out of a dresser; a blue wild-eyed fellow with serrated rows of teeth which Mordent thought he recognised from a Disney movie was in fact a backpack suspended from a curved hook on the back of the door. If Mordent hadn't known the room had been vacated some time ago, that Lola had lived a separate life in the city, that she had been murdered in the most gruesome fashion imaginable, then he might expect her as a fourteen year-old to come running up the stairs, throw herself on the bed, and start texting on her cell amidst the familiar habitat she had created.

He did the math, realised how long George had decided to keep her room as a shrine, saw it had been well attended to. Only now was a thin patina of dust accruing on her belongings.

Kovacs' men had disturbed the diorama. That much was clear when you paid attention, when the initial shock of the completeness had abated. Mordent considered the usual places for hiding a diary, but realised this wasn't George's room. If it remained in the house he had to think like an adult, consider where George might want to place something that disgusted him but which was still part of the Lola he loved. He backed out of her room, again finding his eyes wet with tears. If George was at the heart of the bubblewrap murders, in an attempt to vicariously blame Mordent for her death, then Mordent hoped he would have the opportunity to explain that he loved her.

After a fashion.

He backtracked to the spare room. Anyone ducking their head around the door would have brought the search to an end. Even Kovacs might not have pursued it further. Mordent entered the room, stood in the empty space. The room yawned with himself as the uvula. He walked across to the window, looked out the front of the property to the road where his vehicle patiently waited. A fireplace dominated one wall. He decided not to ruin his suit. Instead he started in one corner and walked vertical to the direction of the floorboards, turned, took a step sideways, and walked back. He repeated the motion one quarter of the width of the room. Then stopped. Rocked back on his heels.

He knelt to the floor. Pushed down hard on the floorboard. There was some give. He brushed his hand over the faint layer of dust that coated the surface. A nail head gleamed new, bent over, its surface shone. A semi-circle of a hammerhead mark indented the wood. It was a recent repair. Mordent guessed George wanted to keep the diary hidden in the house where Lola had lived, that he couldn't dispose of it, and – if he *were* alive – didn't want to take it with him. It was just a guess, of course, but taking the crowbar from his bag, forcing it under the bent nail and then easing it upwards loosened the board and he pulled it free from the floor. Peered into the dark space within.

46
Lola's Diary

People grow older. They grow up. They change.

They lose the patina of innocence that we as adults ascribe to them but which in reality is a natural shedding of no longer required virtue. Sometimes our image of the person we knew and the person they are changes, despite no change to the outward physical appearance. Mordent knew this was the dichotomy George felt between himself and Lola White. Yet no one was to *blame* for those changes. Least of all, Mordent.

He had relocated to her bedroom. Somehow reuniting the diary to the location where much of it had been written had a calming effect on his emotions. Sitting on her bed he flicked through the pages. Lola wasn't a frequent diarist. The earliest entries were dreams, written when she was eleven years old. They held no interest. The dream diary morphed into the usual catalogue of school relationships and break-ups. Again, he skipped through those pages. Around the age of thirteen she became sexually aware - a little late, Mordent thought, but it fuelled pages and pages of self-experimentation and schoolteacher fantasies. Even so, it wasn't until she was sixteen that she first lost her virginity. He didn't read it avidly, was unconcerned by those details. Like most people who read other peoples' diaries the only entries that interested him concerned himself.

Yet he imagined George browsing through the diary, searching for some answers to her death. He could imagine the resultant horror, disbelief. It was an age thing, a pseudo-parental thing. What was perfectly acceptable for one person would be abhorrent to another. Mordent wasn't there to judge. He tried to accept everything for what it was: personal aberrations of what we assumed was a normal life. Only the *normal life* never existed, each of us perverted it in our own ways.

As she got older the diary entries became litanies of expression, of fantasies Mordent knew had been fulfilled:

I want bruises from multiple men.

I want to whore myself out.

I want to be bound / suspended / gagged / blindfolded / no escape. no safeword. NO IDEA what is gonna happen.

I want to be tied down, legs spread. NEEDLES forced through labia / can be soooooooooooooooooooo pretty. laced with ribbon and stuff.

He found himself being turned on by the entries, remembering some of the conversations they'd had, some of the acts they had performed; but also recalling his occasional distress that he hadn't been enough, that he would never be enough, that being enough with him wasn't even what she had been looking for.

Gradually he noticed himself entering the diary. He hadn't been named. In fact, there were no names within the pages once the focus became sexual, but she had mentioned the murder for which she had only ever been an auditory witness, and then his involvement with her was established as *that policeman*.

Having found himself, he now had to force himself to turn the pages. It was clear his existence was arbitrary, a simple conduit for some of her fantasies to become reality. It was with him that the drug she had taken, which immobilised her during sex yet retained her consciousness, was first mentioned. She had wanted total desensitisation coupled with a complete knowingness of her inability to say *no*. Mordent remembered it as an intense experience, akin to the rape fantasy that she mentioned in the diary, although not - of course, essentially - actual rape. Understanding the connections between them, their open and honest discussions of her needs, and the increasing intensity of their relationship Mordent saw this as a safe and natural progression for Lola to experience her desires, yet for George - without that insight - *with* the familial relationship - these diary entries would have been incendiary, confusing, heartbreaking. Mordent could clearly see how George could have connected her behaviour to deviance, how he might mutate her many male experiences into a grooming whereas the reverse had in fact held sway, how Mordent himself - the main player in her experimentation with *Flunitrazepam* - had led to a circumstance where it was used to silence her in that horrific death. Towards the end of her life, her experiences with *that policeman* had been richly detailed.

She had been nineteen, he was thirty-something, and he hadn't been able to believe his luck.

That luck had taken a back seat now.

Mordent had seen the diary before, in an evidence bag, when her body had been recovered. Kovacs had been right, he had suppressed the content without having read it. The diary might have held a clue to her murderer but he had placed his career before that knowledge. Now he read to the last pages, saw no mention of anyone other than himself, simmered down the feelings of betrayal he felt towards her memory, sobbed when he read the final entry:

The funny thing is, I could even love him.

He lay back on the bed, clutching the diary to his chest.

Lola oh Lola oh Lola.

He remembered a metaphor from a poem long forgotten. How a river might run over razor sharp rocks without feeling a thing, without being able to differentiate between those jagged embraces and smooth polished stone. That, for the river, it made no difference, yet if there were a body in the water each jolt would create a tear, a rendering of the flesh.

Mordent was that body in the water.

He closed his eyes. Despite the years he could detect Lola's scent on the bed.

He should have left well alone.

He should have protected her.

He should have done more than he did to avenge her, instead of covering his back.

For now *he* was to be avenged. Girls had died through misunderstanding. George's understanding of fate had been contorted by grief, sex had been made a dirty word that only interested dirty girls. All connections were evident. Right down to the goons.

George wasn't a man familiar with the underworld. And you got what you paid for.

He remembered his first encounter with them in the alley, the reason for Grace Frost, the warning to stay away from Ezra George. It had been enough to implant George's name in his mind, for him to work out those connections. What use revenge if the source was undetermined? But also, what better than to throw someone off the scent than to direct him to a dead man?

He remembered the story of Brer Rabbit. Brer Fox had caught him and was deciding on his punishment, whilst all the time Brer Rabbit insisted he might be tortured by any means so long as he was not thrown into the briar patch. Eventually Brer Fox believed the only thing Brer Rabbit was afraid of *was* the briar patch whereas the reality was that Brer Rabbit wanted to be thrown there. It was where he was born.

Ezra George had created himself as his own briar patch. Something he wanted Mordent to be directed away from, whilst at the same time be attracted to.

Mordent didn't need the coroner's report to understand that Ezra George wasn't dead.

47
For Want Of A Nail

Lola's diary sat snug in his jacket pocket together with the Woolrich book. They were the only things Mordent would take from the house.

He wandered from the back to the front, down the drive to his parked car. The street remained deserted. It was clear he hadn't been followed. He wondered if George expected him to find the diary. He wondered what George had in store.

If the plan had been for the bubblewrap deaths to be pinned on him then George would need to change that plan. Perhaps he would try to kill Mordent himself.

Bubblewrap had been mentioned more than once in Lola's diary. Anyone reading it would clearly have attributed it to him. He only wished he'd had the chance to explain. It was for want of an explanation that those girls had been killed, which reminded him of the old nursery rhyme:

For want of a nail the shoe was lost
For want of a shoe the horse was lost
For want of a horse the rider was lost
For want of a rider the message was lost
For want of a message the battle was lost
For want of a battle the kingdom was lost
And all for the want of a horseshoe nail

Things had a habit of escalating. What was it Grace Frost had said about snowballs? That gave him the urge to see her again. Another snowball, another escalation. If that liaison led to *her* death would Mordent have another disgruntled family member pursuing him? He couldn't be liable for all the crimes and misdemeanours in the city.

Dusk began to fall on the return journey. He considered the similarity between the words *dusk* and *dust,* how on occasion words themselves might fall on a page, in a diary, and settle there: like snow, like the night, like airborne detritus; covering, obfuscating, concealing. Meaning came down to interpretation. Interpretation was individual, harnessed to previous life experience, expectation, breeding, culture, hang-ups and preferences. Really, it was impossible to judge anything from words.

Yet he had been judged, tried, found guilty. All from the words in the diary. Night had fallen on Ezra George like a blanket over the head of a criminal being led to court. Yet there were always lights in the darkness.

He watched them now as the city approached. In the darkness it was easy to imagine he was stationary, that it was, in fact, the city which advanced towards him, on caterpillar tracks, effortlessly, uncontrollably. As dusk darkened into night lights popped into existence, the births of new stars, pinpointing people as easily as police spotlights, showing the world – or beyond the world – that they were there.

People needed light to exist. There were always the exceptions - those that were blind – but even those who claimed to be nocturnal, who embraced the noir-fantastic, needed some form of illumination to penetrate their existence. For Mordent, the multitude of lights which welcomed him back to the city were simply another aspect of noir: their shadows throwing themselves in front of vehicles, against buildings, into the hands of the disreputable and the dispossessed. Without light, there was no darkness. You needed comparison for one to define the other.

His cell rang. He negotiated it out of his pocket and pressed it to one ear, driving one-handed, an eye out for cops.

'Mordent.'

'Hey buddy. It's Marsham.'

'On friendly terms again?'

'Of course. Listen, Kovacs asked me to call you. The plates of the vehicle you trashed were those of a rental company. Those guys have had the car a month. It was rented in the name of Ezra George. Guess they knew if it was tailed back we'd come to a dead end.'

'Only we haven't, have we?'

'You're one smart cookie Mordent. Results of the exhumation are in. The dead Ezra George isn't Ezra George. The corpse is currently unidentifiable but no prints or DNA match from that found in George's home. It seems this George guy is alive and well and on your case.'

'We need to find the goons,' Mordent said. 'Those girls weren't killed by the hands of an eighty year-old. And he's smarter than them. We need to trace *them*.'

'Kovacs has pulled out all the stops.'

'They'll run to ground. They don't need to commit more bubblewrap murders, the reason for those has gone. It's me they'll be after now.'

'You got protection?'

Mordent laughed. 'I bet that's what you say to all the girls. Let me get home. I'll call Kovacs direct. I'll do something, anyhow. I just need to think things through.'

'Ok, buddy. Hang in there.'

'I have no plans to do anything else.'

Mordent killed the call. He lay the cell on the seat beside him. Berenice. She still hadn't responded to his text. This time he pulled over and rang her number just as the last droplet of dusk fell from the sky.

The line rang and it rang and it rang.

He pulled back out into the traffic; a metal box carried on melting tar.

He felt sick. His hands clung to the steering wheel but there was Jello in his arms. He was thinking irrationally, there were a hundred and one reasons why Berenice might not have answered her phone; he was thinking rationally, there was only one reason Berenice might not have answered the phone. Both outcomes were likely.

The coffee had long gone cold. He hadn't taken a bite out of the food. He had been consumed by a different kind of hunger: that of the truth. Now that sickening feeling spread through his body, the smell of the sandwiches that bled through their paper bag added to the nausea. Yet he had to eat. He had to ensure he had strength. What had Napoleon said? That an army marches on its stomach? But then what did Mordent know, Napoleon hadn't said it to him.

He pulled over again. Grabbed a mouthful of warm ham and rocket. From the daytime heat within the vehicle it almost melted in his mouth. The ham tasted like cheese. He felt like pushing the vegetation into his anus – he needed a rocket up his ass. Consuming it hungrily made him realise how hungry he was. He ate the second, more meat less foliage. By the time he got back on the road his belly was full, cold coffee sat like froth in a sewerage plant, and he had the sensation of having been freshly stuffed.

48
Bread Crumbs

There was a light on at the taxidermists but the door was locked and the dead animal had its legs in the air. Mordent banged on the glass.

Nothing happened other than the air pressure on the other side of the door flickered imperceptibly, sound waves buckling the still-life reality. Within the confines of the walls the shop was but jelly in a mould. Something wobbled.

He banged again. Harder. Then banged again.

He thought of smashing the glass, but reason held him back. He took out his cell and rang Berenice, pressing his ear to the door in case he could hear it ringing from inside. Maybe reason *had* left him.

Then he banged on the door again.

A shape shifted at the back of the store. Damian was on his way. He was shuffling, yawning. Mordent checked his watch. It was barely after eight but Damian wore a dressing gown. He guessed he lived at the rear of the store.

He was let in.

'She isn't here.' Damian scratched the back of his head, leant against the polar bear.

'How did you know...' Mordent stopped himself. He was getting paranoid. Why else would he be there. 'When did she leave?'

'She hasn't been here all day. Phoned in sick this morning. Sure sounded sick. I gave her the day off.'

'You have her address?'

'You don't?'

'Damian, we've only just had our reunion. I don't have her address.' Mordent realised he had never thought to ask. Wondered what that made him.

Damian rubbed his chin. 'I don't know if I can give it to you. Data protection. How do I know you haven't fallen out? Can't you call her and ask her yourself?'

'She's not answering her cell.' Mordent sighed. 'Listen, there's a possibility she might be in danger. She tell you about my work?'

'I know you're a PI. You forget things easily. I'm working on *that* for you, remember?' Damian gesticulated to something unseen in the back room. Mordent didn't look.

'Yeh, of course. Look, my head is scrambled. There's guys after me. If they can't get me then they might get her. They might *have* got her.'

'Or she might be tucked up in bed, asleep.'

Mordent sighed. There was no need to get angry, but he found frustration boiling. 'She's a good worker, isn't she. I can tell she loves it here.'

Damian nodded, slowly.

'Has she spoken much about me?'

'She likes you.' Damian spoke quickly, without thinking of breaking confidence. 'She's surprised how easily you guys have hit it off. I had warned her it might be a long process, but she's fine with it all. It's given her an extra spring in her step.'

'So it's unlikely that we would have had an argument. Damian, I need her address. Come with me if needs be.'

Damian shuffled his feet. Mordent looked around

at the animals in the room, all of whom had been transformed from chaos into order. It was clear Damian needed to operate in certain ways.

'As I said, come with me. I'll drop you back here afterwards.'

Damian nodded. 'You really think she might be in danger?'

'I hope not. But it's possible. You want to help me with that?'

He nodded again. 'Let me get changed. You'll have to excuse the dressing gown. I'm never more at home than when I'm with my animals.'

Mordent waited. In the half-light the critters gave him the creeps. He was never keen on waxworks either. There was enough in life that was alive that was already unnerving without needing the dead or the pretend to augment it.

It wasn't long before Damian returned. He locked up the store and they left in Mordent's vehicle. Damian gave him the address.

'You know it?'

'I'm aware of the district. Should be easy enough to find.'

They pulled into light traffic. Damian appeared different outside of the store: smaller, less defined. Out of context he was almost childlike.

They drove in silence. Mordent's palms were damp. Night had locked heat in. They needed something to break the tension.

'I imagine you're the butt of many jokes in your profession,' said Mordent. 'Do you know any?'

Damian shook his head. 'Know any? I'm adept. You've got your usual kind of joke, like this one.' He cleared his throat. 'A New Yorker walks into a bar in the boondocks and orders a cosmopolitan. The bartender looks at the man and says, 'You're not from round here, are ya?' Guy replies he's from New York. Bartender says, 'What do you do there?' Guy says he's a taxidermist and when the bartender looks confused he explains, 'I mount dead animals'. The bartender then hollers to the whole bar, 'It's ok, boys! He's one of us!''

Mordent smiled. 'You'd be good chums with a guy I know at the morgue.'

'At the morgue? Then he'd enjoy the taxidermist classic: 'skinned, tanned, and spread? Just how I like them.''

'You said those were the usual kinds of jokes?'

'Yeh, there aren't any others. They all relate to stuffing and mounting. I guess the public doesn't have much of an imagination when it comes to my line of work.'

'I searched the internet for PI jokes once, came up with an image for the mathematical symbol of pi with a moustache underneath it. *Magnum PI*, it said.'

'We've drawn the short straw with joke professions,' Damian answered.

Mordent nodded. There was little laughter to be had.

They pulled up outside Berenice's apartment building. Mordent offered Damian a wait in the car but he was insistent on coming. *He still thinks I might bash her*, Mordent thought. Berenice was on the fourth floor. They depressed her buzzer but received no response. Mordent pushed a couple other buzzers at random until someone let them in. The magic words were *pizza delivery*.

'There's always someone expecting a pizza in this city,' he told Damian.

They rode the elevator. Mordent's heart in his mouth: a violent hiccup.

Damian edged Mordent to one side. 'Let me knock.' He nodded at the fisheye.

Mordent watched him knock. He looked for a flicker in the fisheye that didn't come and which he probably couldn't have seen if it had. Then *he* knocked. Then he fiddled with the lock with his back to Damian and shortly afterwards they both entered the apartment.

It was immediately clear that it was empty.

Mordent couldn't explain, afterwards, how he knew this.

But empty it was.

Not completely empty. Not *Berenice is not your daughter and never has been and she has rented this address for subterfuge* empty. But simply devoid of her.

They wandered through the rooms. The bed had been hastily made: duvet thrown back rather than hospital corners. A single pillow held the imprint of a slowly disappearing head. In the kitchen, a plate lay in shallow water in the sink, inches above it globules of marmalade floated like bubbles in a lava lamp. A knife crossed the ceramic like an arrow diagonal to a cartoon heart. Slippers were placed neatly by the doorway, the liner in one of them worn thin, almost useless. The apartment was clean but lived in, existed in the stasis between someone having left and someone intending to return. There were no clues either way as to where Berenice might have gone.

Except one.

Damian pointed to a stuffed animal in the living area. A squirrel in fencing pose, little gauze mask made from a tea strainer, a letter opener working as an epee.

'I gave her that,' he said, 'shortly after she began working for me. An introduction to taxidermy.'

A piece of paper had been stabbed on the end of the sword.

Mordent plucked it off.

What's yours is mine, it read. Mordent filled in the blanks: *Just as what was mine was yours.*

'I think,' he said, 'she's been kidnapped.'

Damian sat down. 'Rather an old-fashioned word. Does that still happen nowadays?'

'Possibly. Does this look like her handwriting?' Mordent held out the note, hopeful that it might have a cryptic meaning only Berenice might understand.

Damian shook his head. 'And I see her writing daily,' he said. 'Looks like a man's handwriting, in any event. An old man. You see how shaky that is?'

Mordent agreed.

'It's not a ransom note, is it?' Damian was warming to his PI-support role.

'I don't think they're expecting financial recompense.'

'Are you calling the police?'

'Not yet. Just give me time to think.' Mordent ran a hand through his hair. 'When she called in sick this morning you said she *sounded* sick.'

Damian nodded. 'She sounded like she was about to throw up.'

'Any clues in what she said? I'm thinking they were here, then.'

'I don't remember. Nothing unusual.'

'Wait for me in the car.'

Damian opened his mouth to object, changed his mind. He opened the apartment door. Stopped.

'Look at this.'

Mordent went over to where they had come in. There was another note, one that obviously hadn't been there before, blu-tacked to the door. He pulled it free, slowly, the blu-tack reluctant to give way.

Lose the buddy and we call your phone.

He darted his eyes from the note to either side of the corridor. Quiet.

'They've kept an eye on the building,' said Damian.

'No shit Sherlock.' Mordent clenched the note in his fist. 'Scram. Don't wait by my vehicle. I'll do this alone.'

'Do you want me to call the police?'

'Do you want to get stuffed?'

'Listen, I can see you're angry...'

Mordent apologised. 'It's not you. Please. Let me be.'

He re-entered the apartment, stood by the window. After a moment Damian appeared on the street, walked to the opposite sidewalk and looked up. Mordent didn't acknowledge him. Damian nodded and walked, turned the corner out of sight. Mordent counted towards ten under his breath. At seven, his cell rang.

'Mordent.'

'Fancy a game of cat and mouse?' The voice was old, slightly sibilant through the whistle of dentures. 'You like games, so I've read.'

'Ezra George. We need to talk.'

'Ezra George is dead.'

'That particular game is already up. Please give yourself the pleasure of introducing yourself.'

'Maybe in person.'

'Where is my daughter?'

'She went out into the woods leaving a trail of breadcrumbs. You familiar with the fairytale Hansel and Gretel?'

'Did you tell that to Lola?'

There was a pause.

'If you don't fight fair then neither will I.'

'Berenice isn't a prostitute.'

'All girls are. Or so I've learned.'

'Lola was an independent young woman open to experimentation. No more.'

'She was open to being abused.'

'No. She was *open* to being abused. I've read the diary. You have too. I loved her.'

'Love!' The voice spat. 'Something else that's open to abuse. Don't give me your excuses. Either professionally or personally you should have protected her.'

Mordent bit back on the arguments. The proximity of telecommunications might place George in the room with him, but in reality he wasn't. He had to keep the line open. George held the cards. George held Berenice.

'What do you want me to do?'

'I want you to follow the trail of breadcrumbs.'

'Is that really necessary?'

'Of course. What good would it do to bring you right here? You need to suffer, as I have suffered.'

'Can I talk to her?'

'No.'

'Where do I start?'

'You've already started at the beginning if you've been to the house. Think it through and you'll know where to head next.'

'But...'

But there was no space for *but*. George had hung up. His number had been withheld. Mordent leant against the window frame, the dark of the night and the drop of four storeys beyond. It would be far easier if the glass were to break and he were to fall to his death. Never had the absolution of responsibility seemed so attractive.

49
The Beginning, The Middle, And The End

In Hansel and Gretel the trail of breadcrumbs was eaten by birds. That was the last of the journeys into the woods they had made. In the first journey Hansel had filled his pockets with stones, which glittered back a trail in the moonlight. Mordent couldn't follow breadcrumbs, but he could follow stones. He could follow the permanence of fact.

Yet he needed more than that: a spurious theory which hit all the right sounds without saying anything. He needed a woman's intuition.

He rang Emmeline.

'Well, Sir, I wasn't expecting to hear from you.'

'I take it the word on the street isn't that I'm a free man?'

'I must admit I haven't had the chance to keep up with such an enquiry. I do have other clients, you see.'

'Thanks for your continued interest.'

'There's no need for sarcasm, however playful it might be. How can I help?'

He told her about his daughter, about Ezra George, about the goons.

'So he said the *beginning* was at the house. That was the diary, of course.'

'I got that.'

'Isn't the end obvious?'

'I have a theory.'

'Tell me.'

'The apartment where she died.'

'So why are you contacting me?'

'You've got a different way of looking at things.'

'It's the middle you're wondering about, right?'

'You got it.'

'Let me pause for reflection for a second.'

Mordent listened to empty space. It was getting late. He couldn't help wondering what she was wearing.

'Your end isn't *the* end?'

'Pardon.'

She repeated it. Then she said: 'Your end is the middle.'

'So what's the end?'

'Think about it.'

'Help me out.'

'My time is your money, perhaps I could string it out.' She laughed, a little.

'Berenice, Emmeline,' he said, his voice cracking.

'Sorry. I'm not usually this harsh; long day. So, was Lola buried or cremated?'

'What makes the difference?'

'If the former, you're after a specific location; if the latter you might be chasing the wind.'

'The end is the cemetery.'

'That's the way I see it.'

'Thanks. I'll head there now.'

'No!'

She caught his ear as it came away from the phone, termination in process.

'No?'

'George wants you to follow the story. You can't jump from the beginning to the end. You'll miss something. The middle is just as important. For some reason he wants you to go there.'

'That'll just delay things. Berenice's life might be at stake.'

'Look, I don't know this guy but it's clear from what you said that he wants to play a game. Don't miss the middle.'

Mordent thought it over. Emmeline was right. That was why he had called her. He needed impartial, untainted advice.

'You're right. And thanks.'

'No problem. And no charge. Not this time.'

'You're a sweetheart.'

'And you're on a mission. Let me know how it goes.'

'You may well find out first.'

Mordent left the call. He glanced out the window at the hunkering night. It was his time of the day. It was showtime.

He left the apartment. Outside it was a still, humid night. If this was a movie it would have started to rain, an increasingly thunderous storm signalling the upped pace in action, the race to denouement. Reality did things differently. Reality was always what you didn't expect.

He sat in his vehicle. Put the keys in the ignition. The engine started as if it had been waiting for him, like a virtuous female meeting her husband after a long jail sentence. He knew the address. He couldn't have not known it. He wondered who was watching him as he pulled out into traffic. He wanted a tail. He wanted to pin that tail on a donkey.

Traffic was light. At this hour the restaurants were already full, but not yet the bellies of their diners. Those out for the evening were trapped within entertainment:

the cinema, theatre, occasional burlesque, pubs and clubs. They had gotten where they wanted to go and weren't ready to come home. The evening non-rush hour in the city had begun. His progress unimpeded.

But he was barely aware of the outside world, his eyes focussed solely on the metre-length strip of light in front of him, the forever moving illumination from his headlights. He thought of all the memories of Berenice he didn't have: her sticky emergence from the birth tract, rolling over for the first time, smiling, raising a hand on the sofa to pull to a standing position, walking. He considered her first day at school, her second, her third, her ongoing education. All those interminable school plays made bearable by her presence. Discussion of her first kiss. Her leaving home, finding employment, ramshackle relationships. Her mother's death and resultant tracking down of the father. Her enthusiasm when he was found. The memory of her existence.

He watched them meet. Saw her glance at him on the stool at Bukowski's, the brittle connection forming like hardened treacle, her surprise at how easy it had been. He tried to telescope them into the future but met a blank black wall. Like a marathon runner he attempted to push through that wall, but it held fast. He banged his head against it, repeatedly. Nothing gave. He pushed his foot down on the accelerator and suddenly he was there, at the address of her former apartment; but then he wasn't. It wasn't her. It was Lola. Lola's apartment.

Shaking confusion out of his head he parked and took two steps at a time to the entrance. Paused, breathed deep, took the remaining steps singularly. The elevator was old fashioned, a metal cage. It rattled as he opened and closed it. He had forgotten to check for a tail.

His eyes fixed upwards. He had memories of this journey. Most of them pleasant. He had a gun in his hand. He couldn't remember taking it out of the holster. He breathed deep, needed to control those emotions, to calm down. He had never felt so protective, so helpless, before. He didn't know what to expect.

The elevator stopped, the door slid open like one side of an accordion but made little noise. He stepped out into the corridor. It was quiet, familiar. Six doors were visible, three in either direction. Two down on the left was the apartment within which he and Kovacs had once attended to argue whether a man had blown his own brains out. The one further down had been rented by Lola White.

He moved cautiously, unaware of the reason why. It was clear George wanted the game, the *end* game. No one was about to despatch him now. But even so. And then some.

The door to Lola's apartment was locked. Years had passed since she lived there. He imagined the blackened ceiling of the room in which her life had departed had been redecorated. That a new solo occupant - it was a tiny abode - had taken residence. Like a hermit crab, someone had pushed into her shell. He stood outside it, breathing heavily. Unable to make up his mind whether to knock.

Then he did. Once, twice. He used to have a key. The locks would have been changed. He no longer had a key. No one answered the door.

Forced entry. That might have amused Lola. That he had to force entry into her apartment. He wondered if she were watching. And if she were, whether she pointed an accusing finger.

Inside it was dark, equally quiet. His fingers twitched for a light switch but he held back. He knew the layout of the rooms, but the furniture, décor, was different. A faint smell of burning assaulted his nostrils. He didn't believe his senses. Inside the kitchenette he remembered searching through the cupboards with Lola, looking for anything that could be used as a sex toy. Laughing. Excitable. On the sofa he detected a yawning pizza box picked out in the half-light from the moon through the uncurtained window, 7/8ths empty.

In the bedroom.

In the bedroom.

In the bedroom there was a person-sized lump under the covers.

It felt there was an equal-sized lump in his throat.

It couldn't be. It shouldn't be. It wouldn't be.

He fished the flashlight out of his pocket that he had completely forgotten about.

He pulled the covers back.

50
Melting, Melting

Bound. Gagged. Alive.

Grace Frost.

He stepped back, snapped on the main light. Her eyes were wild, hair ruffled. He held up one hand.

Yellow light accentuated her smooth skin, curled foetal-like on the bed. Her hands were behind her back, wrapped inexpertly in rope and duct tape. Her legs the same. A poorly tied piece of rope linked her ankles to her wrists. There was too much slack in it. Under the strip of tape over her mouth was a bulge where Mordent guessed her panties were held. The whole thing smacked of the goons. There was no artistry in it. They might as well have read a manual rather than perfected it through repetition.

He sat on the bed. He remembered their lovemaking. Inside he was tense, a confusion of emotions. Gently he reached out and began to pick at the edge of the tape across her right cheek that ran across her mouth. In movies this would be pulled off in one action, but it would depilate her. Gaffer tape would have been cleaner. A synthetic petroleum-based adhesive rather than a natural rubber adhesive trumped the choice for kidnappers every time, but because they were amateurs Grace would have to be patient and surrender to further discomfort. Once he had loosened half an inch he slowly rolled it back, pushing against her soft cheek where it connected with the tape, his fingers coming away tacky, her skin flushed and hot.

He was right. They were her panties. Original.

She gasped as he removed them.

With the remaining tape flapping from her left cheek she gulped big breaths. He waited, didn't question her straightaway. Whilst she regained some composure he picked at the tape at her wrists and ankles. He didn't think she had been there long; circulation seemed fine and the rope's indentation on her skin was minimal.

She wasn't even bruised.

'Thanks.'

He nodded. 'Want to tell me what happened?'

'Those guys turned up at the club a couple of hours before I was due to go on. One of them had a knife. I was bundled out of there pretty quickly. I could have argued but I kind of like living, you know what I mean? The threat was pretty clear.'

'They bring you straight here?'

'Yes. They told me to strip. I had the feeling it was going to get nasty, but they kept looking at their watches. Time was on my side. Then one of them said a strange thing: 'Did you remember the bubblewrap?' They stepped into the next room and had an argument about it. Eventually they came back and tied me up just like you found me.'

Mordent kept his thoughts to himself. 'Anything else?'

She nodded. 'They wrote on my body. On this side.'

She rolled over, exposing her flank that had lain on the bed. Black marks spotted the white bedsheet. Mordent thought they would be difficult to wash out.

Written down her side was one sentence: *She is in the dead centre of the city.* Berenice had been right. The graveyard held the answer. He had lost time getting there, but thanks to Emmeline they might have saved Grace's life. Who knew how long she might have waited otherwise? Or if the goons would have returned with the bubblewrap.

She sat up, rubbed her wrists. Turned her head to try and read the writing, but he could tell it was difficult for her at that angle.

'What does it mean?'

'My daughter. Berenice. They've got her too.'

She wrapped her arms around him. He barely noticed her nakedness. Barely.

'Shouldn't you call the police?'

'Only if I don't want to see her again. You know how that works.'

'I'm pretty shook up,' she said.

He nodded. 'I should get someone here for you.' He thought, considered the words on her body. 'Wait here a minute.'

He entered the bathroom. No one used bars of soap any more. There was a cloth lying on the side that he soaked in warm water then returned with it to the bedroom along with a hand wash dispenser. He wondered who lived in this apartment now that Lola was gone. Whether they were on vacation. How George knew it would be unoccupied.

Grace lay motionless as he rubbed his fingers against her skin, then attacked the ink with the rag. It hadn't been an indelible marker, probably just a dry felt pen. The words disappeared without trouble. He wiped his fingers on the bedsheet.

'You going to be ok, here?'

'What are you going to do?'

'I'm gonna call the cops then head out to find Berenice.'

She gripped his arm. 'Let me come, don't leave me.'

'You come and she's dead. They won't be back here.'

He didn't know if either statement was true.

He rang Kovacs. Didn't mention Berenice. Gave him the address.

'Another prostitute? Your stamina impresses me.'

'Cut the crap Kovacs. Just get someone over here. She's pretty shook up.'

'Where are you going?'

'I've some unfinished business to settle.'

'Very dramatic.'

'Sometimes it has to be. Listen. Run a check on the owner of the apartment. I had to be a little resourceful opening the door.'

'Was just thinking it over. That address is familiar.'

'It's where Lola White died.'

Kovacs was quiet. Mordent held his breath.

'Figures.'

'What are you thinking?'

'That there's logic in George's processes. What do you think he'll do next?'

Mordent bit back telling him about Berenice. What good would it do to have the force turning up at the cemetery? It was Mordent George wanted. He had to go it alone. That was how these things worked.

'I gotta go,' he said. 'Get someone here quick. The girl is fragile.'

Grace looked at him as he ended the call. 'Take me with you.'

'I can't.'

'Don't go and get yourself killed. Come back to me when it's done.'

He took her hand. 'Maybe I will.'

He rose from the bed. Grace pulled the covers up to her chin. 'Thanks,' she said again.

Mordent nodded. 'I'll buy you a snowball when all this is done.'

She smiled. 'In this heat? It'll melt.'

He grinned. 'I *will* be back for that drink.'

When he closed the door he glanced at the damaged lock. He could wait for the police to arrive, but it would only complicate matters. He was sure she would be safe just as he was sure Berenice would be safe. But it was Berenice who held sway.

The cemetery beckoned.

It always beckoned. It was always there. It couldn't be avoided.

Mordent just hoped it wasn't expecting a fresh body that night.

51
An Unsavoury Bunch

Darkness discoloured the sky. As Mordent drove through the heart of the city tendrils of lights attempted to harmonise the view: neon, fluorescent, headlight. They reached upwards, fading towards the heavens, eventually lost amongst the blackness of the universe.

At the interstice of the illuminated ground and the expansion of sky the light and dark converged, built a falsely monochrome horizon. Mordent headed towards it. It was a mirage, a Shangri-la noir, a point of reference. As the centre of the city was swallowed in his wake so the light pollution lessened, the sky hardened. By the time he reached the cemetery surrounding lights were at a minimum. There were three cars in the car park evidently unoccupied. The parking area was outside of the actual cemetery and the entrance gates were closed. He parked up some distance away, checked the bullets in his gun, wondered if he was likely to kill someone.

He opened his car door. Somewhere, someone was watching. Should they want to they could open fire right now. He would collapse in the proverbial hail of bullets. Yet he felt safe for the moment. George would need that final conversation. It was up to him to speculate how he might subvert it.

As he approached the main entrance a motion-sensitive security light tremored then illuminated his progress. If his arrival was in any doubt then it was signposted now. He cursed technology, abhorred the negation of surprise. Knew that this Luddite perspective made no difference to his situation, but had to bitch about something as his heart palpitated.

Berenice, Berenice, Berenice.

Her name was a thump to his chest.

He regarded the high stone wall, the spiked railings on top. There didn't seem to be many footholds. No doubt it was designed that way. He imagined the other side to be just as smooth.

There was movement at the gate. The sound of keys. The gate opened without a screech. The cemetery was well maintained, the gate well oiled. The glint of something at the end of a sleeve beckoned Mordent wordlessly into the darkness like Orpheus entering the underworld. He followed, glancing towards the tiny stone office where the nightwatchman could often be found, and he saw him slumped, motionless against a computer keyboard which perpetuated endless *z*'s on a screen in a simulacrum of sleep.

At least, Mordent thought, it explained the third vehicle.

His shoulders were grabbed as he went through the gate. Both goons were silhouetted by the darkness which then fell as the timer on the security light flipped off. He had been counting the seconds away under his breath. Mordent jerked to one side, loosened the grip on his jacket, freed his gun from the holster and pushed it against the head of Gravel-Voice. He wasn't sure where the other glint had gone. He felt sick and frightened, but not for himself. He looped his other arm around the goon's as though they were about to promenade along a seafront.

'Let's do this my way, right.'

'We've got the girl.'

'I know you've got the girl. Where is she?'

He kept an eye on the other goon. The one he had chased along the street from his apartment. He knew he was more nimble than Gravel-Voice. He decided to name him Nimble for the sake of something to call him.

'Back there,' gestured Nimble. He stepped into better light. Mordent noticed there was a gun trained on his chest.

'Better drop that if you want your friend here to live.'

'You kill him I kill you you kill me? I don't think so.'

'Fair enough. But we've reached an impasse.'

'A what?'

'An impasse. A situation where no progress is possible. Deadlock.'

'Why don't you put *your* gun down?'

'And be led like a lamb to slaughter?'

'And be led to your daughter.'

'This is starting to sound like a bad poetry slam. You know George wants me alive, for now. How about I follow you and drag this guy around with me?'

Nimble sneered. 'How do I know you won't shoot me in the back?'

'George is with my daughter. I take it if he hears a shot then she's on a timer. Shall we just get this over and done with?'

Gravel-Voice grumbled behind his ear. 'It wasn't supposed to happen like this. Just do as he says.'

'That's right,' Mordent said. 'Just do what the guy with the gun to his head says.'

Nimble shuffled from one foot to the other. Mordent knew of ways he might already have been disarmed. Yet these guys were amateurs, even if they were amateurs who had already killed several girls. He couldn't rely on their lack of experience, because that also meant a reliance on their lack of professionalism. When it came to the crunch they would save their own lives, their allegiance to George purely financial.

'Ok,' Nimble said. 'Let's get walking.'

Unsurprisingly there were no lights in the cemetery. Mordent knew the way to Lola's grave – or at least the rough direction. He might have been there no more than half a dozen times but it was six times more frequently than the goons. Without a light they headed out under the cover of darkness. The roads gave way to gravel paths which would then give way to stumbling amongst gravestones. His eyes scanned the night for a light, some indication that George was out there, but there was none. Unless the goons were doing a circuit he could tell they were walking in the wrong direction. They were, he decided, both personally and professionally, a wholly unsavoury bunch.

'So George gets you to do his dirty work, right? How'd you get into this game? McDonalds prove too taxing for you?'

'Huh?'

'He's kidding us, Jack. Trying to rile us up.'

Jack? Jack be Nimble? Mordent suppressed a laugh.

'Don't listen to him, Jack. I'm genuinely interested in how you guys got into this line of work. I'm particularly impressed with the bubblewrap deaths. How'd they come about?'

'George had you tailed,' Nimble began. Then Gravel-Voice hushed him quiet. Mordent pressed the nub of the gun just a little harder against his head.

'What does it matter,' Nimble continued. 'There's five of us in the cemetery and not all of us are coming out alive.'

'He don't know nothing yet,' Gravel-Voice hissed. 'Just guessing. Why can't you keep quiet, ya smuck?'

'No he's right,' Mordent said, 'not all of us will be coming out alive. Don't you want to hear how interested I am in you guys before I pull this trigger.'

'You won't do it. Not whilst you dunno where the girl is.'

'But I could, right? I could probably take you and Jack out before you could say Jack Robinson.'

'How'd you know his last name?'

'Jesus!'

'Is that *your* name?'

'What?'

'Jesus.'

'Funny guy.'

'He didn't know my name,' Nimble said. 'It's just an expression.'

'You guys are in the wrong business,' Mordent said. 'You're the new *Amos 'n' Andy*.'

'The new who?'

'If you have to ask then you don't know.'

'Huh?'

They had left the main drag. Mordent could tell that Nimble didn't know where he was going. The conversation had further disorientated him. Even so, Nimble was clearly the smartest and Mordent wished the gun was at *his* head. Gravel-Voice had been easy to disarm, was a caricature of a goon. Nimble was the loose cannon. He was the one with balls.

'So,' Mordent continued, 'you were saying George had me tailed?'

'There was the three of us. We were staking out the sumo club. George knew you would show, he said. Didn't tell us why. When you came out you delivered a peach on a plate.'

'It was his idea for the bubblewrap?'

'Yeh.'

'Had you ever killed before?'

Gravel-Voice opened his mouth. Mordent sensed a tensing of muscle, jammed the gun harder against his head.

'Yeh. Both of us.'

'Where did George find you? Place an ad in *Goons To Rent*?'

'You're funny. You can find anything on the internet nowadays.'

'Used to be word of mouth.'

'Times change.'

'You don't know why George is doing this?'

'We don't know and we don't care.'

'Must be paying you a fair bundle then. Might turn out what you're doing is illegal.'

'Like I said, you're a funny guy. Now keep quiet. You're putting me off.'

'Remember I have a gun to your friend's head.'

'So you might but we know you won't use it. Not yet, anyway. And by the time you do it won't matter.'

'No?'

'No. Cos you'll already be dead. Now shut it.'

Mordent complied. By his reckoning Lola's grave was in the opposite direction. They had turned twice, once correctly, but they had set off wrong from the start. Unless they weren't heading for her grave. Had they made a mistake or had he? But no, he could tell in the half-light that Nimble was scowling. He could see Nimble wanted to check with Gravel-Voice but didn't want to give their idiocy away. The best thing to have done would have been to retrace their steps to the entrance, take it from there. Instead, Mordent saw the light of a cell illuminate Nimble's face which then gave an expression of exasperation at having no signal. He stuffed it back in his pocket, his hand lazy on the gun. Contrary to commonsense they set out diagonally, off the path and through the headstones. Mordent knew he was trying to short cut it, bluster through the mistake. Instead they would make another one.

He knew this part of the cemetery. It was an older section. One that had been given over, with some controversy, as a 'wildlife' area. What that meant was that the authorities didn't see fit to maintain an area that no one visited any longer, because the relatives of these guys were already interred in the newer part of the cemetery. The dates on these stones would be 1800s. No one cared about them anymore. Occasionally you might get someone with a camera and a bunch of family history notes stop for a moment for a photographic opportunity so they might tick off a distant relative, like a railbuff or a birder might do in their equivalent pastimes.

It reminded him that Ian Fleming had taken the name of James Bond from an ornithologist based in the West Indies. The thought had popped up through word association and he pressed it back down again. It was irrelevant to the task at hand.

The 'wildlife' area had welcomed squirrels and rabbits. Mordent wasn't sure what else might be present, but their habitat had thrived unhindered and the ground snaked with Japanese knotweed and brambles. Heavy trees with low-slung branches scraped the tops of the stones, which themselves were mostly covered in moss with their inscriptions illegible.

They stumbled through this set-up; civilisation seemingly miles away. Each time they tripped Mordent could feel Gravel-Voice tense. He had to seize the right moment or his captive would do the same. Nimble ploughed ahead, no longer concerned, just determined to get through to George and to put this at an end. Gravel-Voice grunted, his right foot catching Mordent's left. Mordent thought about that grunt. Waited for it to happen again. Waited for it to become assimilated in Nimble's mind as a natural reaction to the task. When Gravel-Voice grunted the fourth time it was because he'd been slugged.

Mordent bent swiftly, lay the unconscious goon down, body-checked clothing and pulled out a knife. He wondered if it was the weapon Grace had seen. The blade was as long as the handle. He continued forwards, dragging one leg sideways behind him, making a ruckus as though there was two of him. He slipped his gun back in the holster, weighed the knife in his hand. It was an unfamiliar tool: he'd used guns, a crossbow, even his own fists; he'd used furniture, bottles, imagination. He guessed it was time that he learnt to use a knife.

It was darker than dark. The foliage had become dense, the tree limbs closer, lower. Mordent thanked the authorities for their lack of respect for the dead, shielded through environmental concerns. Nimble was proving less so. Mordent watched him trip and fall and in an instant he leapt a few feet ahead and sank the knife within Nimble's shoulder blades. It penetrated no more than an inch. Nimble *Ooofed*. Air pushed out of him. Mordent sat astride, pushed his face into dirt, knees clenched to Nimble's legs. The knife held like Excalibur in stone. Mordent became King, pushed it down again. Two, three inches. The sensation of muscle and bone against the blade was sickening: a scrunch of resistance. Nimble's back buckled, rearing against Mordent's weight. His screams were muffled by earth. He was choking on grass. Mordent tried not to think about the loss of life, of blood seeping into the soil to be reclaimed by the dead, about the absoluteness of what he was doing.

Berenice. He had to focus on Berenice.

And those girls. There was no time to be squeamish.

He twisted the knife. Nimble was taking a while to die, belying his nickname once again. Mordent's wrist ached. Again, Nimble buckled, tried to raise his mouth clear of the dirt. Mordent couldn't risk a shout, a warning to George. He felt about in the dark with his free hand, realised Nimble had fallen close to the stone surround of a tomb. He gripped the hair on the back of Nimble's head and pulled it back sharp. A scream formed in Nimble's mouth with the unexpectedness of a breath. But it was too late. Mordent pushed at an angle, directed Nimble's forehead against the concrete. The force reverberated up his elbow, paused, then petered further along to his shoulder. There was a thud, then a crack, and then Nimble fell still.

Mordent breathed heavily. Spat. Gagged. Spat again.

He had known people who would have gained pleasure from the killing - from *this* killing, specifically.

He was not one of those men.

52
The Girl Behind The Man Behind The Gun

He sat on his haunches. Listened. There were no noises to be had.

It was too dark to see blood. He could feel it on his hands - on *both* hands, the one that held the knife and the one that held the hair. He rubbed them against dry grass.

If Gravel-Voice had risen then Mordent knew he would have heard him. He decided against going back to complete the job. Unlike the last time he had killed this couldn't be hushed up. Too many people knew the situation. *Kovacs* knew the situation. Whilst recent events might indicate Kovacs could turn a blind eye, it was only to look the other way at the wider picture. Mordent could legitimately claim self-defence for one body, but three would be pushing it. And if he wanted to gamble at two then he knew the second one shouldn't be Gravel-Voice.

He stood, slowly. It was himself who was now disorientated. He pictured the cemetery in his mind: the newer sections with their mounds of light brown earth ready and waiting to be turned back into soil, the tiny headstones and teddy bears of the children's cemetery, the recent past, the further back, the wilderness of the wildlife area in which he had just made an offering to gods long forgotten. Overhead, the red lights of a plane winked on and off – *on and off* – and he judged the angle of the ascent, picked out his destination as though using satellite navigation. Wondered how best to approach his elderly adversary.

Truth be told, if the story had unravelled correctly, he felt more sadness for George than anger. The much-loved grandchild, the surrogate father, the devastating death, the discovery of fetishistic tendencies, the closeness to home. This wasn't a happy trajectory for an elderly man. But George had used the proverbial sledgehammer to crack a nut that was already shrivelled and useless inside the shell. Bite into it and it would crumble, a soft paste on the tongue: like moth bodies, like ash. If he had spoken to Mordent then whilst no resolution could have been possible – resurrection not being an option the last time Mordent had browsed for it – then at least a level of understanding might have been reached. For Mordent didn't kill Lola - as much as George might wish to believe – in the absence of the real killer who had never been caught.

If George wanted an eye for an eye then he hadn't stopped short.

Mordent began to walk in the direction of Lola's grave.

Night had sucked the heat from the day, but it was still humid. Mordent glanced at his watch. It had yet to click across midnight. There was symbolism there if he cared to think about it. But whilst such a time in a work of fiction would be a signifier of importance - as though the writer were attempting a high-noon scenario with a noirish twist – here such an hour was purely coincidental. The time carried no more significance than 15.43 or 18.28. Mordent couldn't help but consider mankind trapped by false boundaries, with a focus on a decimal system which invited rounding up dates and times divisible by ten or five or for whole numbers that - in the bigger scheme of things - were totally devoid of rational meaning, purely scripted by the number of fingers on each hand.

If it was true mankind held no importance in the universe it was equally true that for everyone we *are* our own universe. And in Mordent's universe there was someone worth saving.

Easing himself out of the wilderness he located a path. The cemetery was designed on straight lines. Looking to the horizon he saw the sky-shine of lights that denoted the bulk of the city, in the other direction the church-cum-crematorium hulked over the night, its silhouette a Japanese spider crab attacking the Whitehouse in some b-monster-movie. He headed towards the structure, aware of his breathing, of the gravel kicked up under his feet. Now he had time to think, now that the goons were despatched, he wondered about Berenice's emotions. Of whether George had shattered any illusions she might have held about her father. He wondered whether this experience would make her hate him.

He wondered if she was still alive.

He didn't know how to play it. Whether it would be best to sneak up on George, take him by surprise. It couldn't be hard to disarm an eighty year-old man. Mordent thought of Copernicus Fear. He hadn't met George, this was true, but the photos he had seen of him with Lola - even though they had been taken many years ago - hadn't revealed a man of great physique. And Mordent could take out Fear, no problem. George was unlikely to be different.

Yet: he couldn't risk Berenice. And for Berenice to still be with George then he had to make the assumption that George had some kind of hold. Whether a direct physical restraint or a gun. Might he walk towards him, unarmed, offer himself in place of Berenice? Would he lay down his life for his child?

He paused. Clammy night pressed his clothes to pulp with mingled sweat and fear. This was a decision he never had to consider, even hypothetically. He repeated the question in his mind: would he lay down his life for his child?

Mordent considered everyone essentially selfish. Even those who performed the greatest humanitarian acts were driven by this quintessential human emotion. There was always a choice: help others, or don't. For some, the *thought* of not helping others was too much of a burden to bear and therefore they offered their services, usually for free, and eased their conscience because of it. Mordent thought of Mother Teresa, the Albanian woman who had devoted her life to becoming a missionary for the poor of India, who was awarded a Nobel Peace Prize for her efforts. Surely the reason for her devotion to that task was because she couldn't bear *not* to do it; her drive being selfishness? Which was just as honest an emotion as any other when the outcome was the same.

Mordent didn't consider being selfish a bad thing. It was innate, incontrovertible. So long as you acknowledged it and embraced it then you could work with it. If George was to fire at Berenice, then the decision as to whether Mordent would take the bullet for her depended on one thing: could he live with himself if he didn't? A snap decision, on the subconscious level; but it was this that would power his choice, not some altruistic definition or the myriad possibilities that swam inside the quandary of love.

Besides, an individual considered themselves as immortal, but not those around them. Another impulse for Mordent to take a bullet would be his surefire understanding that he wouldn't be killed. He couldn't be so sure about Berenice.

He was stalling, he knew this. Confrontation was at hand and these theoretical decisions might be forced into reality. He couldn't risk Berenice being killed. It seemed the decision was already made for him.

Moonlight painted the blood on his hands black. He still held the knife that he'd removed from Nimble's back with a guttural sucking noise. He slipped it in his inside jacket pocket, but the length rocked against the lining, like someone balancing on a single stilt. It was too evident. He pulled it out and bent down to push it into the dry ground, standing on the hilt until it sank out of sight. Someone would come across that one day, if he wasn't around to retrieve it.

He crept off the main path down one of the narrower side sections, those that vehicles were unable to access. Lola rested down there. Shapes began to resolve themselves at her graveside. Berenice stood, awkwardly. He couldn't quite discern her features but it was clear it was her, instinct affirming their brief familiarity. The other figure sat adjacent to the grave, hands in a lap; one of those hands seemed to be disfigured but the closer Mordent got he realised it held a gun.

He decided to call out.

'George. It's Mordent. I'm alone.'

One of the heads jerked in his direction. The one sitting down. Berenice remained motionless.

Again, that slightly sibilant voice: 'I see you escaped my welcome party.'

'It wasn't much of a party. No streamers, no cake, no candles.'

'You've probably done me a favour. They know too much.'

Mordent walked closer, a slow increase, making no sudden movements. 'Those guys knowing too much? That's a gross understatement.'

'They've served their purpose. Are they dead?'

Mordent flicked a glance to Berenice. Now he saw the reason for her posture. She was rolled, vertical, in bubblewrap, each pod reflecting moonlight like a glitter ball. Only her head was free. Duct tape sealed her mouth.

'One of them is. Jack.' He said the name to confirm he'd seen the goons. He wanted George to understand he was alone. That there was no back up.

'I see. And the other one?'

'Nursing a swollen head. If he shows up it might depend on how much you're paying them.'

Now Mordent was no more than a few feet away he understood why George was sitting down. He was in a wheelchair. George turned to look at him, but the gun did not waver from Berenice.

'Money is no object,' he hissed.

Under moonlight George's face appeared softened, a putty sculpture. Mordent looked closely: wanted to see the signs of ageing. Wrinkles, sallow complexion, liver spots. He wanted to know if George might die of old age before their conversation was over. It would make his job one heck of a lot easier.

'And no funny business.' George jerked the gun. 'I would kill her without hesitation.'

Mordent nodded. There were a few seconds of silence as though they were paying their respects by Lola's grave. He wondered how to deflate the situation. Noted the family resemblance. If he'd had one word to describe Lola it would have been *determined*. That was the expression paramount on George's face.

'I take it you're carrying a gun. Remove it please.'

Mordent slowly opened his jacket, revealed his holster. He picked the gun out between his thumb and forefinger and threw it on the grass at George's feet. It was about as stupid as he could get. Berenice's eyes agreed with him.

'This is easier than I expected. Anything else?'

Mordent slowly removed his jacket, dropped it to the floor, pirouetted with half a thought of a bullet in his back.

'This isn't about her,' he said. 'Let her go.'

George smiled. It wasn't a nice smile. It was infused with bitterness.

'So she can run and call the cops. Unlikely, don't you think. Besides, she needs to hear what I have to say.'

'And then?'

'And then a decision will be made.'

'Any point in pressing you on that decision?'

'Nope.'

George rested back in his wheelchair. Mordent knew these kinds of showdowns usually panned out one or two ways. Having waited all this time George might find he had nothing to say, that confronting who he considered to be his nemesis would be a let down, a negation of the hatred that had simmered. In which case, he might find he relinquished his position. But life wasn't that simple, because to relinquish also meant to give himself up to the authorities and with murder on his hands Mordent knew that wasn't much choice. George might just take them both down for the hell of it.

On the other hand, George might relish in the expansion of their unknown shared history, get fired up with enthusiasm for the kill, and then despatch the both of them to kingdom come. Either way, the outcome was funnelled, almost pre-ordained. There wasn't a great deal of choice in the matter.

The only choice Mordent had was how he handled it.

'Tell me something,' he said. 'Who was the guy they buried instead of you?'

53
Elucidation

George shifted his legs. Mordent noticed his shoes were newly polished, a moon reflected in each toe-cap.

'Just a bum,' he said. 'Some down and out that was going to die anyway. Jack played the role of the son I never had and identified the body. Who would suspect anything. I was just an old man.'

'You're still just an old man.'

'That's as maybe. But that makes me an old man with nothing to lose. That makes me dangerous, doesn't it, Mordent.'

'If Jack was the son you never had then who were Lola's parents?'

He spat in the dirt. Then mumbled an apology under his breath. 'Her mother was my daughter. She was no good. The money I had spent my life earning which I then lavished on her went to her head. Drugs. Cars. Nonsense. The usual. She met some guy from upstate whose name I no longer care to remember. Then she had Lola. Left her with me. Willingly, I might add. The only tears I shed when they hit a juggernaut head on were for those of the family of the other driver. He gave his life to give me Lola. I never looked back. Not once.'

'She was your life.'

'Damn right she was my life.'

'I loved her and I told her and she laughed it off.'

George grimaced. 'Then she didn't love you. She was *used* by you.'

Mordent shook his head. 'That's how you might like to think of it, to take away some of the pain. But the truth was she initiated our relationship. And it was an open, honest understanding that we had. I might have wanted more, but she didn't give it. If anything, she *used* me. Although I didn't like to think of it that way.'

'She was nineteen and you were in your thirties. I know who was innocent and who wasn't.' George looked towards Berenice. Mordent did too. He trusted his expression hid no guilt. It would be fair for Berenice to know the truth.

'She couldn't have been much younger than your daughter is now.'

'You flatter her,' said Mordent. 'This was all a long time ago.'

Spittle formed at the sides of George's mouth. 'You're casting irrelevancies. Regardless of the *nature* of your relationship with Lola you were in a position to protect her. But you didn't. You made her vulnerable, weakened her. You led her into danger. You might as well have set fire to her yourself.'

Mordent dropped his eyes to the ground. 'Is that a good enough reason to kill all those prostitutes? Because I didn't do the job that you could no longer do.'

There was a loud crack: a gunshot. Mordent couldn't pinpoint the direction of the bullet, but it was close, real close. His eyes flickered over to Berenice. She was still standing. In the aftermath of the afterburn he realised she was duct-taped to a tree which had previously blended into the night. She couldn't have fallen if she wanted to. When she looked at him her eyes were hopeless, wild; but alive.

George spoke slowly. 'Next time you think to criticise, don't. I was Interstate Champion 1957, Firearms.'

Mordent knew competitions sprung up all over the place, with all kinds of bogus categories and prizes. The award meant nothing. The shot itself meant George wasn't to be messed with.

'I was part of the investigating team...' Mordent began, but he knew it was weak; he changed tack: 'and we failed you on that.'

'Damn right you failed.'

'We never had a good lead on the investigation. The original murder that it was assumed she had witnessed was originally going to be classed as suicide if it wasn't for my input. We had no reason to believe that killer might return. There wasn't a case for police protection. There were several apartments on that floor where the occupants might have seen or heard something. Lola was just unlucky.'

'You don't think her relationship with you might have fuelled the killer? Maybe he believed you were interrogating her?' Mordent heard the sneer in George's voice which couldn't be wiped off as cleanly as a smear on a windscreen. Mordent was battling years of frustration that an argument wouldn't abate.

'It's possible. If the killer had been watching the area I guess he might have believed what you're saying.'

'And that drug you were using, the one in her diary, the one which then allowed her immobilisation. You don't see you were instrumental in that?'

Mordent felt tired. Truth was, he *had* considered these things. He had considered them at the time and he had considered them recently. What he couldn't do was change the past so he had buried it. None of this was going to bring Lola back. But that wasn't an argument George wanted to hear.

'We experimented together,' he said. 'Everything else is coincidence.'

'Not good enough!' Again, Mordent was drawn to the white spittle at the corners of George's mouth. He tried to change tack.

'You mind if I sit?' Without waiting for the answer Mordent bent his knees then sat cross-legged on the grass. George could now look down on him. Mordent hoped it assisted in negating threat.

'Let me get this straight,' Mordent continued. 'You cared for Lola from when she was a baby. You felt a great affiliation for her. Not only as a grandchild but as a surrogate daughter for the one who turned out bad. But she grew up, became a teenager. All children betray their parents eventually, they have no choice. She kept her deviant side hidden. The first thing you knew about it was her death. That in itself must have been a great shock. Particularly the nature of the death. Investigations lead nowhere, so you sit on it year after year. Cancerous thoughts contaminate. You can't get away from what happened.

'Then, the police ditch any hope of continuing the investigation. Lola's personal belongings are returned to you, including the diary. You discover a side to her that you didn't know, wouldn't accept. It *can't* be Lola's fault. Blame comes to me. That isn't my fault. You become obsessed with me, wanting revenge for something I didn't do, simply because you have no way of finding the actual killer. The actual killer.' Mordent let the words sink in. George's face remained impassive. He might not even have been listening.

Mordent continued, wondering that if a film was ever made of his life whether this denouement would be rendered black and white, *a la* Monk, with grainy flashbacks.

'You're getting old, decrepit, maybe you haven't got long to live. Somehow you hire those goons, you get a plan in your head that you can't deviate from because to do so would negate what you've already done. Your *own* killings. When I spoke to Grace Frost she talked about snowballs, how they get bigger and bigger when rolling downhill. That's what happened to your plan. You have to follow through. You have to kill both me and my daughter otherwise everything will have come to naught.

'But I'm getting ahead of myself. You see in Lola's diary that I developed a bubblewrap fetish. You had me tailed to one of my regular whores. Coincidentally you were aware of the sumo club. A plan forms. You don't care about killing prostitutes because they're an easy target, they're on the downward spiral that your own daughter helter-skeltered her way through. I'm not sure about the first death. I think the goons got lucky I slept in the car. The second and third deaths were easy, straight tails. You get Grace and the goons to warn me off, dropping your name casually into conversation so I know that it's you. What's the point of revenge if it isn't appreciated? Besides, you're already dead. Kidnapping Astrid went wrong, was ill-thought. Kidnapping Berenice makes sense. You want to hurt me as much as you think I've hurt you.

'But let me tell you this. You're after the wrong guy. Lola would tell you that. Lola wouldn't want this. Lola doesn't need her death avenged by senseless death. And you know this, but you have no one else to direct the anger against. And you're too far gone, there's no turning back. As I said, you have no choice but to follow it through, because if you don't then those three prostitutes who also had loving mothers and fathers will have died in vain. Even though I can tell you now they died in vain anyway.'

He stopped. It was hurting his eyes to keep staring into the dark, into the darkness of the gun barrel that remained directed towards Berenice.

George tapped his free hand against his gun hand, a weak clap. 'That's quite some speech. But you're masking the truth. You were partially instrumental in Lola's death, however unwittingly that might have been. And you could - as a police officer - have taken that investigation further. In fact, Lola would have wanted you to do that. But you had to hide your relationship with her in order to further your career. That's where you come unstuck, Mr Mordent. That's what justifies my actions. That's why you have to feel my pain.'

'I already do. I carry the pain of Lola's death daily.'

'But it's not enough. Originally I thought I'd get those murders pinned on you, then I realised your kind would protect each other but at least there'd be some embarrassment about the bubblewrap. Eventually I realised there were no other options: your daughter, and you, dead. It's simple, isn't it. There is no other way.'

Mordent nodded. 'Seems you got it all figured out.'

'And yet you're still talking, trying to dig your way out of things, trying to persuade me to change your mind. It won't happen. You're going to watch me shoot this girl and then I'm going to shoot you. And you're going to take the bullet like a man. Accept your guilt.'

'But...'

'There's no time for buts. We're done.'

Mordent watched George raise his arm. The end of it wobbled, like he was shaking hands with the gun. Mordent calculated whether he could rise and race across to the wheelchair in time. Whether he might rush to Berenice and topple her, faster than a speeding bullet. Whether he might reach his own gun without being shot first. Wondered if the sky might fall.

All these wonderings took place within a bubble of time, slo-mo fashion. Then the bubble went *pop*.

54
Band Aids Won't Fix Bullet Holes

The noise was deafening, louder than the previous shot.

Mordent's senses were heightened.

He sprang from the ground, kicked oncoming cramp from one leg, tripped, rolled, fell onto the wheelchair.

His right hand gripped George's gun hand. The flesh was cold and weak, chicken-skin texture. Mordent twisted sharply, attempted to dislodge the gun, then heard the unmistakable crack of a bone breaking. George grunted in pain through clenched teeth, kicked at Mordent from the wheelchair, connected with his shins. Mordent wrestled the gun free, threw it to one side where it chipped Lola's headstone, then tilted the chair back and forth until George was dislodged and he fell to the ground.

Mordent panted, swore, bent his right leg for a kick at George's chest but held back. He checked the surrounding ground, found his own gun, picked it up. George lay in pain, clutching his broken wrist with his left hand. Mordent watched him awhile, pity or empathy or something violently unknown to him cruising in his head. He extended his hand holding the gun. Thought. Didn't pull the trigger.

It was all procrastination because he barely dared to look at Berenice.

Eventually, in what probably was no more than seconds, he did.

She was slumped forwards, held to the tree by the duct tape's embrace. He accessed the tiny flashlight which was part of his cell. Shone it towards her. Globules of blood were reflected in the bubblewrap, they looked pretty in the light. Jewelled beads. He walked towards her slowly, lifted her chin where it had slumped to her chest. There was a pulse in her neck. He shone the torch downwards, saw the blistered remains of wrap where the bullet had entered her side. George was right, he wasn't a bad shot. The bullet had penetrated just below the ribcage. The heat of its passage had melted the wrap into the wound. It might be enough to save her. Already blood coagulated around the hole. The blood on the wrap had been sprayed on impact, wasn't still flowing. Some of it had already dried in the heat of the night.

He took time to carefully peel away the tape from her face.

Her breaths were shallow.

He checked his phone, had a signal. Dialled 911. If the operator considered there was humour to be had in being called to the cemetery in the middle of the night then they didn't show it. Mordent name-checked Kovacs as insurance against it being dismissed as a prank call.

He whispered *I love you* in Berenice's ear. Couldn't decide whether keeping her vertical or laying her horizontal was the better idea. He stroked one side of her face. Then he turned back to George.

The old man had wriggled onto Lola's grave, presumably to reach the gun Mordent had thrown, but the effort was too much for him. He lay, splayed, in a concrete embrace. His head touched her headstone. It might have been a headboard.

Mordent walked across, crouched.

'If she dies, so do you.'

He ran a finger over Lola's name on the headstone.

'I'm sorry,' he said.

And he was.

He remembered their first meeting.

He had just stepped out of the doorway of a dead guy's apartment. Saw her leaning against the jamb of the adjacent. She was dressed in blue jeans and wore a black band t-shirt that he didn't recognise. Her skin moved under the shirt with a very *fleshy* movement. Mordent would describe her as *chubby,* later she would call herself *fat.* But either way it made no difference. There was an almost visible crackle of attraction. Mordent had stepped back, as if it were him who had been shot; the 'bullet' ricocheting inside like a bee trapped in his heart.

That was the start of it.

George rolled over. 'You fucking hurt me you shit.'

'That's no language for someone your age. Make the most of the night air, you won't be feeling it much longer. The only breeze you get in jail is from some guy's farts you share a cell with.'

George coughed, a hacking motion as though he already resided within that confined space.

Once he'd finished Mordent listened for the siren that would accompany the ambulance. He heard something else.

Movement on the path.

He picked up the gun that had been out of George's reach. Considered things.

George had instigated the bubblewrap murders out of a distorted sense of revenge. He couldn't fault him for consistency, couldn't absolve him from the crime.

But the goons were the guys who had carried them out. One was dead and the other was wandering. Was it his moral right to defend himself or should he let it lie?

The moon picked out Gravel-Voice in relief. It wasn't much of a relief.

Mordent righted the wheelchair, sat in it head down. He dangled his gun hand towards George's slumped body and told him to shut it. As though aiding the subterfuge a cloud decided to skate a path across the moon. Darkness darkened.

Raising his eyes upwards Mordent made out Gravel-Voice picking his way between the headstones.

'Sorry boss. Guy jumped me. Knocked me clean out. Those shots woke me. We might have some trouble on our hands.'

Mordent grunted, kept the tone as indistinct and guttural as possible.

Gravel-Voice glanced towards Berenice. 'She fallen asleep?' He laughed. Turned back to Mordent. 'Guy got my knife. S'okay if I take your gun and hunt this guy down?'

Mordent nodded a yes. He pressed the nub of it hard against George's body in the shadows as a warning then held it out for Gravel-Voice to take. He remembered as a boy his mother telling him to never hand over scissors with the sharp end extended. Gravel-Voice obviously never had such a good mother. He reached out for the gun barrel-end first.

Once he had gripped it, Mordent held fast. With his head still down he nodded over to Berenice.

Gravel-Voice did too. 'Gotcha. You want me to take her out first? No problem.'

Mordent depressed the trigger.

Gravel-Voice leapt back like a cat jumping away from a burst balloon. He clutched his chest automatically, the other hand waving about with a burn that almost glowed in the dark. As he receded, the incredulity on his face faded. As he fell, Mordent looked up, hoped Gravel-Voice would understand why he'd been shot.

'You bastard,' said George on the ground. His words quivered with an ill-disguised frisson of fear.

'Takes one to know one.'

Mordent was tempted to place the gun against George's temple, to burn a circular brand against his skin. But he held back. He could hear sirens in the distance.

'It was self-defence,' Mordent said. 'You want to stay alive then you agree with me. You've got enough on your plate as it is. Death won't make it any easier. Stick with that story and I'll try and use this little escapade as a way to re-open Lola's case. I want justice for her too. We didn't just sit on our laurels, you know. There were other ways for you to kick start the investigation than this.'

George simply groaned, the impetus gone from his campaign.

Mordent saw the security lights illuminate the entrance, accompanied by flashing blue. Strong torches glared their way. He stood and shouted, waved his arms. As they came closer, their lights lifted the manifold of darkness, made the situation all too real. For the first time he allowed the thought that Berenice might not make it. The lights from the ambulance crew were an ascending dawn lifting him out of dream. He wanted to sleep, to get back under the covers, to discover that life wasn't in fact as dreadful as he might think. Somewhere, in the recesses of his mind, a hitherto dormant part of his upbringing awoke and began to pray.

55
The Happiest Finish

Mordent rolled off. Grace Frost gazed at him with post-climatic eyes. *Wonderful,* she mouthed.

He couldn't resist a grin. 'That's the way it works.'

She pulled a thin bedsheet over her body. The heat remained intense. 'I needed that.'

Mordent tried to force the smug expression off his face. He held back on saying *snowball.*

He had hooked up with Grace after her performance at the club. He had braved a second meal there, solo this time, enjoyed watching her from a distance. There might be something there, he thought, just as he knew that was unlikely. Still, he had saved her life. There had to be a fuck in it for that.

Grace leant over to her bedside cabinet, pulled it open. 'Do you mind?' she asked. He nodded over the cigarette, didn't fancy one himself. She lit it, sucked on it, blew smoke out into her room. 'So,' she said, 'everything's resolved?'

He nodded. 'No one will be tying you up again.'

Her expression froze. He imagined the words, *that's a pity,* were hanging on her lips, but equally he might have initiated some post-traumatic stress disorder. Then her face softened. 'The less wc talk about that the better,' she said.

'Those goons are dead.' He decided to be abrupt.

To kill the thoughts of repercussion. 'All in the line of duty.'

'By your fair hand?'

'Yes.'

She shivered. Maybe he had gone too far. Maybe she wouldn't see him again.

'It's not machismo,' he found himself saying. 'It was just how it panned out.'

'That's what makes me worried.' She took another drag on the cigarette, blew out a crescent. 'I could never do those things.'

'Those things?'

'Blow a smoke circle.'

'Oh. Ok. You know all this anyway, don't you. Didn't the police fill you in?'

She laughed. 'Not the way you just have.'

'I'm serious.'

'They came and made sure I was okay after you left me alone. Then they took a statement. I haven't heard anything more. You weren't that quick to check up on me.'

This was true, Mordent thought. It had been two weeks.

'Berenice, my daughter, she got caught in the crossfire. I've been busy.'

'She's ok?'

'She is now.'

'Good.'

Mordent didn't elaborate. Grace wouldn't have wanted to hear how the bullet had ended up in the tree Berenice had been taped to. That she was lucky it hadn't hit any vital organs. That the stress of her ordeal had almost destroyed their relationship. That whilst she was in hospital Mordent had bribed one of the doctors he knew to take a DNA sample and that he had been positively confirmed as the father. Grace didn't need to know any of that. Berenice only needed to know half of it. Mordent felt sick remembering any of it.

Grace blew out more smoke. If Mordent were feeling generous he might view it as a question mark.

'So, this Ezra George, he was behind it all?'

'In a nutshell, yes. Personal vendetta against me for something I didn't do.'

'Hmmm.'

No doubt Grace believed he was holding back. He couldn't disagree that he wasn't. But it was true. What he *didn't do* included not being instrumental in initiating Lola's practices but also not following through properly with the investigation. He couldn't deny there was some culpability.

He reached under the covers, stroked the top of her thigh.

'You won't be getting any more at my age,' she said. 'Nor at yours.'

'Just being tender.'

'Then love me so.'

'You serious?'

'Just wordplay. Tell me more about Ezra George.'

'He's been charged with conspiracy to murder, amongst other offences. He won't see life again outside of jail.'

'I guess that's a good thing. Although it makes me kinda sad how people throw their lives away. Forever is a very long time.'

'You're being charitable. He could have got you killed.'

'I know. I'm surprised I've not been asked to be a witness.'

'I leant on Kovacs – he's high up in the department

– to leave you out of it. We've got enough dead bodies as evidence without needing a live one.'

'Helps your cause too, no doubt.'

'No doubt.'

He had moved his hand away from her thigh during the burst of conversation. She reached out and replaced it.

'Tell me more.'

'There's not much else to tell.'

He slid his hand closer to her pubis, extended a finger. Truth be told there was more to tell. Nine days after the cemetery incident a guy had been arrested as part of a drugs bust the FBI had initiated. One of those dawn swoops where doors were hammered to splinters and guys were hauled out of beds beside unsuspecting wives and girlfriends – and in some instances, both.

Fingerprint searches had led to a match for someone who had previously escaped the system. Not just once, twice, or three times, but for as many times as he had fingers and toes. One of the matches had been for a print recovered from Lola White's door jamb. The guy had been indicted for her murder.

'There's never any escape,' Kovacs had said, according to Marsham who had filled Mordent in over the phone. 'We're like the Canadian Mounties. We always get our man.'

'Sounds like Kovacs is appropriating success,' growled Mordent.

'You know how it is,' Marsham said.

'Whereabouts is this guy being held?'

'I can't give you that information.'

'C'mon Marsham, you must know how much this means to me.'

'So the guy can get kneecapped before he goes to trial? Or worse?'

'Both of us have done worse.'

'Both of us ensured our necks were out of the noose, buddy. There'd be an audit trail on this one.'

'Spoilsport.'

'Either way, you got to be happy, right?'

'That's a funny way of putting it. Would have been better if this happened a month back, or years back. Lives wouldn't have been lost.'

'*If only* is a dead end journey.'

'Argh Marsham, don't go all philosophical on me. Doesn't suit.'

Marsham laughed. 'No worries. Laters buddy.'

'Laters.'

They woke mid-morning. Grace's legs across his. A pincer movement. The day was already hot. Mordent was becoming disaffected by the weather. It didn't suit him. Grace blinked: once, twice. He wasn't sure of his feelings. It was a night time relationship. Daylight did neither of them any favours.

Grace sensed it. 'Morning you. Want some breakfast?'

'Eggs over easy?'

'No eggs.'

'No eggs, huh?'

'Nope.' She smiled.

'I guess I can't stay here any longer.' He made a show of getting up, looking for yesterday's underwear.

She became serious. 'Are we just on again off again.'

'You tell me sweetheart.'

She shrugged. 'Maybe we could play it by ear. Neither of us are teenagers.'

He nodded. 'No rush?'

She smiled. 'No rush.'

He bent over and kissed her. Lips closed against morning breath.

'I've gotta be on my way.'

'Business?'

'You could say that. And pleasure.'

She raised an eyebrow.

'For once, it's both business *and* pleasure.'

'Lucky you.'

He finished dressing, left her apartment. Wondered if he would see her again. Warmth hit him like a breezeblock as he opened the door of her building, almost knocking him back inside. Maybe that was fate lending a hand.

He had a couple of calls to make and most of the day to waste before the fun began. He drove across the city to his office. Cyclists painted in day-glo lycra damaged his eyes. Sun-reflections off slanted windows in non-air-conditioned offices burnt his skin. Expanses of flesh insulted his intelligence or aroused his interest dependent on size and sex. He wished he had tinted windows. He wished he wore sunglasses.

In his office he left the door open a crack. It was so humid he needed scuba diving equipment. Leaving the door open didn't help matters, but gave him a clear view of the temps heading to the agency down the corridor who raised his temperature in their summer-appropriate clothing. There were few perks to be had in that office. This was one of them. He didn't mind turning up the heat.

He leant back in his chair, put his feet up on the desk. Dialled a number.

'Benedict Holmsworth.'

'Ah Benedict me old chum, it's Mordent. Your friendly PI.'

'Have you been taking stimulants, Mr Mordent? Can we not keep this professional?'

'Apologies, Holmsworth. It's just that a weight

was recently lifted from my mind and I'm lightheaded as a result. What have you got planned for this evening?'

'Let me check my diary.'

Mordent didn't know anyone who had to check their diary for less than three days ahead. Unless they were doing so for a purpose, to imply importance. Nevertheless, he waited patiently.

'I seem to have had a cancellation. What is it you have in mind?'

'Fear,' said Mordent. 'I'm going to crack a case and I think you should be there when I do so.'

'Sounds very Agatha Christie to me. Inviting all the participants for a drawing room showdown.'

'Agatha Christie would be right up your street. You're going to see where your money has been going. Meet me outside The Fear Institute at ten. You can park on the opposite side of the road. And be discreet. It'll be a blast.'

'I do believe you're appropriating my mode of diction as some form of chameleon ingratiation,' said Holmswoth. 'But nevertheless, I will be there.' He hung up the phone.

Mordent smiled. Perhaps Holmsworth would be a gas in a social situation; not his cup of tea, but entertaining for an hour or two.

He dialled again. Drummed his fingers on the desk. Emmeline was quick to answer.

'Mr Mordent. How goes it?'

'It goes very well.'

'What can I do for you this fine morning?'

Mordent coughed, phlegm suddenly crowding his throat like The Blob at a bus stop. 'I was wondering if you would care for a drink. To celebrate your input into the case that I solved. To mark the successful start of our new working relationship.'

'The keyword in that spiel, Mr Mordent, is *working*.'

'Surely one drink wouldn't hurt?'

'It's not the drink that I'm expecting will hurt.'

'Do you have such a low opinion of me?'

'It's not that. But you forget that I'm in the information business. And because of the recent case against you not only am I painfully aware of your sexual peccadillo and preference for those on the game, but I also happen to know that only ninety minutes ago you were seen leaving an apartment building containing one Grace Frost, nightclub singer, with whom you had left from that nightclub the previous evening. Far be it for me to suggest that you spent the night in her apartment doing anything other than playing canasta, but under the circumstances I find it less prudent for me to accept your invitation.'

'You've been tailing me?'

'I find it useful to know of my client's whereabouts.'

'Interesting.' Mordent sighed. 'So we still have a professional relationship?'

'But of course!' There was a pause. 'And it was nice doing business with you, Sir.'

Mordent found himself smiling. 'Until next time?'

'Until next time.'

He disconnected the call. Women were like buses. They all tended to come at once.

He re-thought that thought.

If only he should be so lucky.

56
Fright Night

The lights were on at *Get Stuffed!* Damian let him in with the usual nod to the rear of the shop.

'She's almost ready.'

'Has she settled back to work ok?'

Damian looked startled. 'I didn't mean Berenice,' he said, 'But yes. Yes. She's fine.'

Berenice stuck her head out from behind the dark. 'Hey Dad.'

'Hey daughter.'

She came over and gave him a hug, a little awkwardly.

'It still hurts?'

'Just a bit. I tense when I probably don't need to. Anyway, you know they said there'd be a full recovery.'

'No thanks to me.'

'No, we've been through this. Thanks to you.'

'You wouldn't even have been there if it wasn't for me.'

'I would rather know you than not. Besides, it spilled all your skeletons out of the closet at once.' She winked.

Mordent flashed back an uncomfortable smile. Truth was, he had a whole army of skeletons, enough to battle Jason and the Argonauts and win bones down. But Berenice didn't have to know everything about him. And hopefully that wouldn't come with time.

'Can I look?' He gestured towards the back room.

'Of course,' said Damian. 'We're going to need a hand getting it out of here anyway. I've rented a van.'

'Keep the receipt. My client will reimburse you in full.'

They headed out back. At first, perhaps surprisingly, Mordent didn't see it. The lighting was low. A desk lamp illuminated objects of the trade: a cavity syringe, bone cutters, a brain scoop, clamp forceps, and a variety of needles, hooks, and chains. On a nearby shelf clear packets held what initially appeared to be drugs, but Mordent made out labels for horse glue crystals, borax powder, alum, and plaster of Paris. Blocks of beeswax and modelling clay sat alongside taxidermy soap, lined up with bottles of formaldehyde, optimalin, and a selection of enamel paints in tiny tins Mordent had last seen when assembling aircrafts kits as a boy. This, together with the disorientation, lumbered him into memory, and when he finally saw the creature he took a reflexive step back.

'Ouch! My toe!'

'Sorry Berenice.'

Mordent admired their handiwork. A flurry of logistical possibilities crowded his head but he dismissed them. The creation was a masterpiece.

He turned to find both of them beaming, almost ghoulishly in the half-light. If he hadn't known them quite well then he might have taken a second step back.

'Beautiful, isn't it?' said Damian. 'I hope it will remain intact.'

Berenice smiled. 'It does have a certain aura to it. Mind you, it's this kind of thing that proves problematic in our industry.'

'Oh rubbish!' said Damian. 'You can't knock good craftsmanship. The business has enough detractors without you joining in.'

'I'm not. I'm just saying something like this fuels the fire.'

'A fire of ignorance.'

She laughed. 'Let's not argue. We both know we love it.'

The three of them looked at it in awe some more, then Mordent glanced at his watch. 'We better get it out of here.'

Damian nodded. 'I put it on wheels,' he said. 'Shouldn't be a problem.'

They manoeuvred it out to the van.

The evening was balmy. Mordent wasn't a great passenger. Damian drove with due care and attention, but Mordent's hands itched for something to do. They were three abreast in the vehicle. He was reminded of the Three Stooges, wondered which one Berenice would be. Knew which one Damian was. Realised which one *he* was. Went round the circuit again.

It was fully dark by the time they parked opposite the Institute. Mordent spotted Holmsworth's vehicle instantly. It appeared affronted to be parked in the lot. Mordent eased himself out of the van and wandered over. Holmsworth's electric window rolled smoothly downwards, a silent slave.

'I hope you haven't brought me here on some ridiculous pretext?'

'Not at all. I fully expect we will unmask Copernicus Fear this evening. Where do you stand on breaking and entering?'

Holmsworth raised his eyebrows. 'A means to an end, Mordent. A means to an end.'

'Good. Fear lives above his offices. We're going to set up a little surprise for him.'

Benedict nodded. 'And your companions?'

'Just some help that's required. Trustworthy folk. It's going to be a bit theatrical. Can you suspend your disbelief and keep quiet until the denouement? Everything will make sense.'

Benedict shrugged. Being told what to do was anathema to him. Then he nodded and started to roll up the window. 'Good god!'

Mordent noticed in the window's reflection that Damian and Berenice had started unloading the van. He held a finger to his lips.

'Remember what I said.'

The heavy door of The Fear Institute wasn't an easy obstacle but with some persistence Mordent manoeuvred the lock to his advantage. The wheels Damian had installed were well oiled, barely made a *ssshing* noise on the hardwood flooring. Mordent directed them along the narrow hallway, unimpeded, until they were installed in Fear's office. After the construct had been positioned to his satisfaction, Mordent bade Benedict crouch on the floor opposite the doorway, behind Copernicus' desk. Berenice confirmed he wasn't visible, then left with Damian to wait in the van.

'Are you ready?' Mordent asked Benedict.

'More than.'

'Then let's see how this pans out.'

Mordent wandered across the room to a pedestal holding a vase. He gave it a cursory glance, decided not to question its worth, then hurled it towards the wall. The impact resonated within the room, then multiplied as the vase shattered on the floor. He assumed his position.

He knew it would take a while. He hoped Copernicus was alone. Truth be told, he hadn't made provision for anything but.

Benedict was getting antsy. Mordent held up a finger. Not that finger.

A beam appeared on the other side of the door, as though Copernicus was using a light sabre as a draft excluder and it had just been activated. Mordent swivelled.

A rectangle was cast against the opposite wall.

Copernicus' voice wavered: 'Is anyone there?'

It was the type of question to which no one wanted an answer.

Mordent heard the first gasp at the smashed vase. He anticipated Copernicus judging the distance from the pedestal to the fragments on the floor.

The main light came on.

The second gasp wasn't a gasp. More a strangled scream.

Mordent heard a crump as Copernicus fell to the floor like a bag of laundry thrown downstairs by a lazy hotel maid.

He swivelled the chair around, faced the scene.

Copernicus caught sight of Mordent from the corner of one eye. His other eye, and the remaining percentage of the first, was fixed on the manticore towering over him.

Get Stuffed! had performed a magnificent task.

The manticore had the body of a lion. Whether it *was* a lion Mordent remained to be convinced, but the torso they had used, together with the red dye, gave it an authentic look rather than fabricated. It stood on two feet. Bat wings extended from just below the shoulder blades. Actual bat wings would have been miniscule, but Mordent knew these were composites, their thin membranes stitched from a multitude of bats. At the rear, another composite – a succession of scorpion tails placed one against another against another against another – reared in a question mark. The pièce de résistance was the human head, baring three rows of sharp teeth. Mordent hesitated to speculate how Damian had achieved this creation, and to a layman it might appear ridiculous, sideshow bizarre; for Copernicus, however, the effectiveness was made evident by the smell that permeated the room.

'I expect you're wondering why I've invited you here this evening,' said Mordent. 'Fear is a psychological phenomenon which is best treated - so I understand - by radical exposure to the object which is feared. Hence, in your case, the manticore.'

Copernicus clutched his chest, left-hand side. He was wheezing. 'Greener.'

'So the grass is, on the other side. Your grass made particularly so by the greenbacks you've pocketed in the name of the cause. I know the reference is anachronistic, but you might be old enough to remember the American Civil War. Let me introduce you to a relative of a former client.'

Benedict stood, on cue.

'This gentleman is the nephew of Benedict Holmsworth, who I believe you were attempting to cure from a phobia of rats. His name is also Benedict Holmsworth which is where the gentry differ from you and I. Either way, his assertion is that his uncle was effectively murdered by your organisation and financially coerced into funding it beyond his means. I'm sure the details could be argued over whether it could be proved as constructive manslaughter or criminally negligent manslaughter, but my assertion would be that Benedict Holmsworth senior was literally frightened to death by exposure to the creatures of which he was terrified following advice given by yourselves in much the same manner as you gave advice to me.

'Being scared to death, as I'm sure you now appreciate, is a realistic possibility. How are you feeling?'

Copernicus remained clutching the skin close to his heart. 'Greener,' he repeated, his eyes glazed.

'Actually your pallor in this light suggests otherwise,' Mordent continued. 'It is my assertion that by advising your clients to tackle their fear head on you are in fact perpetuating their fears. It becomes a vicious circle fuelled by money and greed. Extortion isn't something to be proud of. Would you claim otherwise?'

Copernicus puffed out breath, gradually regained his composure. He edged away from the stuffed monstrosity, but even shivered when it was to his rear. Mordent waited.

'You've made your point. What do you want?'

Mordent looked to Benedict. 'You've heard his confession. What do *you* want?'

Benedict's brow furrowed. Mordent wondered how he might respond, delicately. He knew what Benedict wanted.

'I...' Benedict began.

'I think what my client is trying to say,' interrupted Mordent, 'is that criminal proceedings might be messy, could even cause some family embarrassment. Also, he's not a ruthless man. He appreciates it wasn't your intention to kill his uncle, but that the death was a by-product of greed. Incarcerating yourself, in advanced years, wouldn't be of great benefit. Instead, he proposes a two-strand solution.

'Firstly, that The Fear Institute immediately suspends its operations and ceases to function, and secondly, that all monies paid by Benedict Holmsworth senior be refunded to my client.'

Copernicus stood. Regarded them both, shakily. His pyjamas were wet. 'Do I have a choice?'

Mordent shook his head. He looked to Benedict. 'Would that conclude the investigation in a satisfactory manner?'

'Oh yes.'

'Then it's a deal. I suggest you two shake on it. You're both gentlemen after all.'

Copernicus extended his hand, Benedict took it.

Mordent's gaze returned to the manticore. Where *had* Damian got that head?

Outside, a warm breeze had picked up. Litter spiralled in mini whirlwinds. A lone plastic water bottle tap-danced on the sidewalk. Mordent nodded to Berenice who leant nonchalantly against the side of the van, and she beckoned to Damian. Together they returned inside to retrieve their work. Benedict shook his hand.

'Job well done. Quite a display.'

'Glad you liked it. I thought it was inspired.'

'I'll see you're all adequately reimbursed. Thank you for restoring my family honour.'

Mordent grunted. It didn't do to displease a satisfied client. But then Holmsworth's family honour was no doubt built on money: restoring money *did* mean restoring honour. He knew it would be the outcome recognised by his class. Benedict wanted no further retribution than that.

He watched him walk around his car, check it remained intact in this less than salubrious district. He had the audacity to pip Mordent as he drove away.

Berenice and Damian returned.

'What are you going to do with it?' gestured Mordent.

'Back of the shop I think,' Damian said. 'It's too beautiful to dispose of, too frightening to display.'

They wheeled it into the rear of the van. Damian secured it with rope whilst Berenice came out and unexpectedly wrapped her arms around Mordent. She winced.

'It's good to know you,' she said.

'Even if it gets you kidnapped?'

'Even if it gets me kidnapped. Just not often, ok?'

'I'll do my best.'

They stood side by side. Mordent was aware of the warmth of the night, of the warmth of her body.

Warmth. He was aware of her warmth.

57
A Happy Finish

He pulled up outside Astrid's apartment.

She had elected to remain in the area, the whiff of scandal blown out of the district via a diversion regarding her husband's employment. He admired her for the tenacity, for the willingness to get back in the game. In some respects they were similar, in others miles apart. The booking was made over the phone. She sounded surprised to hear from him. But also grateful. He could understand that. He had helped save her life.

The brownstone flaked in the heat. Tiny particles of grit dislodged by a light wind fell like dry rain. He looked up at her window, became eye-speckled. Taking a handkerchief from his pocket he blinked rapidly then wetted one corner and curled it into a cone. Carefully he removed the grit from his eye.

She let him in the ground floor on the buzzer. He glanced, automatically, at the corner of the hall where the police officer previously guarding her had been found slumped. No blame had been attributed to him. Slowly, he ascended the stairs.

He couldn't help noticing the smart interior of the building.

At her door he rapped three times. There was a slight discolouration in the fisheye and then she let him in.

'How's it going?'

'Fine. Just fine.'

'Would you like a coffee?'

He looked around. Shook his head. 'Actually, can we just get down to it?' He found himself looking towards the bedroom, aware how awkward words were in his mouth.

She smiled. Her fingers removed his jacket from his shoulders. He shrugged out of it as she pulled it off him as though undressing a child. She was beautiful, he realised,. The fingers on his right hand began to subtly shake.

He followed her into the bedroom. The curtains were closed. A red lamp imbued the bed with a cherry-cola glow. A variety of toys stood upended, unashamed, on the bedside cabinet. He realised she had begun to unbutton his shirt.

She smiled again. 'Feeling comfortable?'

He stammered a yes. Slowed his breathing. Was fourteen all over again and Maisy-Lou was alone with him in his father's shed, her panties by her ankles, his cock in her hand. A memory of something illicit.

Leather whipped through his belt holes when she might have simply undone the buckle. He stepped out of his trousers, kept on his socks.

'Lie down,' she said.

He sank onto the bed. It was a whore's boudoir, it was a dentist's chair, it was his sofa in front of the television, it was a psychiatrist's couch, it was his mother's bosom, it was comfortable. He found himself relaxing.

'Over the phone...' he began.

She put a finger to his lips, quietened him. Ran the same finger down his torso and hooked it under the elastic of his underpants. He assisted her pulling them down by raising his hips and then his bottom.

She opened a cupboard and removed a roll of bubblewrap. He watched as she picked at a strip of Saran wrap binding it together then pulled it off and rolled it between her fingertips until it lost its stickiness. She dropped it into the bin, then let one end of the bubblewrap drop until it touched the floor. Her legs, encased in sheer pantyhose, mutated with the wrap's distortion. He became fixated in locating her knees within two of the bubbles, barely registered her reaching for the scissors.

A section of wrap fell to the floor. She bent - there were those knees - and picked it up. Bent again and crouched by his head on the bed. He lifted it at her command, then held his neck steady as she wrapped it one, two, three times around his head.

'I'll have to be quick,' she said.

He nodded. His vision a fly's eyes.

She picked up some more Saran wrap, clear but thick. Then wrapped it around his head securing the bubblewrap. He slowed his breathing again, the air became stuffy, his hands reached out and gripped the bedclothes. Then he realised one of them had caught the end of her skirt.

She reached behind herself, unzipped it. Stepped out. He could barely see this.

Quickly she wrapped more of the stuff around her hand. His penis remained limp. She cajoled it with her fingers, ran the tips along the underside of his anus, felt him stiffen in her palm. Glancing at his muffled face she climbed onto the bed, sat on his face, leant forwards and took him in her mouth until he was hard enough to get a result.

As fast as she could without damaging the shaft she pumped her hand up and down, hearing some of the wrap pop both between her fingers and against her thighs, until she felt his body tense and he ejaculated swiftly, grunting gutturally that transformed into a cough.

She swung her legs back onto the floor, cut through the tape and removed the wrap from his face. He breathed hard. His eyes struggling to focus, then she came into view standing over him, her smile intact.

'Thank you,' he said.

'Any time.' He watched as she pulled disinfectant wipes from a container like white elephants connected trunk to tail. She wiped him clean.

The experience had been over within fifteen minutes. Through parking outside until restoring his clothes. He felt disconnected, dislocated from reality. Deep inside him, hastily being buried, a miniscule element of shame recognised itself and nodded.

He handed over the money.

'Come again,' she said. He was aware of the irony.

As her apartment door closed behind him he paused for a moment, leant against the wall. So *that* was a happy ending. He hadn't even had a massage. What was the attraction other than a fleeting experience, the discovery of something new? A trace of semen dried on his thigh. It was hard to see what the fuss was about. There was no joy in it. Yet there was always someone who would get off on something and Mordent was no exception. He allowed himself a smile. If nothing else the experience had revealed an aspect to the man which he might be able to use in a future encounter. Sometimes it proved useful to step inside someone else's mind, someone else's shoes.

Kovacs reached the bottom of the stairway and pushed himself out onto the street. Despite the fifteen minutes there was a change in the air. Fall, that most delirious of seasons, was finally on the way.

The heat in the city was about to break.